The Silly Season

The Silly Season

by Bernard Shrimsley

ROBSON BOOKS

First published in Great Britain in 2003 by Robson Books, The Chrysalis Building, Bramley Road, London, W10 6SP

An imprint of Chrysalis Books Group plc

British Library Cataloguing in Publication Data
A catalogue record for this title is available from the British Library.

ISBN 1 86105 667 2

Typeset by FiSH Books, London
Printed by Butler & Tanner Ltd, Frome and London

For Norma Jessie Alexandra,
and to our memories of Tony

Prologue

It is Investiture Day at Buckingham Palace. Fleet Street's most tabloid editor is about to be knighted. In the gallery of the ivory-and-gold ballroom, the Royal Marines orchestra is playing Sondheim. Two bars into 'Something Appealing, Something Appalling', the baton commands a pause for the Lord Chamberlain to proclaim the citation.

'For services to journalism.' His lordship's eyes roll. 'Jack Stack.' His lordship's nose, which until now seemed retroussé beyond further disdain, turns up to display nostrils like a sawn-off shotgun. 'To receive the honour of knighthood.' His lordship's lips form a silent word. 'Asshole.'

Jack Stack's lovable-cockney face glows and his shoulders see-saw as he advances up the red carpet to the throned dais. That electric-blue morning suit, with toned-in cravat and polyester carnation, has last been hired for a jockey's wedding. He kneels at the gilded footstool to await the ritual tap of royal sword upon shoulder that will dub him Sir Jack and admit him to the company of Galahad and Drake.

The blade trembles in the hand of the sovereign whose family this creature has comprehensively shat upon. The six royal corgis rumble and bare their teeth. So do the four royal heirs – Princess Victoria and Princes Nicholas, Michael and Richard (aka Vicki, Nicky, Mickey and Ricky).

Now the sword begins its descent, gleaming in the light of the great chandelier as it hovers about Jack Stack's bowed head –

But to begin at the beginning . . .

1

Wink-wink

The bells of St Clement Danes said 'Oranges and Lemons' as the Aldwych traffic lights across the road changed to red. From the pillion of his chauffeured Kawasaki, a moon-helmeted Jack Stack nipped to the pavement kiosk. It was his custom at news-stands to lift handfuls of whichever tabloid he was now with and sit them on whichever he had most recently left. So, yet again this Monday morning, Jack Stack made a pile of Globes invisible under a layer of Mercurys. He squared them up, patting paternally this first front page of his new editorship.

'Berk.' The baseball-capped man in the kiosk replaced the newspapers.

'Leave my religion out of it, sunshine.' Jack Stack's foghorn tones blared through his visor.

He sat Mercurys back on Globes and himself back on the pillion, turning to offer two fingers as the lights changed to green. The bike vroomed him down the street called Fleet, still the label for the London press of which it was for centuries the heart, though now only the Mercury lingered on at the foot of the hill.

Dismounting outside Mercury House, Jack Stack exchanged glances with the bas-relief head on the wall plaque commemorating the local hero who sold still-warm Mercurys on this pitch at the age of eleven and went on to fame and fiction:

EDGAR WALLACE • REPORTER
Born London 1875 • Died Hollywood 1932
To Fleet Street he gave his heart

'Wanker,' said Jack Stack.

An hour later, Humpty (born Humphrey) Baynard tumbled through the revolving doors like an empty canoe shooting the rapids. It was much the way he had inherited the role of chief executive last year when a stroke retired half-brother Toby to the Bahamas and brought Humpty in from exile at their new printing plant down river.

He crossed a lobby marble enough for the good old days when the Mercury was king of the middle market, had evening and Sunday sisters – and there was never an out-of-order sign on the directors' lift.

Humpty turned to wait in line with the busts of the first, second and third Viscounts Baynard, as though reserving a plinth for when he became the fourth. Thanks to another weekend on the boat, his face was already as bronze as theirs. But it was nothing like as serene. Their editors lasted twenty years. Humpty was bracing to fire his after twenty-four hours.

Jack Stack hadn't even been due to start until today. There was to be a boardroom lunch to welcome him and begin the countdown to a life-saving relaunch in the autumn. Humpty had scheduled thirteen weeks to get the new format right, showcase it to advertisers and line up a multi-media campaign to win readers. But bloody Jack Stack couldn't wait. Aware that Mercury directors hallowed the sabbath (Christian, Jewish and, if the sun was shining, Muslim also), he had sneaked in to run the skull-and-crossbones up the mast on Sunday before anyone was around to hold him back on Monday. Overnight, he had switched the title to red-top and the rest to match.

At the lifts, two temps were absorbed in the result. Today's Mercury was devoted to the first kiss-and-sell in its history. Pages 1, 2, 3, 4, 5, 6 and 7 were filled with Top TV Weathergirl Tina's account of her date with the Prince of Wales; warm fronts, ridges of high pleasure, isobars and all:

Sexclusive!! My nookie with Nicky
TINA'S ROYAL
WEATHERCOCK

His picture, in Garter robes, was captioned: *HRH Nicky, 20...Seven times.* And hers, in garter belt: *TV Tina, 29...What a scorcher.*

'Seven times?' echoed Temp No. 1. 'On a first date?'

'He did used to be a frog,' said Temp No. 2.

Humpty finger-combed his wings and slipped into a waistcoat pocket the bifocals that made him, at 44, look old enough to be their father. A smile polished his face as he stood back for them when the lift doors opened. They gave him a look and shuffled in, one turning to **KNICKERLESS WITH NICHOLAS** across pages 2 and 3 while the other craned to **WHETHER FORECAST: REIN-IN THE HEIR?** across 4 and 5. Humpty was still waiting for them to budge up when the doors closed him out.

The next lift was stuck at the top floor. He sighed. It had seemed such a nice day as he set off from his home on the Hamble before the papers arrived. Motorway empty. Porsche hood down. Sun on his back. But when he stopped to pick up a Mercury, he thought he'd been given a Globe by mistake. Then the car phone had started trilling 'Rule Britannia'...

'It's meltdown, Humpty,' said the marketing director. 'Even non-readers are cancelling.'

'It's shit, Humpty,' said the advertisement director. 'I can't sell space on used toilet paper.'

'It's brilliant, Humpty,' said the management consultancy chairman who had persuaded him to plant this kamikaze pilot in the editor's chair. 'Who dares, wins...' He was still pitching as Humpty pitched the phone out on to the hard shoulder.

Damn consultants. Damn their focus groups and their psephobabble, their nubile PAs and their Dom Pérignon. Damn them for convincing him half-brother Toby's bid to survive as a nice tabloid was a no-hoper. What you need, they said, is a young editor with the full-blown tabloid virus. One who says bollocks a lot and doesn't believe in days off. Our head-hunters have found you just the man. Sure-sure, they said, Jack Stack ain't exactly Eton and Oxford but this ain't exactly the Boat Race. To prise him from the Globe, Humpty had to pay the earth and promise the moon. Massive TV spend? You've got it, Jack. Big bucks for big buy-ups? Name of the game, Jack. Editor on top, management on tap? No prob, Jack. Fire 50 old farts? Music to my ears, Jack. And replace them? Er, sure, Jack.

When the lift eventually delivered Humpty to the boardroom floor, secretary Maxine was waiting with hands at prayer and the usual message from Dumpty (born Daphne) to ring home the moment he got in.

He crossed an office like a stately home drawing room with french windows open to the roof garden. A harpist would not have been out of place amid its columns and cornices, its Adam fireplaces and Turkey carpets. He slumped into his swivel throne and lifted the antiqued brass phone on his ormolu desk.

'Let me guess, Dumpty. Percolator on the blink again?'

'Ha bloody ha. Thought you'd like to know I've rung the newsagent to stop the Merc. Join the club, he said . . . '

Humpty was grateful when Maxine bustled in, open mouth and urgent forefinger prompting him to switch on his TV.

'Must go, Dumpty.'

'What about the percolator?'

'Just get a man in, eh?'

The screen was filled by a pink pussy-cat face below floppy grey hair and above floppy bow-tie. The caption read: Francis Franklin CBE, Mercury ex-editor. This was the safe, liver-spotted pair of hands Humpty had fired on Friday to make way for Jack Stack. The man had reacted by dashing into the roof garden and straddling the rail until Humpty doubled the pay-off he first thought of. Just look at Francis Franklin CBE now, all puffed up for after-life as a media pundit.

'. . . I edited the dear old Merc for dear old Toby Baynard for twenty years. Loved it. Loved him. But when his successor chose to take it into the gutter, I said over my dead body . . . '

'Should have let you jump,' bellowed Humpty.

'. . . Now his new Merc has sabotaged Fleet Street's solemn undertaking to cease hounding the young royals. How soon we forget. Is another generation to be sacrificed on the altar of tabloid competition?'

'Should have pushed you,' bellowed Humpty.

'. . . Is this goodbye to the self-restraint that has saved the press from state restraint? It surely is – unless readers hit the Merc in the only place that hurts . . . '

Humpty thumbed the mute button as the marketing director burst in, flapping printouts at him.

'No need to look so damn pleased.' Humpty's words hovered like a cartoon bubble above his head as he swung away to frown at the fountain farting into the goldfish pool.

'I'm pleased because I was wrong, Humpty. Wrong, wrong, wrong. We sold out.'

'No need to sound so damn surprised.'

'God, Humpty, if we can sell out before we've even begun our campaign, just think what we'll do when we get going. You're a genius, man. A bloody genius.'

'Who dares, wins,' said Humpty, swivelling to wave him away and flip the intercom.

'Great paper today, Jack.'

'How the fuck would you know, Hump?'

The line went dead. The little sod had hung up.

But what to do? Fire the man whose insolent genius was going to save the paper and make Humpty rich? Fire him back to the Globe to smother the Merc at rebirth? Restore the self-restrained Francis Franklin CBE? Humpty flipped the intercom to risk offering further encouragement.

'Good news, Jack. We sold out.'

'Good news? Bollocks. You didn't print enough.'

Again, the line went dead. Again, Humpty chanced it.

'One small favour, Jack – just tip me the wink next time you're about to trigger World War Two-and-a-half.'

'Wink-wink.'

'Oh, no.' Humpty crumpled.

'I'm firing the First Lady of Fleet Street – '

'Marina Marshall? I can't believe I'm hearing this.'

' – and I'm bringing in a new star columnist. Born of the age we live in and sexy with it.'

'No go, Jack. Marina's fireproof. You know perfectly well why.'

'I know perfectly well her crap column is the symbol of everything that stands between us and success.'

'Steady on, Jack. Talk to Marina when she gets back from the States. Surely you can work something out.'

'No time for foreplay, Hump. Paper to edit.'

Again, the line went dead. For ten minutes, Humpty moved only to put his bifocals on or off and swivel his throne clockwise or anti-clockwise.

He had his orders about Marina Marshall. Issued by half-brother Toby as he lay tranquillised and tubed in the ambulance plane to the Bahamas. Toby was unlikely to return other than in a box, but the chairmanship and the controlling financial interest remained in his hands. Humpty could still hear those huge sighs, those audible silences:

'You and me, Humpty, we're just ten-a-penny managers. The journalists are the heart and soul of the paper. Cherish them. Especially Marina...'

But Humpty rarely roamed below the boardroom floor and had been within cherishing range just once. He and Dumpty had found themselves sharing the revolving doors with Marina. Dumpty identified her right away although, apart from that teasing glance, Marina was no longer much like the Lord Snowman portrait still ornamenting her byline after fifteen years. Humpty saw a tall goddess in a saffron trouser suit; thirty-something and so exquisitely groomed and scented that he took her for a client of the fashionable divorce lawyers on what used to be the Sunday paper floor. Dumpty saw a ship's figurehead of a woman; forty-something and with big feet.

Of-course-of-course, Humpty had said before Dumpty tugged him away. He did not mean of-course-of-course, our celebrated columnist. He meant of-course-of-course, brother Toby's mistress.

Of-course-of-course, Dumpty had mimicked. She meant of-course-of-course, the bitch who would have robbed the Humpty-Dumptys of their inheritance, had Marina got Toby to a register office before the affair fizzled out.

Dumpty's orders did not make it easy for Humpty to follow Toby's orders. She renewed hers every Thursday, the day the Marina Marshall column appeared. Underlined them with a hyperthyroid glare across the All-Bran. Spat them out over the rear end of her hunter as she spurred off on her dawn gallop:

'Don't go within four-and-three-quarter inches of that scheming slag. She'll be after you now. She's not fussy.'

Humpty closed his eyes and brushed up his forehead with the back of his hand as Maxine buzzed to put through Lord Bull, chairman of the Globe and Jack Stack's employer until last Friday:

'Bet the little shit didn't tell you I killed that Tina's Royal Weathercock rubbish last week. Nearly killed him too. He'd paid her a hundred grand. So – ha! – I'm billing you for a hundred and fifty.'

'...six, seven, eight...'
Jack Stack was pacing out Marina Marshall's handsome office suite under the gaze of lifesize blow-ups of her with the great and the grateful. In each cameo, as in each of her columns, she was the star.

The co-stars were upstaged by such actressy devices as lowering her glass to look as though they were raising theirs to her.

'...twelve, thirteen, fourteen...'

The deputy editor readied clipboard and looked on through fat glasses from his perch on her desk. His rump displaced a photo of Marina with her twins in Harrow boaters and blazers new enough to proclaim their first day at father Toby's old school.

'...twenty-eight, twenty-nine, thirty.' Jack Stack clapped his hands. 'Raze it to the ground. I want every trace of that bloody woman removed.'

Clop, went the deputy editor.

Bish Bishop knew that a click of the tongue was the smart contribution to the editor's monologues. As at the Globe, the deputy's was not a speaking part. He was the oldest among the posse of executive cowboys Jack Stack had roared in with from the Globe. At 47, Bish could give him ten years and settle for being the deputy who never deputised.

'Her secretary's office will be plenty big enough for my new star columnist – born of the age we live in and sexy with it. Mustn't spoil the kid, must we?'

Clop, went Bish.

'I'll need the rest of Marina's space for my new departments. The Mercury CID. The Whistle-blower Freephone. The Royal Watchdog Desk. The Jack Hughes Page.'

Clop?

'Jack Hughes – *J'accuse*. Geddit? We'll expose a miscarriage of justice a week.' He looked through the window to the gilded figure balancing scales and sword atop the Old Bailey. 'Pity about the view.' He yanked venetian blinds shut and knotted the cord. 'What view?'

Clop, went Bish.

Jack Stack sniffed around Marina's dressing room. He sampled her swansdown seat, switched on her bulb-encircled make-up mirror and counted her assembly of cuddly little teddies. He looked into drawers. He slid open the mirrored wall of wardrobes, and the toecaps of 50 size 7s peeped at him below rails loaded with look-at-me outfits. Each hanger was collared with a card recording where and when Marina had worn the garment. From the shot silk at the Royal Yacht Squadron Ball to the Nassau Wildcats baseball shirt at the Notting Hill Carnival. From the Hunting Stewart cloak at the Edinburgh Military Tattoo to the cream safari suit for a guest spot on *Sunnyside*, the nation's favourite soap.

'Tell the Salvation Army to send a couple of vans round.'

Clop, went Bish as the door of Marina's loo slammed shut. He kicked his heels until it opened and Jack Stack emerged, zipping up.

'Cor, that's some bog. Make it *en suite* with my office. Her bidet will be my bidet. Think about it.'

Bish thought about it. Clop. *Clop.*

Jack Stack's head swung with his to the doorway – and a sharp-kneed secretary with a glossy shopping bag in each hand. The face was not as young as the promise of the rah-rah skirt. Or the yah-yah voice:

'Who the fuck are you?'

'Who the fuck wants to know?'

'I'm Marina Marshall's personal assistant actually.'

'I'm Marina Marshall's new editor actually. Jack Stack – rhymes with sack.' He snapped fingers at her. 'Name?'

'Claudia Carr – and please don't snap your fingers at me, OK?' Her confidence was that of the PA who assumes her boss's status.

He tapped his watch. 'Always come in this late?'

'If you must know, I'm halfway into my hols. Just popped in to firm up a couple more American interviews for the new book.'

'When's she due back?'

'Two weeks, OK?'

Clop.

2

The First Lady

Harry Chacewater's niece came running from the portico of the stately colonial Virginia mansion that still commanded an entire bend of the James river. Her ponytail and her Juilliard music academy T-shirt stopped bobbing for a moment as she pondered where to search next. On one of the William and Mary tables in the hall, the phone lay where she had parked it, the earpiece spluttering despair from Marina Marshall's personal-assistant-actually, holding the London end of the line with another phone at her free ear while her free hand redialled and re-redialled the mobile that Marina always switched off during interviews.

That dated Sloane drawl had Li'l Mizz Chacewater squirming yet. 'Believe me, Honey – fab name, lucky you – if we don't get my boss to the phone, it'll be the end of civilisation as we know it.' And in Sloane italics, *'At the very least, OK?'*

It was two hours since Marina Marshall had descended in lemon silk from the Chacewater Inc. helicopter to interview Uncle Harry for some book on press barons. At 27, he was the youngest on her list: president of Chacewater since his father died five months ago. The pair had disappeared after a lubricated lunch which Honey spent watching Uncle Harry wanting Marina, perspiration pearling his forehead as she dealt with the asparagus. He had topped up her Chablis over the brim rather than drag his Garfield eyes from that corn-blonde mane burnished back from that classy head, and those freckles dancing at that peachy neckline. She had him thrilling to that B-flat voice and thralling to that perfume you had to be her age to wear, dammit.

Honey had sniffed the trail around the house. No Marina Marshall, no Uncle Harry. She had bounded up to the Sky Room and focused the resident binoculars on the gallop, the orchard, the boxwood maze and the pet cemetery. No Marina Marshall, no Uncle Harry. She had scanned the tennis court, the croquet lawn, the old rose garden and the new pool. No Marina Marshall, no Uncle Harry.

Downstairs again, she had picked up the still-spluttering phone.

'Sorry, Claudia. Guess they've taken off in the golf buggy. Why don't I just have her call you back when she shows up?'

'Listen, Honey darling. Her life's in my hands. I'm absolutely not budging. Even if I pee myself, OK?'

Now Honey Chacewater lifted her mountain bike from the shingle forecourt. The breeze wafted a sweet cigar-box aroma up through the cedars as she bumped down the mile of old plantation terraces to the river. Maybe they'd taken the boat out. She hoped so. Otherwise that left Uncle Harry's bandstand. She hoped not.

This was a century-old original which he had transformed into a summerhouse and equipped with much hi-fi and every convenience, not least a phone he could unplug. Here Uncle Harry shared his bourbon and his music with the lucky sonsofabitch who hadn't had to give up a career in the Navy: the family had made him quit when a car crash killed the big brother groomed to take over. And here Uncle Harry brought his babes. Honey could hardly forget the sights and sounds that awaited her last vacation when she had to intrude on such an interview. That time, the bandstand guests were two easy pieces from a journalism faculty and half this one's age. The trio hadn't seen or heard Honey. They were in no position to hear, above the Mendelssohn violin concerto, anyone coming except themselves. Honey had retreated in mid-cadenza and sat in the shade of the old oaks through andante, allegretto and final allegro. Delivery of the message had waited until Uncle Harry emerged, followed by the two easy pieces patting their hair as though to check their heads hadn't come unscrewed.

At this moment, Marina was at the landing stage, looking out to Harry's white-and-gold *Miss Print IV*, fringed canopy fluttering invitation as she strained at her deep-water buoy. He was shinning down fourteen feet of ladder to untie her cutely matching dinghy, *Miss Print IV*$^{1/2}$, and ferry them aboard.

'All set, Marina,' he called up as her Ascot hat and the gloved hand securing it bent into view. 'Champagne on ice. Caviare in the fridge. Mendelssohn in the hi-fi.'

Molasses vowels doubled from the merry mouth. Decadence glowed from the easy-go face with the smile creases about the baggy brown eyes. The planter hat plus chewed cheroot added a touch of the *Gone With the Wind* forefathers whose empire Harry Chacewater had inherited without, alas, the genes that made it mighty.

'Uh-uh.' The Ascot hat shook with each syllable.

'Uh-uh?'

'Uh-*uh*.'

God, he was young. Couldn't he see she was hardly dressed for sheer ladders and heaving dinghies? God, he was obvious. The hands that loaded the champagne, the caviare and the Mendelssohn had no doubt been instructed to turn down the master cabin sheets and centre a gold-foiled chockie on each pillow. God, he was dumb. She hadn't got a quotable quote out of him yet.

'Aw, come on down, Marina.'

'Aw, come on up, Harry. Let's get to work.'

'So screw work.'

'So screw *Miss Print IV* – and *IV$^{1}/_{2}$*.'

'So screw the interview.'

'So screw you. Call me a cab.'

'Jeez.' He shrugged like a thwarted teenager and came muttering up the ladder.

'Wasting my time anyway. You'll be back in the Navy before my book's out.'

'No way. Hung up my flying helmet for good. Had it mounted in the hall alongside the moose heads – just one more family trophy.'

At last, she felt a chapter coming on. But Harry hadn't given up on his agenda either as they got back in the buggy and headed for the bandstand.

'Say, Marina, who fed you that garbage about me rejoining the fleet?'

'Lord Bull of the Globe.'

'Lord Bullshit.'

She smiled. What Johnnie Bull also told her was, *Watch it – ha! – they don't call him Horny Harry for nothing*.

'And who'd you check me out with, Harry?'

'Lord Bullshit, would you believe?'

He grinned. What Johnnie Bull also told him was, *Watch it – ha! – give her half a chance and she'll eat you alive.* Harry Chacewater's nature doomed him to take this not as a warning but a hint.

'Got to tell you, Marina – I aim to be a real big chapter in this book of yours.'

Her hazel eyes widened as they came to the bandstand. It gleamed white, like some giant wedding cake, on a lawn that gleamed green under a battery of sprays.

'Like it?'

'Love it.' Though she'd have it less Disney, more Palladio.

At the stacked bar inside, Harry filled two tumblers with half-and-half Rebel Yell bourbon and water and presented one to her. She set it aside and fixed herself a drowned single as he looked on.

'Hey, lighten up.' He raised his glass. 'Get me nice and loose' – he took a swig – 'and I sure give great quote.'

He conned a smile out of her by twitching his eyebrows and tapping his cheroot in a Groucho lurch across the floor to load a collection into the stereo. He motioned her to take a seat. She chose one of the club armchairs rather than the hammock or the various couches with room for him to cosy up.

He sat alone in the hammock and set it swinging gently. Boy, she looked tasty in those outsize spectacles she was fishing from a handbag big enough for a bride's mother. Maybe she'd keep them on once in a while.

'Come on, Honey. Come on.' The phone back at the house was spluttering away. 'Oh, sod-bugger-damn, come on . . .'

Honey juddered over the corduroy path by the landing stage to find *Miss Print IV$^{1/2}$* still tied up. She put her tongue out at the Red Cardinal perched on the radar bowl of *Miss Print IV*, braced herself and set off for the bandstand.

'My favourite piece, Marina. Know it?'

'Mendelssohn?'

'Nice try.'

'String octet. E Flat. Opus 20.'

'Ouch.'

'Harry, do you imagine I got where I am without doing my homework? Your Forbes Magazine profile mentioned you're a

Mendelssohn nut. So I invested in a *Best of* CD to tap into your soul on the plane over.'

'Bet you just loved every chord.'

'You lose. The Wedding March makes me want to throw up '

'I can't believe that.'

'You could if you were seventeen and holding a posy and a dinky white Bible.'

'Shotgun wedding?'

'Popgun wedding. An hour before marrying the deputy head's son, the head's daughter turned out not to be pregnant after all...'

Switching roles in the confessional was Marina Marshall's artform interview technique. I reveal all. You reveal all. The difference is that your stuff gets printed.

'...Threw myself into my career. University mag. North-country daily. Young Journalist of the Year. Toby Baynard was chairman of the judges. Snapped me up.'

'Snapped you up?' Johnnie Bull had put it rather differently.

'Christened me the new First Lady of Fleet Street. I loved it – and I loved him. And he loved me. But he'd been through a couple of ruinous divorces. Nearly had to sell the Mercury. So never again. I didn't care – until Olly and Nolly. Eventually I walked.'

'Olly and Nolly?'

'Here.' She dipped into her bag for a print of the photo on her desk. 'Oliver and Noël.'

'Great kids. I see you in them.'

'I see Toby. And I'm glad. I owe him everything, Harry. This book's dedicated to the man. He's my ticket to most of the oddballs in it.'

'Will Toby get back to Fleet Street?'

'Doubt it.'

'Still... see him?'

'No.'

She was intrigued by the pause. She was intrigued by Harry. Sure, he was eight or nine years younger. OK, eight or nine or fourteen. So what? He was a warm and sexy guy she could work like a glove puppet. A billionaire glove puppet.

Bourbon refill in one hand, cheroot as baton in the other, Harry rose to conduct Mendelssohn's eight strings in their race round the bandstand.

'Right now, Marina, we could be the only people in the world hearing this. Like Felix wrote it for us. Imagine.'

'Doing my best.'

'Reckon he got off on it?'

'Reckon you're going to tell me.'

'*Con fuoco* – that's what the man said.' He offered her the CD sleeve. 'There. *Con fuoco* – with fire, passion. How does that sound to you?'

'Like an Italian anagram.'

He closed in. His toecap came on to her toecap.

'Marina, you're a beautiful woman...'

'Harry, go *con fuoco* yourself.'

He offered a weak laugh as he put up his hands and backed away to make a little drama of flicking off the stereo. It was Mendelssohn's fault. He exiled his glass to the far side of the table. It was Rebel Yell's fault.

'Sorry wrong number, Marina.'

'Sorry wrong woman, Harry.'

His eyebrows and shoulders signalled can't-blame-a-guy-for-trying. Hell, it was more of a buzz to be put down by Marina Marshall than to be put up by any of the many.

'*Mea culpa.*'

'Five Hail Marys.'

Plus one Hail Marina. She took a tape recorder from her bag and set it between them, as though the interview was only now beginning and he need not worry his little head about the destiny of anything said when the tape wasn't turning. He would not know about the other recorder inside the bag and wired to the clasp that was also a mike. This was the secret of the nuanced dialogue that lifted her column above the rest. She would retrieve every cough and comma of the *Miss Print* and *con fuoco* sequences. They said so much about the essential Harry Chacewater even if, as usual, Marina Marshall had the best lines.

'OK, Marina. Got the message. Let's go to work.'

'Fine. So tell me all about yourself. Begin as far back as you can remember. Falling out of your pram. Or into the girl next door's.'

'How long you got?'

'Long enough if we fast-forward the Navy and skip the Mendelssohn. I need to be in Toronto tomorrow in time for dinner with my next chapter.'

'Toronto? That wouldn't be Max Magnus?'

'That would be Max Magnus. My book won't be complete without him.'

'But he ain't a press baron. He's a porn baron.'

'A porn baron who wants to be a press baron. Which is why he's out to buy up a respectable outfit. Just like yours. Just like ours.' Marina snapped finger and thumb. 'Just like that.'

'Just like Wild Wives? Just like Eager Beavers? Jeez, Marina, ever see that stuff?'

'When I can't get the Richmond & Twickenham Times.'

'Y'know, Pa always called him Skinmagnus.'

'Skinmagnus, mmmmm.' Now she had her next chapter heading.

'Listen, stay over. I'll fly you to Toronto in the morning. And maybe rustle up a fighter escort.'

'He's that dangerous?'

'He's that dangerous. Take out extra life cover ' Harry dipped to the tape recorder. 'I never said that. Quote: Max Magnus is a real wonderful human being. Unquote.' He depressed the pause button. 'Max Magnus.' He sucked air through clenched teeth. 'Have you met the guy?'

'Has anyone? He's just a sincere Aberdonian accent on the phone. Used to call Toby now and again to add a few million to his standing offer for the Mercury.'

'Did Toby's boat blow up just before he rang?'

'No, Harry.'

'Just after?'

'No, Harry.'

Marina looked hard at him. Like all the others, the Chacewater chapter was going to be one for the psychiatrist's casebook.

'He sure blew up our *Miss Print II*. Then rang to warn Pa off bidding for a chain of papers in Maine. Been manoeuvring to gobble up Chacewater Inc. ever since.'

Through the open windows they began to hear someone whistling *Dixie*, in perfect pitch. Harry got to his feet as Honey Chacewater fell up the steps and gasped out the message. Harry went to plug in the phone.

'Gosh, Marina.' Claudia was in a state. 'Thought they'd never ever reach you. Going to pee myself any minute.'

'That what you rang to tell me?'

'Listen, we've got a new editor – Jack Stack. He's saying the Merc's going to be a multiple orgasm every day.'

'Jack Stack? I can't believe it.'

'Please yourself. He's about to pull down your office – '

'Is he fuck.'

' – and bring in a new First Lady of Fleet Street. Quote: Born of the age we live in and sexy with it. He says you're dead as a dildo.'

'Dodo.'

'I'm telling you what he says, OK?'

'Hang about, darling – you sure it's not a wind-up?'

'Marina, it's for real. God knows who he's moving in, but he's asking Lord Snowman to take her byline portrait.'

'Snowman? That does it. Cancel Toronto. Book me on the morning Concorde home. And cancel Olly and Nolly. Disney World will have to wait.'

'Not again? Poor little chaps.'

'I'll make it up to them. Take them to Wimbledon.'

'They absolutely loathed it last time.'

'Did they? Fix for the Jag to pick me up. And for my solicitor to be in it with a copy of my contract – '

'Right.'

' – and a blank pad of death warrants.'

'See you tomorrow then.'

'Bless you, Claudia. Now skip to the loo, my darling, before it's too late.'

'It is too late.'

3

Holy Effin Communion

Jack Stack's permasmile glowed as his audience of conference executives shuffled in. Nine jacketless men and three jacketed women sagged into the old leather couches lining the walls, and set legs sideways to maintain laps horizontal enough for clipboards and notepads.

They were followed by an overalled man parading a mounted blow-up of the Mercury's red-top debut front page. He banged a hook into the wall behind the editor, squared up the picture and clapped approval on behalf of the non-editorial underclass, no longer working for a paper they wouldn't pay to read.

TINA'S ROYAL WEATHERCOCK updated the new editor's CV, which already occupied the opposite wall. Illustrating a dozen Fleet Street years refreshed by a Florida sabbatical on the National Exposer, it proclaimed his genius at producing tabloids throbbing with pizzazz, phwoaar, glee and gorblimey. There were Jack Stack classics from the Echo, the News and the Globe: blockbuster spreads, knockout Page Threes, grabber Page Ones. His patent 'double ejaculation mark' qualifying **END OF THE WORLD!!** reflected concern for readers of a nervous disposition who might not guess that the story was England's World Cup soccer elimination.

On the drinks cabinet stood twin Editor of the Year awards, with photos of him being presented with one by Prime Minister Beth Macbeth and the other by the Prince of Wales. The PM, eyes open, was giving Jack Stack a kiss. HRH, eyes shut, was granting a handshake at arm's length.

Conference watched as the editor opened a humidor and picked out a Havana. This he sniffed, rolled, listened to, disavowed – and put back to take another. This he sniffed, rolled, listened to, approved – and decapitated, seared and sucked at, taking his time as though that of his department heads had no value. He made smoke idly for a few moments more before coming round to take the apron stage for his one-man show.

From his desk, he lifted last week's Marina Marshall spread, holding it away between thumb and finger as he made a performance of letting it float to the floor.

'Absolute crap.'

He scoffed and, since editors do not scoff alone, the four executives who had come over with him joined in. The old-regime colleagues, who had thought the piece delicious, wondered whether they would survive the day.

'Swans off for a millionaire fortnight in America. And fits in this Brits-on-Broadway bollocks so she can stick us with the bill. Who gives a stuff about Dame Betty Bottyface, aged 75? Sell more papers with three actresses aged twenty-five—'

The phone went. It was his secretary, who had been told to ring at ten-past and just listen.

'What? Humpty's bloody secretary says what?...Tell her to put the moron on the line.' He blew smoke as he waited. 'Listen, Hump. One – my conference is as uninterruptible as holy effin communion. Two – never, ever, summon me to your presence. Three – don't try power games with me, sunshine. I wrote the bleeding book.'

Jack Stack banged his phone down. Outside, his secretary looked at hers as though it had bitten her. Applause sounded through the closed door. The Mercury had never known such a display of editorial supremacy. The ex-Globe quartet clapped hardest, having shared Jack Stack's humiliation at Lord Bull's frequent ploy of sending for him in mid-conference.

'Have to spell it out to that plonker. Told him, Hump, she's past her sell-by. Know what he said? Can't sack the mother of the chairman's twins, Jack. She's on a ten-year rolling contract, Jack. God, what a scam. Fat-cat salary geared to the Swiss franc – and by now treble that of the prime minister. Penthouse flat on Green Park. Chauffeured white Jag. Personal-assistant-actually. Personal car for the personal-assistant-actually. Company gold cards. Trips all over the known world – as the result of which she is on first-name terms with every Concorde pilot, second pilot and chief steward in the sky and every five-star maître d' on the ground. Fabulous office, complete with bidet and chaise longue, and immediately identified by Bish here – a man who knows about these things – as a tart's boudoir. Right?'

Clop, went Bish.

'And that's not all, folks. Marina wrung out of poor Toby the right to fill her Thursday spread with any old doodoo she chooses – never mind the bloody editor. To dictate the headlines – never mind the bloody editor. To select the pictures – never mind the bloody editor. To veto the layouts – never mind the bloody editor. Listen Jack, said Hump, you can't touch her. Listen Hump, said Jack, we can't stop the sacred cow walking out when I give her sacred spread to the one and only Heidi Hunt.'

Who Heidi Hunt? The ex-Globe executives knew. The soon-to-be ex-Mercury executives did not, since they hardly glanced at the red-tops. They glanced at each other. Who Heidi Hunt? And they glanced at Jack Stack, to find him already glancing at them like an arrow at a target.

'Heidi Hunt, the Poet Laureate? Nah. Heidi Hunt, the three-time winner of the Nobel prize for literature? Nah. *That* Heidi Hunt – '

He levelled his cigar at the wall displaying his last Globe blurb. The page was dominated by an unashamed borrowing of the classic Tennis Girl poster, with Heidi sporting impish cheeks. The blurb shrieked:

HERE COMES HEIDI HUNT!!
Fasten your seat belts for
a dazzling new Globe column
by a dazzling new Globe talent.

Make a date every Wednesday
with the Adventures of Heidi Hunt.
She's the new First Lady of
Fleet Street. Born of the age we
live in and sexy with it.

'Tomorrow we run that same page in the Merc – with two minor improvements. For Globe, read Mercury. For Wednesday, read Thursday. And, Eddie – ' the cigar jabbed at the picture editor.

'Boss?'

'You're getting Snowman to do a classy portrait for the Heidi byline, right?'

'Right, boss.' Eddie trembled for fifty per cent more pay than he trembled at the Globe. He had yet to get beyond Lord Snowman's answering machine.

The editor's phone rang again.

'...Sure. Put her on.' Jack Stack flipped the loudspeaker switch so they could all listen.

'Morning, Jack.' The headmistressy tones of Beth Macbeth straightened slumped spines all round the room.

'Morning to you, Prime Minister.'

'Want to wish you the best of British. Great challenge. Great opportunity.'

'Trust you to find time for a kind word when you've got the world on your plate.' He put a hand over the mouthpiece. 'And a general election any day, ho-ho.'

'Off to Rome – as you were, Paris – in two ticks. We must talk soon. You're my line to the great British public.'

'Beth, I'm with you all the way. No other bugger's got your vision. Your guts.' Again, he muffled the phone. 'Your balls.'

'Look, pop down to Chequers on Saturday. Must fly. Bye.'

'No can do, Beth. Aussies at Lord's. Make it Sunday. Bye.'

Jack Stack milked the moment as he studied the prematurely expired end of his cigar. Bish sprang to take it from him, knocked an inch of ash into the bowl, handed it back and lit the required match.

'Shouldn't be leaping around at his age.' Jack Stack spoke through smoke.

The phone again.

'Palace press secretary. Says it's urgent.'

'OK...Morning, Admiral.'

'You alone, Jack?'

'Sure.' He mimed a chortle as the loudspeaker broadcast Admiral St John Standfast's confidences.

'Don't want to be a pain in the stern, Jack. But about your TV Tina story. Seven times? HRH was only alone with her for four minutes.'

'Wish we'd known. Better story.'

'HRH swears she's a liar.'

'But is HRH ready to swear it in the High Court? Because Tina will sue for libel if we slag her off.'

'Jesus. If I go back with that answer, I'll be flogged round the fleet.'

'Can't have that, Admiral. Want me to run a clarification? Palace asks us to make clear that the Prince of Wales shagged Tina only the once. No problem.'

'No thanks.'

'Listen, take my advice – tell them the Merc's done Nicky a favour. Pulled the chain on all that nudge-nudge confirmed bachelor gossip in the quote-unquote quality press.'

'I'll buy that. Let's lunch. Friday at Boodle's?'

'Make it McDonald's. I've got a reputation to think of.'

The moment Jack Stack grounded the phone his secretary interrupted holy effin communion once again.

'BBC on the line. MPs screaming about intrusion into the private lives of the young royals. *World at One* want to interview you.'

'Bollocks. I don't speak to journalists. They twist everything. Tell the Beeb I'm addressing the nation on Page One tomorrow. I'll fax it to them in an hour – and they have my permission to quote the lot.' He replaced the phone. 'OK, Bish. Headline: **OUR FREEDOM IN PERIL**.'

Clop, went Bish as he made a note.

'Nah' – Jack Stack shook his head – 'that's not it. New headline: **YOUR FREEDOM IN PERIL**. First par: Let MPs dictate what you are allowed to read about Royal Highnesses today – and MPs will dictate what you are allowed to say about Royal Highnesess tomorrow. Second par: Would Nicky's behaviour improve if he could keep it out of the press? Third par: Fat chance...'

Twenty minutes later, all but the senior executives shuffled out, their schedules derided with an invitation to come up with something fantastic for afternoon conference or swap jobs with their deputies.

Clop, went Bish as he set up six glasses on the drinks cabinet. From the fridge he took a bottle of champagne and ceremoniously uncorked it.

'Highest-paid barman in Fleet Street,' said the editor.

The men laughed. So, in spite of herself, did Maria-Teresa, the all-in-black associate editor with the naked face. Things were improving in one respect: Francis Franklin CBE had looked to her

23

to do the pouring. But she wasn't planning to stick around. Even into the twenty-first century, editorship of a national daily was widely regarded as an unnatural job for a woman. She needed a publisher with a Sunday paper chair.

Women had come a long way in her fifteen years in the Street. That old double-glazed ceiling was crack'd from side to side, though those women who crack'd it were seen as very much blokes of the other sex. They displayed and demanded the same widow-making 24/7 commitment. They raged and bullied like backbench gladiators of legend. But they had beavered up through features rather than news – and news remained the big difference. News was why dailies were daily. And news was macho still. News was hard. News was hairy. News was right now, darling; shouldering aside your lovingly gift-wrapped pages, violating your immaculate conceptions. If women could bring themselves to get off on news and not wish it would fuck off, every throne in Fleet Street might be theirs.

'Tell me, Ma Teresa' – Jack Stack had been mocking her name since she rolled her eyes at his weathercock headline – 'why don't you wear make-up? After a part in a video nasty?'

'Already got one.'

'Here' – he beckoned her to his screen – 'be my guest. The Adventures of Heidi Hunt. You'll love it.'

'You're slipping, Jack.' Tsk-tsk. '*My night as a lap-dance star* – and you've got her with her hands over her tits?'

'Eddie?' The cigar stabbed at the picture editor.

The man trembled as heads swivelled to him. 'Shooting it again tonight, boss. I'll have my best man there.'

'Make it two best men,' said Jack Stack. 'One per tit.'

The heads swivelled to Maria-Teresa.

'Grow up, Jack. You're talking about a woman, not a piece of meat. Someone's daughter. Someone's sister.'

'And you, Ma Teresa, are talking like someone offered a twenty grand rise to join the Globe – right? Someone playing for a pay-off from me in the bargain – right?'

He was right all right. She had sent Lord Bull her dummy for improving his Sunday Globe. Impressed, he had invited her over as No. 2 on the daily. Unimpressed, Jack Stack had persuaded her she'd be a fool not to hang on for the pay-off that could wipe out the mortgage on her Barbican flat. But that was then. This was now.

She watched as he dialled his old private line number to reach his successor at the Globe.

'Pissed again, Kev?'

'Never mind, Jack. So am I.'

'How about an exchange of prisoners? Your clapped-out sports editor for my multi-talented associate editor.'

'Pay her off, Jack – and it's a deal.'

'Done.'

'Lucky you. She could take your job.'

'Lucky you. She goes like a train.'

As he put the phone down and made going-like-a-train motions at her, Maria-Teresa reversed two decades of downward modulation.

'You – you sad little man.'

'Sad? Little? Bollocks.'

'I'll take your word for it.'

Maria-Teresa turned to walk out. Jack Stack put two fingers up to her back. They were still up as she turned at the door and strode to challenge him head to head across his desk.

'I'm going to do you for sexual harassment.'

'Not if you ever want to be an editor, you aren't.'

'Rotten shit.'

She lifted a glass from the desk and hurled the contents at him. She missed, splattering Bish, who went clop.

'Rotten shot.'

Jack Stack raised his glass to her, took a sip and threw the rest in her face. Tears raced the champagne down her cheeks as she turned and stumbled out.

'One down.' He pushed his chair back. 'One to go.'

He led the way to the door. The team followed, shoulders slouched, necks shortened and legs buckled within trousers to avoid looking taller than the boss. He ground a heel into the Marina Marshall byline picture on the spread that still lay where he had dropped it.

Back at Jack Stack's flat, a size eight blonde was yawning in his bed. She stretched an arm, edging aside a cigar box as she fetched the bedside clock into focus. Christ, 12.35. Not that she would be late for work. She was at work. She had been since she buzzed his entryphone last night and said she needed a hand with her column, and he said what a coincidence.

Heidi Hunt sat up in his pyjama top and waved to her reflection in the dressing-table mirror. She was so happy that he wasn't leaving her at the Globe to write her dazzling new column all by herself. She could do with a bit of help with the words. It was only two weeks since he had talent-spotted her shuffling handouts in the showbiz department.

She found him terrifying but lovely with it. She appreciated that unexpected snooze before midnight while he devoured a mountain of rival early editions, along with champagne and a Corona. He made the usual demands of her only after much time on both phones making unusual demands of his night editor, news editor, features editor, sports editor and picture editor.

Heidi used his bathroom, where two Airwicks lay slumped in defeat. Peeking into the medicine cabinet, she counted five varieties of hair growth promoter. How come so many little guys with deep-pile chests were thin on top? She moved on to mix instant decaf and take one of his Globe mugs for a tour of the flat.

The fluorescent sitting room – all mirrors, crystal and chrome – was like the inside of a bookie's cocktail cabinet. Nosing around, Heidi came to a side-table drawer with a few family photos. She drew out one of a proud couple with a boy of about eleven. Both lad in Scout uniform and dad in clerical collar had the look of Jack Stack. Another, a dozen or so years on, showed that same trio plus an almond-eyed bride. Then a picture postcard from Singapore. Heidi turned it over: *Did you even notice I'd gone?*

She picked up a phone and fed in his number.

'Me, Jack. Must have overslept. Oo-er.'

'That's OK, star. You're working late tonight. Those lap-dance club pix didn't come out. This time, we'll have our two best men there.'

4

Bullseye

With Harry at the controls, the Chacewater Inc. helicopter lifted off the croquet lawn. The Chacewater Inc. 757 would be at Richmond to fly Marina to Washington, and Concorde would have her back in London in three hours forty minutes.

'See our pool?' He leaned to her ear as they circled his estate. 'When Harry C the First played host to George Washington, that used to be the kitchen block.'

'Quite a hike to the dining hall.'

'Which is why he had the waiters whistle 'Amazing Grace' all the way. Can't whistle and nibble at the same time, right?'

Harry diverted over the Second Fleet base at Norfolk to show Marina the USS *Enterprise*, the massive carrier from which he had flown Hornets.

'There – the Big E. Ain't she something? A movie star too. Top Gun. That's what I did. Used to call me Bullseye.'

'Think they'd have you back, Harry?'

'Think Mom'd let 'em?' He banked low over a pine-clad island, startling herons out of the marshes. 'Say hi to Jamestown. Pocahontas country. Where the first English colony took root. Where we really all began.'

'Not the way they tell it in New England.'

'Oldest Yankee lie, ma'am. We'd been up and running thirteen years before *Mayflower*. Could have been there waiting on Plymouth Rock. Hi, Pilgrim Daddies! Welcome to the New World. Have a nice day.'

As Concorde levelled out ten miles above the Atlantic, Marina settled into the inky-blue leather. These people were her scene:

Who's Who, Rich List and The Ivy, but for the odd long-haul hooker and incentivised time-share salesman. She could expect hi-Marinas from a dozen celebs, most still wondering just how they had enabled her column on them to be quite so revealing.

In 20C and 20D, dear Sir David was running through tonight's talk show with dear Sir Mick. In 4C, dear Lady T was warheading a speech to nuke her latest successor's election prospects. Up front in 1A was dear Rupert, already a powerful chapter in her book. Alongside sat dear Dr K, who seemed to be giving him the lecture on shuttle diplomacy he had given her. And darling Joanie was in her usual 12D – right by the toilets so she wouldn't have to stand in line to re-gild her face for the Heathrow cameras. Well, we all had our re-entry problems. For the First Lady of Fleet Street, it was coming down to the world of Jack Stack.

Lifting her bag to the empty seat beside her, Marina took out laptop and tape recorder to work on the Chacewater chapter. She fitted an earphone to play back the cassette of dinner last night with a very different Harry to the guy in the bandstand. Their candle-lit corner at the Tidewater Inn, the Krug on ice, the Haut-Brion decanted and the Armagnac warmish had encouraged the unbuttoned dialogue she was after. She tapped the keyboard:

Harry's hand flew towards my lap when much too much of my wrapover evening skirt unwrapped as I fitted myself into his red Ferrari. Was this why they called him Bullseye? Nope. He wrapped the skirt over again. Was he out to wreck my Con Fuoco *chapter? That decadent* ante-bellum *look had gone with the wind. Here was an earnest suit, button-down white shirt and shiny shoes. Ten minutes at the barber and you couldn't have told him apart from those naval officers over there, boyishly celebrating not being civilians.*

'...I'd have made lieutenant-commander by now. Maybe one-star admiral before they beached me. And been a darn sight happier fella.'

'You seem a pretty happy fella tonight.'

'That's on account of you... you picking up the tab.'

'Come on, you're not a bit happy with me insisting my American Express card will do as nicely as yours.'

'I'm not a bit happy with anyone calling the shots.'

'In particular?'

'In particular, Mom. Put the heat on me to quit the Navy. Still can't forgive her. Pa wasn't going to let me run anything. I was shipped out to the bureaus for a year. New York, LA, Miami. Frigging in the rigging until Pa dropped dead...'

By then, Harry' had frigged overlong. There was polo and there were chukka babes. Yacht-racing and regatta babes. Skiing and piste babes. And babes and babes. He reckons that if he goes without for three days it gives him backache.

He had also tippled overlong. I find it difficult to picture him without a Rebel Yell in hand.

Harry didn't have the fifth-generation heart to throw out that first-generation pigeonhole desk and all it symbolised about Chacewater Inc. Easier to throw himself out. He fled from the torrent of printout. He left unread the avalanche of newspapers and magazines from across the state, the nation and the globe.

He had his traffic reduced to need-to-know summaries, maximum one side of one sheet of A4. He delegated all he unreasonably could to the legendary Ed – that's Edgar Segal, aged 80 – and the other old faithfuls who'd promised the dying king they would watch over the unready Prince Hal. The legendary Ed saved it for Harry's Pa and looks like having to save it for Harry.

The fear was, and is, that Harry will sell his holding that keeps the family in control. And they do not fancy their chances of surviving a new regime bound to see potential way beyond the horizons of old man Chacewater or the capacity of young man Chacewater. They go along with his disinclination to attend the office daily, or even for whole days. They accept his rejection of the mobile phone that would enable them to consult their president any time, any place. That matters less to Harry than being let alone (which usually means not alone). Aboard Miss Print IV. Or on the bandstand. There to confirm his faith in the pulling power of Opus 20, though the parade of pushovers at his feet, his fly and his fortune would spread as eagerly for the Woody Woodpecker song.

'...Hey, I told those guys, I'd sooner let Max Magnus in than let you put a ring through my nose...'

Nothing Harry said to me displayed much insight into publishing. Everything he said begged the question: what is such a man doing in this jungle? He has no hunger for power. No thirst for *blood. No appetite for mischief. No need for money. As a publisher, Harry is a meal lying in wait for a tiger.*

He's in the wrong game, all right. I don't think he told me a fib all the hours I was with him. He is honour-code to a fault: an Annapolis halo is, alas, a cosmopolis noose. His self-mockery is enchanting, and very often fully justified. He is well travelled, well read and, by all accounts, well hung. It was clearly routine politeness (I don't flatter myself) to present me with the opportunity to make my own appraisal. He really has been spoiled by too many forgettable females. If he remembers me, it'll be because I hit him where it hurt most. In the bandstand . . .

Marina lifted fingers from keys but continued to watch the screen as though her thoughts were continuing to appear. She laughed at herself for wondering if he might yet be redeemable. Oh, yes, and just who might do the redeeming? And would that be before or after the *Con Fuoco* chapter hit the fan?

She fished from her bag the packet Harry had slipped in as he said goodbye with a Navy salute and a peck on the cheek. His gift was a CD of Mendelssohn's *Midsummer Night's Dream*. His note said:

I will remember you by this piece. Especially those woodwind chords. They make me dizzy with delight. I never heard anything like them. And I never met a woman like you.

Marina Marshall added it to her chapter.

A sheaf of gladioli was thrust at her as she came from the fast-track Concorde channel at Heathrow.

'My dear Marina,' said the bald, round solicitor with the hairy Adam's apple.

'My dear Arnold,' she said. 'Such gorgeous gladdies. You sure I can afford them?'

Her chauffeur held open the door of the Jaguar and relieved her of the gladioli in exchange for that morning's Mercury. Arnold savoured the scent of her as they moved off and she homed in on the Heidi blurb:

'"Here comes Heidi Hunt!!" Two exclamation marks, for fuck's sake. "Dazzling new Thursday column. Dazzling new talent."' She pitched the paper into Arnold's lap. '"The new First Lady of Fleet Street." God almighty, he's burying me alive.'

And God almighty, looking at that Heidi picture was like looking at herself twenty years ago.

'You,' he said, 'need a solicitor.'

'I,' she said, 'need a contract killer.'

'So who'd draw up the contract?' Arnold patted her arm. 'Pity you weren't my client earlier. I'd have sealed that unfortunate gap in your own contract.'

'Unfortunate gap?'

'No Jekyll-and-Hyde clause. Sure, you're laughing if they sack you. But you don't have the right to elect for a pay-off on change of regime. New owners...paper going downmarket... hostile editor.'

'Does that leave Jack Stack free to call someone else the First Lady of Fleet Street? Pull down my office? Pronounce me dead as a dildo?'

'Dodo.'

'I'm telling you what he said.'

'My bet is that he simply can't get Humpty to write you a seven-figure cheque. So he has to provoke a walk out.'

'My bet is that the switch to red-top will fail. The Merc will be gobbled up by Max Magnus or whoever – and the options Toby gave me will make my fortune. But they come and go with the job. So, no matter what Jack Stack does, I'm not walking, am I?'

'Listen.' Arnold raised a hairy hand. 'First thing tomorrow, I deliver a letter to Humpty demanding that he repudiate his editor's clear intention to destroy you.' He wagged a hairy finger. 'I warn that if no such undertaking is received by noon we go for a High Court injunction.' He shook a hairy fist. 'I spell out that we'll be after monumental damages for conspiracy and aggravated breach of contract.'

'Sounds great to me, Arnold. But I've flown back to confront Jack Stack. And confront Jack Stack is what I'm bloody going to do.'

'Be careful.'

'There's always a first time.'

Marina took Harry's Mendelssohn CD from her bag and loaded it into the player. The Chicago Symphony Orchestra began to fill the car. 'Listen for those woodwind chords. They'll make you dizzy with delight.'

'There's always a first time.'

'Well?'

'Was that it, then?' Arnold displayed neither dizziness nor delight.

'The response I'm used to is – I never heard anything like it before, and I never met a woman like you.'

As they emerged from the Heathrow tunnel back into early evening sunlight, Marina closed her eyes and did not open them for almost twenty minutes. Then she laughed as the soprano came in with 'You spotted snakes with double tongue...Come not near our fairy queen.'

'Huh!' Marina picked up the car phone and called the spotted snakepit.

'Hi, Claudia. I'll be swinging my handbag at Jack Stack in fifteen minutes.'

'Hard luck, darling. He just lurched off.'

'Shit. I could have been on a yacht in Chesapeake Bay with a billionaire bachelor who fancies me something rotten. Are you sure Jack hasn't just popped out for his kebab and double chips?'

'Said he was going to his club.'

'Club? People like him don't have clubs. Listen Claudia, tell his secretary I'll be in to castrate him at ten in the morning. Anything else?'

'Max Magnus phoned to say how sad you had to cancel. Kindest regards and would you call him.'

'Glad somebody loves me.' He'd be itching to hear what she had from Harry that might be turned to advantage. And eager for her update on the state of play at his other known target: the Mercury.

'He's not the only one. About a million roses just arrived. All yellow.'

'And the card says?'

'I'll be in London for the Ambassador's Fourth of July party. And for Harry's Fifth of July party. Please be my guest. Can hardly wait to see you again.'

'Mmmm. Have to check if I'm free.'

'Smitten, is he?'

'Head over heels.'

5

The Spoiler

Jack Stack had scoffed when the Globe first edition was biked to him last night. The splash was 'close friends' of the Prince of Wales rubbishing TV Tina's story. It looked pathetic against the Mercury's own follow-up, triumphantly putting her through a lie detector test – and challenging HRH to take one.

But when the finals dropped this morning, the Globe had struck back. Alongside the title was a panel displaying a cigar-chomping head of Jack Stack and the cross-ref: *Boss who made office girl strip for promotion!! Exclusive Page 7*. Dominating that page were the champagne glasses and champagne grins of Jack Stack's lap-dance club table as the spotlit Heidi Hunt swished her diamanté bra at the audience.

Clop, went Bish as he studied the story over the editor's shoulder:

HEIDI'S CAREER
IS TAKING OFF!!
By Rosie Gee

Blonde office girl Heidi Hunt, 22, bared all for promotion last night. Her boss had challenged her to show what she was made of.

She did a guest spot at a smart Soho lap-dance club. And got a big hand from balding boss Jack Stack, 37, and his party of male executives from a London rubbish recycling factory.

Heidi's reward? An office with her name on the door, a bigger pay cheque and a smaller mobile phone.

Said Heidi: 'I also get to keep these diamanté knickers. Jack said they'd go down on expenses.

'It was fun. The girls taught me the tricks of the trade. Like perking up my nipples with an ice cube.

'Yes, I suppose my mum Tara, 44, would tear me off a strip. But I was only showing my initiative.'

Said dad Gustav, 49, a karate instructor in Hornchurch, Essex: 'I'll be having a word with that Stack bloke.' He declined to say what the word was...

'Trust Ma Teresa to tip them off,' said Jack Stack. 'There's gratitude for you. She can forget that pay-off.'

He dialled his successor at the Globe.

'Kev, you're a disgrace to journalism.'

'Screw you, Jack. You'd do the same.'

'No I bloody wouldn't. I'd give it the whole of Page One. Sorry, Kev, old son – you're never going to make it as a serious editor.'

He buzzed his secretary to get him the director-general of the industry's pet watchdog, the Press Complaints Commission.

'Morning, DG,' said Jack Stack in a Yorkshire accent. 'This is Reg Bishop, deputy editor of the Merc – '

Clop, went Bish.

' – complaining about the Globe story. Under Clause 1 for distortion and failing to distinguish between conjecture and fact. Clause 2 for denying a fair reply. Clause 3 for breach of privacy. Can't a man pop into his club without his face being plastered all over the gutter press? Mrs Bishop went mad – '

Mr Bishop went clop.

' – Clause 4 for harassment. Clause 5 for intrusion into grief... Where's the grief? Having the editor's personal double ejaculation mark nicked by jackdaw journalism – the man's inconsolable. Clause 11 for subterfuge. That Rosie Gee didn't tell Miss Hunt she was a reporter... What do you mean – have we complained to the Globe? That's like the police asking have we complained to the burglar.'

Clop, went Bish as the phone went down.

'Didn't mind, did you? Couldn't complain myself. I'm on the bloody Commission.'

Bish readied notebook and pen for battle orders.

'That Rosie Gee. Smart operator. Hire her.'

'Rosie? She's knocking on 60.'

'Well hire her – and fire her.'

Clop, went Bish.

'Now... we're not going to dignify their spoiler with a reply, are we? Let Heidi's brilliant spread speak for itself. An award-winning insight into the psyche of the skin game today. Significant. Compelling. And with diagrams. Ice cubes, eh? What do you use?'

'Oxo cubes.'

'We'll have the strippers baring their souls to Heidi. But don't be sexist. We're talking about women, not pieces of meat. Someone's daughter. Someone's sister. Marvellous stuff – can hardly wait to read it.'

Clop. Can hardly wait to write it.

The editor riffled through the Heidi pictures and pushed one under Bish's nose.

'Her dad's a karate instructor,' said Bish.

'Yeah, well.' The editor settled for an earlier frame, with diamanté thong still in place. 'Run her the full depth of the page.'

'Life size.'

The editor held out his empty glass. The deputy editor filled it, and one for himself.

'You haven't got time for that, Bish. Get moving. And make it sing. Heidi needs a little technical assistance on the writing side. Get a journalist to interview her.'

Clop.

'Hell, Jack.' Humpty quivered on the intercom. 'Just had Lord Bull on. Laughing his fat head off.'

'Laugh even more if he could hear you. Don't panic, Hump. I'm on my way.'

Secretary Maxine was waiting, hands as ever at prayer, when the lift doors opened. She wrinkled her nose at the advancing cigar and pointed to the no-smoking sign.

'No problem, kid.' He handed her the remaining five inches of his Havana. 'Look after it for me. Don't be afraid to give it the kiss of life.'

Humpty was standing before the crested firescreen, flapping hands at his back and blinking behind his bifocals. The rattle of the roof garden lawnmower came through the french windows.

'God.' He marched to his desk and tapped the Globe's Page Seven. 'Worse every time I read it.'

'Not going to fall for that, are you, Hump? Cheap attempt to discredit me. Johnnie Bull's shit-scared of what I'm doing for the Merc.'

Johnnie Bull wasn't the only one. 'All lies, you mean?'

'Worse. It's a spoiler.'

'I see.'

He didn't. He couldn't. Jack Stack was the Mercury's first editor to generate thunder worth stealing. The chief executive sat and counted his cufflinks as the editor, flattering him by waiving simultaneous translation, delivered an address on the art and mystery of the Fleet Street spoiler. The ecstasy of zapping an enemy project and seeing all that investment of time and money, energy and emotion, crumple on the launchpad. The agony of having it done unto you. The glee of converting their spoiler into your trailer – which was just what he was about to do to unspoil Heidi Hunt's dazzling debut.

'Well, there we are,' said Humpty, who now knew better than to offer an editorial judgement.

Maxine burst through the double doors with the letter from Marina's solicitor.

'Mr Baynard, you'll want to see this right away.'

'Christ, Jack' – Humpty paled as he read – 'what are you doing to me?' He shoved across the desk Arnold's letter, with its attached copy of Marina's service agreement. 'Breach of contract . . . conspiracy . . . injunction . . . monumental damages . . .'

Jack Stack took in the four-page document at the speed of a High Court judge. He recognised that he wasn't going to be able to kill off Marina with one blow. It was going to take at least two.

'Monumental bollocks.' He shoved the letter back.

'I can't reply, *Monumental bollocks*.'

'Hump, you asked me to sort things out with her when she got back – remember? That's exactly what I'm doing. She's on her way in now for a cuppa. I'll have her eating out of my hand – and do you a reply before conference, OK?'

'But what's all this about demolishing her office?'

'Told you, I need a bigger newsroom.'

'Steady on. We produced a broadsheet in the existing space. Surely we can do a tabloid.'

'Leave the gags to me, Hump.'

'This is no joking matter.'

'Oh, yes it is.'

Humpty smacked his forehead, once in despair and once for inspiration. Jack Stack was inspired.

'Doesn't say her office has to be on my floor.' He waved the contract. 'So move it up one. Tell her the council's condemned the plumbing. An eel could come up her bidet.'

Humpty's eyes followed the editor's exit. He looked at the letter again and smacked his forehead again.

As Jack Stack came out, Maxine picked his still-burning cigar from its perch and held it out.

'Thanks, kid,' he said, taking it like a relay baton and tapping ash on to her carpet.

On the fifth floor, the advertisement director was phoning the media chief of a top-ten agency:

'...Trust me, Barry. You can schedule autumn with absolute confidence. Your clients will love you – getting a quarter-million more readers than they're paying for...No, I wouldn't categorise us as dumbing down. More widening our appeal. Now, to serious matters. I'd love you to be my guest at the Arc de Triomphe. On condition you bring the lovely Lucy...OK, the even lovelier Olga...'

On the fourth floor, the circulation director was phoning the MD of a nationwide chain of newsagents:

'...Over the moon, Stu. At last I've convinced Humpty the only way to increase circulation is to sell more papers. Get Jack Stack, I said. He'll never come, he said. Will if I ask him, I said. Been mates for years. Knew him when he only had one eyebrow...'

Marina Marshall was in her dressing room preparing for the ten o'clock showdown. In a buttonhole of her designer-camouflage combat suit, she planted one of Harry Chacewater's yellow roses. She looked to the mirrors for approval, and got it.

'Surprise, surprise,' said Claudia. 'His secretary just rang to put us off for twenty minutes.'

Marina groaned. The delay would give him an exit line five minutes later on the grounds that he couldn't keep a dozen highly paid executives waiting for conference.

'Assholes to that,' she said. 'The moment I go round his corner, ring her to say you can't find me.'

She charged through the editor's door while his secretary was taking Claudia's call. He was leaning back in his chair, feet up on the desk. He looked round them at her.

'Long time, no see,' he said.

'Not long enough,' she said. 'Only ten years.'

'Still the same old Marina. But never mind.'

She took the chair facing him. He put his feet down and swivelled full circle, pausing at the cupboard behind him to collect a bottle and two flute glasses.

'Hardly a champagne occasion.' She flapped dismissively.

'I could put the kettle on.'

'Jack, I haven't broken the sound barrier to discuss fuck-all squared over a Nescafé.'

'Wasn't expecting you back for a couple of weeks.'

'I know you weren't, you rascal. By then you'd have crowned Heidi Hunt the First Lady of Fleet Street.'

'Who feeds you this bollocks?'

'You do.' She thumped the paper on his desk. 'That's what it says in your bloody blurb.'

'Oh, no.' Jack Stack shook his head as he read. 'The berk.' He flipped the intercom. 'Bish, you shit-brained old fart. Dropped me right in it. I told you to call Heidi the First Lady in her Globe blurb last week, didn't I? I did not tell you to do it in her Merc blurb this week, did I? Marina's here, spitting blood. And I don't blame her. She could walk out any minute. If she does, mate, you'll follow her through the door – '

'He got the day wrong too, Jack. Thursday's mine.'

'And Heidi's Wednesdays, you twat. Thursdays are Marina's. Everyone knows that.'

He uncorked the champagne anyway and poured for two anyway. She shook her head. He raised both glasses.

'Here's to you, Marina.' He sipped at one and raised the other. 'And here's to your solicitor. What's he charge for threatening letters?'

'Less than you're paying Snowman to snap Heidi.'

'More bollocks. It's not Heidi I want Snowman to do, sweetheart. It's you.'

'Oh, yeah?' Her eyebrows were question marks.

'Give us a break, Marina. I'm trying to be tactful.'

'Don't you dare.'

'Believe me, I speak as your greatest living fan. That old picture dates you. Doe eyes, for God's sake.'

'And when I phone my old friend Tony Snowman, he'll confirm that it's me you've asked him to do?'

'Jesus, Marina, it was only an idea.' He threw up his hands. 'I wouldn't approach your old friend without first getting your OK, would I?'

'You're a fucking liar.'

'You do need a drink. Here.'

'Stuff it. What about the dazzling new column...the dazzling new talent...the dazzling new bum.'

'The dazzling annual set-piece bollocks on the Soho scene, that's all.' He yawned. 'Yawn-yawn.'

'I did enjoy the Globe spoiler.'

'If you're happy, I'm happy.'

'I will be once my lawyer gets the letter we want.'

'In his hot little hand by noon. Promise.' He turned to his computer, stroked a few keys to call up tonight's Page Five, and beckoned to her over his shoulder. 'Take a look. Four-column shadow box. Your old Snowman pic, with stamp edging, top right. Looks like a postcard home. And – in copperplate – our message to the readers: *Marina Marshall, the one and only First Lady of Fleet Street, is on holiday. Her irreplaceable Thursday column will be back soon.*

'No double exclamation mark for me?'

'In copperplate?' He rolled his eyes like an art editor. 'You're a class act, kid. Oasis of culture in a desert of titillation and botillation.'

'You said it, Jack.'

'You and me, Marina – we'll make a great team.'

'Don't hold your breath.'

'And thanks for saving Bish's job. Never get another one at his age. You're a real pro, Marina.'

She went to the door, opening it, shutting it behind her and opening it again to deliver a parting shot.

'Oh, and you can pick up the bill for repairing my holiday. See you in a fortnight – if you last that long.'

Heidi Hunt had been waiting on the couch in the secretary's office outside. She rose for Jack Stack like Venus for Botticelli. Tongue curled under chipmunk teeth as she smoothed dinky skirt and tugged shrinky top towards winky navel.

'Oo-er,' said Heidi to Marina.

'Been at the ice cubes, I see,' said Marina to Heidi.

6

The Firing Squad

Heads bent to keyboards as Jack Stack swooped the length of the newsroom. Bish caught up as he fell upon a mouse of a man waiting at the vending machine for milk to trickle into his coffee.

'Small world,' said the editor.

'Too sodding small,' said the mouse. He had found refuge on the Mercury Postbag Page three months ago when Jack Stack fired him from the Globe Postbag Page.

'What was it you called me on your way out that time?'

'Can't remember.'

'Pity. You could call me it on your way out this time.'

After two weeks of Jack Stack, the editorial floor was heavy with fear. You could smell it. The run of sackings, early retirements, redundancies, demotions and internal exile proclaimed how unwise it was to displease the editor or the executives who feared to displease him. Exhibit doubt: you're a wimp. Double-check: you're a wanker. Knock a story: you're a private part. The Page One exclusive this morning was an other-woman photo snatched from the lid of a grand piano by a cameraman told to come back with one or not at all.

Already, Jack Stack had collected 32 scalps, most of them grey or Grecian 2000. So bloody what about their historic scoops, their Homeric odysseys? By now, they were smelted. Their priorities had become time off in lieu and pension arithmetic.

The gaunt figure Jack Stack now targeted had weathered many changes. Been on six different papers, he would grin – five of them the Merc.

'Who the hell's this?' The question was addressed to Bish, who shook his head.

'Mr Stack, I'm Hugo Cunningham. Diplomatic corr.'

He got uneasily to his feet, attempted a smile and put out a waxwork hand. When the editor ignored it, Bish was moved to shake it for him.

'Never see your name in the paper,' said the editor.

'Nine weeks in dock, I'm afraid.' He ran a finger inside a shirt collar now two sizes too big. 'First day back.'

'Diplomatic illness, eh?' He nudged Bish.

'Not exactly.'

'So, Hugo, what sexy exclusives have you got for me?'

'Nothing quite like that. Not my line of country.'

'Not his line of country.' The editor winked at the deputy editor. Got a right one here.

'Busy enough day though. Briefing from Our Man on the state of play in Saudi. Lunch at the Aussie High Commission. Might get a clue as to what torpedoed our submarines deal. And tonight, Italian Embassy do. Item on the Christian Democrat fiasco, I imagine.'

'My-my, Hugo, you have been away a long time. Fact is, Hugo, your stuff's too good for the Merc. Frankly, Hugo, you ought to piss off to a decent newspaper. I would.'

'Been here . . . 30 years.' Hugo sat down heavily.

'Take my tip – don't stay anywhere that long again.'

Jack Stack moved towards a flickering screen on the sports subs' table. The man sitting like a heap of old tyres at his keyboard heard a voice over his shoulder, reading the screen with a German accent:

Exclusive to *Süddeutsche Zeitung* . . . Secret Manchester United bid for Munich's World Cup striker . . . The English champions were last night poised to capture . . .

'Oh, hello – ' The sub desperately flipped the screen to a Mercury story.

' – and goodbye.' Jack Stack switched off the terminal. 'If you're selling our secrets to the Germans, you're not bloody working for me. Bish – firing squad.'

Clop, went Bish.

The pair passed through the Lifestyle department, whose editor had scorned Jack Stack's idea for a feature on Y-fronts. Bollocks, she said. Right first time, he said. Her departure was marked by a

Lifestyle spread with six female soap stars saying **Y They Turn Us On** and six saying **Y They Turn Us Off**. The subject of the next conference rant was Y The Lifestyle Editor Had To Go.

Other regular faces had departed the department. The Agony Aunt who declined to be born again as the Ecstasy Aunt. The fashion editor who found asylum where it was not treason to deny the editor another suspenders spread already. The gardening editor who transplanted herself rather than allow her column to be fertilised up. And the cookery editor who refused to confine her ingredients to those Bish's mum could buy in her Pennine village store.

But there were enough new faces for Jack Stack to boast that he was creating more openings for women than any other editor. In a moment there would be one more.

Like his mother before him, Cerise l'Escalier seemed to have been coming in every other Tuesday for ever to deliver his next batch of horoscopes. Looking into the past confirmed his belief that if you looked after the future the present would look after itself. So, day after day after day, the star sign of the editor would radiate optimism. This morning, Cerise was promising Capricorns an encounter to enrich their lives.

'Remember me?' The editor was at his elbow. 'I'm your favourite Scorpio.'

'You can't fool Cerise,' chirped Cerise. 'Pretending to be Scorpio – typical Capricorn trick.'

'Go on, you looked me up in *Who's Who*. Bet you can't tell Bish's sign. Not easy. He doesn't have a date of birth.'

Cerise studied the man. That Adam's apple, Virgo. Nose, Aquarius. Forehead, Aries. Ears, Libra. Dimples, Leo. Lips, Scorpio. Teeth, Cancer. Chin, Taurus. Eyebrows, Pisces. Eyes, Gemini. Glasses, Sagittarius. The only safe bet was that Bish wouldn't be a Capricorn: no Capricorn boss would pick a Capricorn deputy.

Cerise offered the other eleven signs in calendar order, confidence ebbing as Jack Stack shook his head at each. But the final guess was delivered in triumph.

'Capricorn!'

'Wrong. Try Uranus.' He said it *your-anus*.

'But Uranus isn't a sign.' He said it *yerer-nuss*.

'It's the exit sign.' Two fingers. 'Up yours, Cerise.'

Jack Stack returned to his office and the door that he proclaimed ever open. But, open or closed, he was rarely there. His style for much of the day and night was editing on the run. He roamed the floor, asking everywhere, what have you got for me? Transmuting base material into golden words. Feeding a reporter the mischievous question that would produce a headline answer. Telling a feature writer what improvements to a boring quote she could get away with. Pushing an art editor to crop and blow maximum impact into a minimum picture. Dictating a phoney come-on letter to generate a page of phobic replies. Finding a path through a legal minefield. Leaning over a sub's shoulder to witticise a flat caption. Breathing life into tombstone layouts. Striking out unsurprising feature ideas to concentrate on the ones that would give him reader-grabbing blurbs. Promoting and demoting stories and pictures to inject a surge into every page of his paper.

By the time he came back from each walkabout, half a dozen people would have been told to see him later. Since such an invitation was a command, the approaches to his ever-open door were like a medieval court. Applicants and supplicants would lurk before the presence chamber in the hope of a moment of his attention. They would scurry to his elbow, waving papers or pictures as they skipped forwards, backwards or sideways to match his progress.

He threaded through the throng, jabbing a finger at each selected target.

'*You* – get those wrinklies off the diary page or I'll give it to news. *You* – if the bugger won't die in time for the edition, bung his obit in anyway and call it a tribute. *You* – out of my sight. *You* – tell their PR one more squeak and I'll let the water out of that pic of them in the bath. *You* – drop our bid ten grand each time the greedy bitch says no. *You* – what do you mean, old story? Ain't old till it's been in the Merc.'

Bish just made it as the editor closed his ever-open door behind them and met the eyes of the five men and one woman on his conference couches. The political editor's knuckles showed white. Neil Robinson's team had been waiting an hour.

'I'd say sorry for keeping you, Robbo' – the editor shook his head at them all the way to his chair – 'except you lot do eff-all anyway. Eighteen pars of politics yesterday – three pars apiece. You're pathetic.'

'With the greatest possible respect' – a pompous voice issued from the pompous head of Neil Robinson – 'you are comprehensively misinformed. We filed ten times that – '

'Bollocks.'

Nobody at Westminster spoke to Neil Robinson like that. Beth Macbeth sought his advice on the election date. The shadow chancellor had him run an eye over his budget day speech. Chief whips preferred his soundings to their own.

'Jack, take my word that the team files day and night. News, features, background, comment, leaders, sketches, diary pars. Simple truth is, they're just not making the paper since you arrived.'

Jack Stack caught the eye, under an unplucked eyebrow, of the twenty-fiveish woman in Neil Robinson's team. 'What are you called, darling?'

'I'm not called darling.' She twitched her black jacket. 'I'm called deputy political editor. Or Gloria. Or Mrs Mundy.' She crossed legs under her long black skirt.

'OK, Mrs Mundy. Got the message.'

Clop, went Bish.

'Might we perhaps get back to the point?' Neil Robinson stood to interrupt the by-play. 'It seems reasonable to ask – do you give a damn about political coverage?'

'Give a damn? Course I give a damn. But not about the crap they feed you. Lobby bollocks. Spin-doctor hype. Ministerial kites. Give me the stories they don't want to see in print – and I'll give you the biggest bylines of your life. We all know what hypocrites the bastards are.'

'And the hypocrites all know what bastards we are' – Neil Robinson smoothed his hair – 'or rather some of us are.'

'Yeah, but some of us aren't in this game to conceal the truth from the readers. Call that good journalism?'

'When you were at the Globe, Jack, you stuck a tape recorder under a hotel bed to trap a minister with a bar girl. Call that good journalism?'

'Sure. Beth Macbeth had just been whipping up another great morality crusade at the party conference.'

'And the lip-smacking extracts from the tape? And the sexy shots you paid the girl to pose for? And the half-page pic of the unmade four-poster? And the readers' competition to win one just like it? Call that good journalism?'

'No, Robbo, I call it brilliant journalism.'

'Well, you need not look to the political team for such material as long as I am in charge.'

'Brave speech, Robbo.' He applauded. 'Even braver if you hadn't already signed up for the top lobby job at the BBC. I'm happy for you.'

'Thank you so very much.'

Clop, went Bish.

Gloria Mundy was the last to leave, only to return as though she had stayed in a revolving door for the round trip.

'Ah,' said Jack Stack, 'the loyal deputy. Come to beg me to beg Robbo to stay.'

'Not exactly. Just wanted to say I'm sorry he gave you such a hard time.'

'He'd appreciate that.'

'I appreciated him. He did give me my big break.'

'Trouble was – '

' – he's so respectable.'

'And – '

' – that's not my style at all. I got stories he sat on because they'd upset Beth or the Palace or whoever.'

'So – '

' – I'm praying your arrival means I'll be able to get some sexier pieces into the Merc.'

'You've come to the right shop, Mrs Mundy.' He waved for her to take a seat and left his desk to pull up a chair opposite, bringing them almost knee to knee. 'Tell me, do you dress down to please Mr Mundy?'

'I sent Mr Mundy packing. Useless plonker. And I mean useless. And I mean plonker. I dress down to calm down randy MPs. Of both sexes.'

'Thought perhaps you had a wooden leg.' He waved over his shoulder as Bish identified the moment to mouth an excuse and leave.

'Don't think so.'

Pointing her toes, she drew her hem to her knees. She watched his eyes glaze at the cancan flash as she lifted the skirt clear to let it fall back to her ankles.

Jack Stack knew a job application when he saw one.

'Dear Mrs Mundy,' he replied. 'Re political editor. Thank you for showing an interest. The vacancy will be filled by the first candidate to bring me an exclusive big enough to win a place on my walls. Yours et cetera.'

'Hallelujah!' Gloria clapped hands. 'Wait till you hear my Princess Xenia scoop.' Her face lit up. 'Sensational secret of Prince Ricky's bride-to-be.' She drummed flat heels. 'How about that?'

'How about letting me into the sensational secret?'

'Princess Xenia does voodoo. Nasty things happen to everyone who gets in her way.'

'How nasty?'

'Terminally nasty. They jump one bungee too many. Vanish in the Channel Tunnel. Drop out of Ferris wheels.'

'Why lay it on Xenia?'

'I've got hold of her diaries. Written in red ink . . . '

The British royals had run out of European royals willing to marry them. Beth Macbeth had come up with a solution in the spirit of the age: a bride from the Commonwealth. Aware that the stud book was top of HM's reading list, the PM had advanced the clinching argument that what Arab thoroughbreds had done for the British bloodstock line, Princess Xenia could do for the thinning blood royal.

The remarkable Xenia was the daughter of a Zulu prince and a Guyanese princess. She had science doctorates from Cape Town and Cambridge, where she first enchanted Prince Ricky. At 148, her IQ was almost twice his. Xenia got a double first in haematology and Romanian literature. Ricky got a grace-and-favour pass for failing English history. Xenia played harp, bassoon and trombone. Ricky played snooker. Xenia was fluent in English, French, Nilotic, Romanian and backslang. Ricky spoke elementary Sloane and Caribbockney (*Nicky and Mickey were 'me bruvvahs', Vicki was 'me sistuh'*.) Xenia stroked the Cambridge women's eight. Ricky watched Millwall.

Xenia was hardly a bride to ease the royal family's hereditary anxiety about marrying beautiful, brilliant and lovable women. But she was squeaky clean enough to be a squeaky queen – should the heir and the spare happen to drop out of Ferris wheels.

'Of course,' said Jack Stack, 'we'd have to get round the Code. No intrusion into the privacy of the young royals, unless there's an over-riding public interest.'

'Like My Royal Weathercock by TV Tina?'

'Doesn't count. Wasn't true.'

'Well, this is true, Jack. And it's got constitutional implications. Once Xenia marries Ricky, it'll take only two voodoo hoodoos to clear his path to the throne.'

'King Ricky the Thicky? Bollocks to that.'

'You'll be doing the nation a favour, Jack.'

'Know what I'm thinking?' He asked and answered. 'I'm thinking of the Hitler diaries. How'd you know this isn't another scam?'

'Whoever heard of a scam with nobody asking for money? My sister isn't asking for a penny.'

'Your sister?'

'Jenny shared rooms with Xenia at Cambridge for three years. They were both doing Romanian literature. And the diaries got mixed into the bags of junk Jenny brought home. Xenia was into Creole cuisine. Had her own cauldron. Did sweet and sour eye of newt. Aromatic crispy toe of frog. Stuff like that.'

'Washed down with?'

'Don't ask. And she'd stick pins into wax images of people who crossed her. Like Ricky's first fiancée, the late Lady Clarabel.'

'The one a grouse fell on at Sandringham?'

'A pheasant – grouse are Balmoral.'

'Just testing. Carry on.'

'Like the University Air Squadron instructor who denied Xenia her wings – his dropped off at 4,000 feet. Like the leading lady in the *Footlights* – broke a leg. Like the anchor woman of the 4 x 100 – overtaken by a javelin. And like 30 more in Xenia's first-year diary alone.'

'Can you finish off the other two tonight?'

'Need more time than that, Jack. It's all in microscopic Romanian. Had to be microscopic to get the spells in. Year One took me a month, even with Jenny translating.'

'Any sex? Microscopic even.'

'She had aphrodisiac rhyming ingredients flown in from her auntie's delibatessen in New Orleans. Lizard's leg and howlet's wing, adder's fork and blindworm's sting...'

'They're a turn-on?'

'If correctly double-bubbled. Just one helping, and Beth Macbeth's son – '

'Beth Macbeth's son?'

'Was at it through the cat-flap with his moral tutor.'

'Drop everything, kid. You're on this night and day. Check out every name. Accident reports. Missing persons registers. Zombie clubs. Go to New Orleans – bring back two of everything from auntie's delibatessen. Don't come in the office. Don't put a word into the computer. Don't trust a soul – living, dead or undead.'

'Cross my heart, Jack.' She crossed her legs.

He took her hand and led her to the gallery of Jack Stack triumphs on the wall.

'Just what I need for the set. **VOODOO PRINCESS!!** It'll double the sale.' He thought for a moment. 'Mind you, **VAMPIRE PRINCESS!!** would treble it. Now Gloria – '

' – am I sure it's red ink?'

'Written in blood is more – '

' – symmetrical?'

'Would God be that good to me?' He lifted his eyes.

7

The Fourth

The US Air Force band was into *West Side Story* as Marina and Harry joined the receiving line at the ambassador's Fourth of July party. Harry crooned 'I've just met a girl called Marina' into her ear and they beamed at their reflections in the gilt mirrors: Harry's in white tuxedo, Marina's in simple sea-water silk that set off emeralds at neck, ears and wrist.

'We sure look an item,' said Harry.

'In your dreams,' said Marina.

The Foreign Secretary's new wife, seven ahead in the line, mouthed, Who's Marina's sexy man? The Magnus bureau chief said Harry Chacewater, the playboy who thinks he's a publisher, and wasn't it something to see him with a grown-up date. The Chacewater bureau chief said lay off my boss, and wasn't it a fact that Magnus took real blood in his Bloody Marys. The Magnus man said not only real but still warm.

'Hi, Marina, Harry,' said Ambassador and Mrs Charles T Bergdorf as one.

'Hi, Janie, Chuck,' said Marina. 'Your excellencies are excelling yourselves tonight.'

'Hi, Sis.' Harry embraced Janie.

'Mom's here,' she whispered. 'Be nice to her.'

Heads turned as they moved into the vast reception hall of the neo-Georgian mansion that Woolworth heiress Barbara Hutton had donated to the US Government for a token dollar. Marina lifted a flute glass from a proffered tray and waited for the waiter to fetch Harry a Rebel Yell. They walked their drinks across the oak parquet and through the open french doors to the terrace looking out over a garden second in size in London only to Buckingham Palace.

'Thought you liked that stuff,' he said as she made a face.

'I like the stuff you call French champagne. This is Californian.' Another sip. 'Tastes like aerated ice.'

'You're not an easy woman to please.'

'I'm not an easy woman to anything.'

'Which reminds me. Sis wants me to say hi to Mom. Hi is about as far as we get. But you'll love her. She's like you – half Scotch.'

'Half Scottish. But if she's like you, she'll be three-quarters bourbon.'

Harry led Marina to a corner table occupied by a duchessy figure sitting as straight-backed as her gilt chair. Alice Chacewater held a glass in one jewelled hand and a stick in the other jewelled hand.

'A kiss wouldn't come amiss,' she said. She patted Harry's cheek as he bent. 'There, darling. That didn't hurt, did it?'

'Mom, I want you to meet Marina Marshall.'

'Ah, Marina.' She shook hands. 'Janie tells me you're putting Harry in your book.'

'We're working on it.'

'Found some nice things to say about him?'

'He's not giving me too much help.'

Mom tapped her stick. 'Harry, I like this one.'

'This one?' Marina laughed. 'There are others? How many writers is he stringing along, for heaven's sake?'

'I wasn't thinking about writers.'

'You weren't?' said Marina.

'She wasn't.' Harry tensed up. 'And I guess I didn't introduce her as a character reference.'

'Who else have you got?' Mom shook her head.

'Aw, give me a break.' He tugged Marina's elbow. 'Let's rejoin the fleet.'

'You rejoin if you want.' With the prospect of adding a dimension to her chapter, the lady was not for tugging. 'Catch up with you later. Maybe.'

She sat by Mom, positioned her evening bag to provide maximum advantage for the mike and went into her act. Candour encouraged candour. Indiscretion encouraged indiscretion.

'... You see, Marina, I'm the one who made him quit the Navy – so I'm the one who's ruined his life. To keep on believing that, he has to keep on believing he isn't up to it as a publisher.'

'Alice, he isn't.'

'Marina, he could be. All he needs is a win. To show himself he can make it without the legendary Ed alongside.'

'It's hell out there. I don't see our boy surviving on his own.'

'Nor do I, Marina. But he could' – Mom lifted an eyebrow at her – 'with the right woman.'

'Don't look at me.'

'I look at the way he looks at you. He's madly in love.'

'Madly, as in wham-bam? Let's face it...'

'Those girls?' Mom sighed.

'That's not what worries me.'

'My dear, they don't mean a thing.'

'That's what worries me.'

She kissed the cheek Harry had kissed, patted the jewelled hand that held the stick, and set off to rejoin the fleet. She docked alongside Humpty Baynard.

'Well then, Marina. Editor behaving himself?'

'Yes, like Attila the Hun.'

Humpty slipped into his top pocket the bifocals that made him look older, as did screwing up his eyes to peer anxiously over her shoulder. She knew the signs.

'Just about to form a search party,' said Humpty as his low-bottomed Dumpty cantered up.

'Working late?' She gave Marina the look wives give mistresses.

'It's what we do,' said Marina.

'Yes, well.' Humpty waved life on. 'Hardly know a soul here. Who are these people?'

'Get Marina to give you a guided tour. She knows everybody. I'm off for a nosebag.'

Humpty tightened his elbow on Marina's hand as she steered him into the throng. For her, this was like cruising through her cuttings, only to find the subjects now curling their edges at her. In a month under Jack Stack, the Mercury had got up a lot of noses. There was disenchantment tonight in the nods, waves and hi-Marinas.

'... And, oh, here comes the Cardinal... Thank you, Eminence. And I'm sure Mr Stack will be including you in his prayers too...'

She side-stepped **ROYAL ARTIST WHO DIDN'T DRAW HER CURTAINS**, only to meet the eye of the sports minister who cancelled lunch when the Mercury blew the whistle on **ENGLAND SKIPPER SCORED 10 MINS BEFORE LOST FINAL**.

'...and here's the Palace press secretary...Cross with you, Admiral. Should have given me that Xenia birthday interview. Nobody reads dear old Glenda...'

She evaded the reproachful finger of **KING LEER!!** whose Arts Council grant had been queered by a full-frontal Jack Stack campaign against his house-full-frontal production.

'...and here's Beth Macbeth...Well, there's a handy coincidence. You're his favourite prime minister.'

Humpty freed his elbow as Dumpty rejoined them, plate of wobbly gateaux in one hand, fork in the other.

'Look,' said Dumpty, 'There's dear Princess Victoria. Taught her dressage. Better say hello.'

'Tries so hard to look like Vicki, doesn't she?' Marina spoke sweetly. 'But it's only her lady-in-waiting.'

'Amazing resemblance.' Dumpty sniffed. 'Amazing.'

'Now here's the real thing...Hi, ma'am darling.'

Princess Victoria looked right through Marina. Dumpty began to enjoy the party.

Two things told Jack Stack his deputy was bringing good news. First, Bish never brought bad news but got an underling to deliver it. Second, Bish's thumb was up as he came through the door.

'Hacked into Marina's computer at last. None of the usual passwords worked. Birthday. Car number. Kids' names. Star sign. Bra size. You'd never guess the one that clicked.'

'Bollocks.'

'Right again, Jack.'

'So who's she planning to puff in this week's spread?'

'Fanny and Danny, your favourite chat show couple.'

'Not any more, pal.'

'It's a year since their wedding. Marina's got a sexy interview. Plus pyjama pix of them in the studio's anniversary present kingsize bed. Great stuff – '

'Great stuff? You mutinous dog. It's crap.'

'That's what I mean. Great stuff – if you like crap.'

'Bet she leaves out Danny's bit on the side.'

'Didn't know he'd got a bit on the side.'

'They all have. Go wave some money around. Buy me the truth.'

Clop, went Bish.

Cornered by Lord Bull, Harry Chacewater was leaning back against a column, looking for escape.

'Get your leg over?' The Bull eyebrows twitched twice.

'Got my ass kicked. Last time I ask you to mark my card.'

The band was playing 'Some Enchanted Evening'. Across the crowded room, Harry caught Marina's eye and willed her to come to the rescue.

'Ah,' she said to Humpty and Dumpty, 'there's Harry Chacewater. You'll love him, I promise.'

Dumpty smiled. 'One from your private collection?'

'Wouldn't say no.' Marina smiled back. 'Would you?'

She guided them over and did the introductions.

'Hi there, Dumpty.' Harry's Virginian vowels melted her. 'And hi, Humpty – how you doing?'

'One publish-and-be-damned thing after another.'

'Damned all right,' said Dumpty. 'Those Adventures of Heidi Hunt are enough to guarantee it. Doing streaks at Glyndebourne and the Guards Polo Club. Whatever next?'

She did not need to ask twice.

Three hundred gasps engulfed the hall and drowned the band. Through the french doors streaked Heidi Hunt in an Uncle Sam topper and high white boots, plus star-spangled bow tie and matching G-string. Jack Stack's headline was already written: **YANKEE NUDLE HEIDI**.

She was illuminated by a salvo of flashes that at first appeared to come from the squad of US Marines right behind her, but turned out to be rapid fire from the squad of Mercury cameramen right behind them.

'Stay cool, folks.' Ambassador Chuck took the mike. 'Everything's under control.'

As though this was standard drill procedure, and to a sympathetic drum-roll from the band, the Marines wrapped Heidi in a tablecloth, 1-2-3; elevated her to the horizontal, 4-5-6; sat Uncle Sam's topper on her tum, 7; and paraded out, 8-9-10. The ambassador led the applause.

'Guess that must've been the nothin' we ain't seen yet. Wonder what Mr Stack will come up with for Thanksgiving.'

'How embarrassing,' said Dumpty. 'I didn't know where to look.'

'Humpty knew,' chortled Lord Bull. 'Better phone Jack Stack, hadn't you? Tell him to kill it. Can't upset the Special Relationship.'

'You run your rag, Johnnie. I'll run mine.'

'Well, at least keep tomorrow's Merc away from the Bahamas.' He sucked in air. 'This'd finish Toby off.'

'As it happens,' said Humpty, 'I'm flying there the day after for a spot of fishing with him. Don't worry, he never reads the papers. Leaves everything to me.'

'Do give him my regards. And say I'm immensely grateful to you for taking Jack Stack off my hands.'

'Sour grapes, Johnnie.' Humpty rocked on his heels. 'Stack may be a bit of an idiot – but he's no fool. Since I pinched him from you, we're gaining 20,000 readers a week.'

'You've lost this one.' Dumpty tossed her head. 'The Merc stinks. Wouldn't line the bloody parrot's cage with it.'

'Steady on.' Humpty forced a laugh.

'Switch to the Globe, Dumpty,' said Lord Bull. 'I'll phone your newsagent myself.'

'I'll switch – if you persuade Marina to switch. She's looking for a new asylum anyway.'

Lord Bull moistened his lips. Dumpty whinnied. Marina's eyes flashed. Humpty put his bifocals back on.

'Marina, Humpty, Dumpty.' Harry loosed one nod at all three, and moved to ferry Lord Bull elsewhere before the Ambassador's Fourth of July fireworks were further upstaged.

'Time we weren't here, Dumpty.' Humpty took her arm and explained. 'She's out on the gallops at dawn.'

Harry rejoined Marina as she watched them go.

'Jeez, how'd that guy ever get to be a publisher?'

'Same way as you.'

'Ouch.'

'Goodnight, Harry.'

'Goodnight, Harry?'

'Column to get ready for the morning.'

'No supper with Harry? No Annabel's with Harry?'

'No anything with Harry.'

'But you will be at my little Fifth of July party?'

He put a hand on her shoulder and bent to say goodnight nicely. After the soft kiss, he left his cheek against hers for half a minute. He closed his eyes. He took in her scents. He ached for her.

'Wouldn't miss it for the world, Harry.'

Back at her flat on Green Park, Marina slipped off her shoes, took the tape from her evening bag and went to her laptop to add to the Chacewater chapter:

'Bye, Harry,' said Mom. 'See you next Fourth.' Her eyes followed him as she spoke to me. 'He's a good boy, really.'

'Meaning he's a bad boy, really.'

'It's my fault. I'm clairvoyant, did he tell you? Saw the car crash that killed his brother. Saw it seven times. Then it happened for real. Soon I began seeing Harry's plane in flames on the deck. The coffin with his cap and medals. The honour guard commander handing me the wrapped flag. Saw it five, six times. Just had to get Harry to quit the Navy before the seventh. He can't forgive me . . .'

After an hour with the chapter, Marina replaced it on screen with the draft of her Fanny and Danny spread. She cut and polished until she was delighted with the piece. Pity it would also delight Jack Stack.

Now she headed for a slow bath and her Mendelssohn homework for Harry's little party tomorrow. She loaded his *Midsummer Night's Dream* into a portable and took it into the bathroom with a malt whisky nightcap. Soon, she began to capture Harry's dizzy delight at those woodwind chords. And to recapture hers at that sweet parting kiss tonight. He hadn't wanted it to end there, had he? And she hadn't wanted it to end there, had she?

There was heavy silence for fifteen minutes in the back of the company Bentley as it rolled the Humpty-Dumptys home to their place on the Hamble. Then Humpty leaned forward to pull down the blind and shut out the chauffeur. Dumpty got in first.

'Not very pleased with me, are you? I can always tell.'

'So why do you always do it? The Merc may be shit to you, darling, but it's my bread and butter.'

She made a little-girl face. 'Dumpty says sowwy to Humpty. It's that howwible Mawina I was getting at.'

'I'm sure we all got the message.'

'She's after you.'

'Rubbish.'

'Get rid of her.'

'Toby wouldn't wear it.'

'You're the chief executive. Pay her off. Leave the cash on the mantelpiece – isn't that the way it's done?'

'Knock hell out of my bottom line.'

'Humpty.' She batted eyelashes at him. 'Take Dumpty with you to the Bahamas. Please?'

'No can do. I've banned picking up the bill for spouses.'

'I'll pay my own bloody fare.'

'I'm booked on Concorde. You'd be looking at seven thou.'

'Marina flies Concorde.'

'Marina's Marina.'

'Humpty, you wouldn't be a man if you didn't fancy her. You do, don't you?' She tried to nudge some response. 'Dumpty's jealous. And Dumpty's worried 'cause Dumpty knows what a stoat Humpty can be.'

'Those were the days.'

She linked arms and went all mellow. 'Dumpty's so extraordinarily fond of Humpty.'

She flicked off the light. Her hands ferreted. Her fingers stirred. Nothing else did. Her head went down. He was more grateful for the silence than the service. Eventually, she gave up.

'You used to like that.'

'Long time ago.'

Flicking the light back on, he reached for the radio and turned up the volume on 'The Ride of the Valkyries'. Dumpty settled into her corner. She was smiling. Marina would get no joy out of this one. He was filleted beyond fellatio.

The message awaiting Harry at his Savoy suite was to call Edgar Segal. The legendary Ed.

'Where's the fire, Ed?'

'Only smoke yet, Harry. A few more per cent of Chacewater Inc. snapped up today. Max Magnus is on the prowl.'

'Better start checking my boat for bombs.'

'All that was a few years back. Guess he's legit now.'

'Maybe. I'll still be checking.'

'Harry, this guy's after a bargain – so why don't we stop shaping up like a bargain? We're earning more from bonds than from publishing. That juicy cash pile makes us too easy to swallow.'

'You mean put it back into newspapers?'

'Not just any newspapers. Buy up some outfit that makes us indigestible. One that needs more patience than Magnus has before it can turn in good profits.'

'Makes sense to me, Ed.'

'There's another way. Beef up the profit forecast so Chacewater stock shoots out of his reach. But we'd have to do to our guys what Magnus wants to do to them.'

'Don't like the sound of that.'

'Slash the payroll. Junk real nice people.'

'Couldn't do it, Uncle Ed. Let's go the other way.'

'Good for you, Harry. Soon as you're home, we'll talk properties. Might just find us something in Washington.'

'Might just find us something in London . . .'

Harry poured a bourbon and took it to the window, looking out to a Thames as black by night as the James by day. He was amused to catch himself thinking like a Chacewater. Sure, Marina's crack about publishing families had got to him; the more so because Marina had got to him. But it was encountering the absurd Humpty that did it. If the Mercury could stay afloat with that dummy at the helm, what could it achieve with Ed Segal's touch? So Harry would chase his hunch and come up with an even better reason to buy the Mercury than that Marina Marshall came with the territory.

He would go about it the Navy way. Reconnaissance/Plan/ Action. The Chacewater bureau chief in London should be home from the party by now. He dialled him:

'Well hi, George Theodoulou's answering machine. This is Harry Chacewater's answering machine. Sorry I didn't catch you and Sally-Jane at the ambassador's. But I'm having a little Fifth of July party. Drop in on me at the Savoy around eight-thirty, OK? Now listen, Theo, I want a fast rundown on the Mercury outfit. Financial appraisal. Circulation charts. Ad revenues. The whole bit. Tell

Richmond you're on a confidential assignment for me. Love to Sally-Jane. See you.'

He dialled the Chacewater bureau chief in Miami:

'Hi, Clarence C Campbell. It's Harry Chacewater...Yeah, great. They keeping you busy?...Don't give me that bilge, I did three months as your sidekick, remember? Listen, CCC. Get over to Abaco for a couple days. I want to know all about Lord Toby Baynard. Publisher of the London daily Mercury till he had a stroke. Still owns it...Tell Richmond you're doing a confidential for Harry. Love to whoever. Call me Monday. Bye.'

Harry felt unusually good about himself. This was one of those magical moments in life when suddenly you could. Suddenly you could whistle. Suddenly you could swim. Suddenly you could ride. Suddenly you could fly. Suddenly you could fuck. And suddenly you could be a publisher.

8

The Fifth

Marina screamed silently as she called up her spread on screen and found it now headlined **DANNY JUST CAN'T GET ENOUGH FANNY**. She buzzed the new features editor.

'Change it back, Wendy.'

'Jack likes filthy headlines.'

'Marina doesn't.'

'But the spread's already away.'

'Don't bullshit me, child. Just restore **FANNY AND DANNY'S BEDTIME STORIES**.'

'He doesn't like the pyjama pic either. Too buttoned up.'

'Well hard fucking luck.'

It was gridlock time, with early news pages running into the back of late feature pages. Wendy couldn't be trusted with such a handy excuse. Better stand over her to see the page away. So would Claudia be a darling and get the hairdresser to hang on. And ring to tell Harry she'd get to his party before the band went home.

'Funny,' said Claudia, reporting back.

'Glad something is.'

'Harry was out. So I asked the Savoy to see he got your message. They said the party's off – he'd already given them his guest list to notify. I said so why hadn't they rung us? And they said – '

' – my name wasn't on his list.'

'Gosh,' said Claudia.

'Yeeee-ha!' said Marina.

Jack Stack tapped cigar ash over the picture of Fanny and Danny in the kingsize bed. He held out his other hand to Wendy for the shots Marina had vetoed.

'Why not this one? Or this? Or this?'

'You know what she's like, Jack.' Wendy shrugged. 'Told me the price for our exclusive shoot was her promise not to use anything tacky.'

'And you let her? You're no use to me. Try the Methodist Recorder. I'll give you a reference.' He turned on Bish as Wendy went out. 'Jesus, who hired that?'

Clop, went Bish.

'Make sure they know it was your headline Marina pissed on. Better for staff morale.'

Clop.

'So, where's my story about Danny's bit on the side?'

'Danny doesn't play away.'

'Creep.'

'But we might be on to something about Fanny...'

Marina Marshall was getting ready for the party at which she was to be the only guest, and no doubt the cabaret.

Since Toby, her sex life had been nothing much. Maybe there would have been more but for her known habit of noting passes in her pieces. She had been faithful in the years as Toby's mistress until the exasperated time that triggered the final break. It was seven months before she let her libido loose again. She had gone to Venice to profile a precocious prodigy in the palazzo that Broadway had bought him. He sat her alongside at the grand piano, looking into her eyes for a just-for-you performance of his new album. She had quite forgotten the just-for-me sex. What she remembered was the view. From his ducal bed she had gazed upon not only his Canaletto but the Canal panorama it depicted. The masterpiece was propped on an easel by the thrown-back shutters, before an empty stool as though the master had popped out for a Cornetto.

And tonight, Harry. Here was a nice warm guy who was never going to break her heart. She guessed he would be pretty good. And she would be pretty good too. Pretty good in black wrapover evening skirt and one-button silver jacket. Pretty good in front-fastening bra and french knickers. And pretty good in cobweb suspender belt: tights were cones in the fast lane. She studied her mirrored self at various stages as she dressed, envying Harry the images she was rehearsing.

Clop. 'We've tracked down Fanny's bit of rough. And he's coughed the lot for five grand.'

'Thank you, God.' The editor lifted eyes to the ceiling.

'On your screen now.' Bish leaned across the desk and tapped the keyboard.

'Lovely.' Jack Stack bobbed on his chair as he scrolled through the reporter's story. 'Move **ROYAL CORGI ORGY** to 3. We'll give Fanny the whole of 1 and turn her to 4 and 5.' He pulled a layout pad towards him, took a fat felt tip and wrote the headlines:

EXPOSED: LOVE SHAM
OF PHONEY & DANNY
I'm her bit on the side
says passionate plumber

Now he turned to the keyboard to compose his rewrite, gleefully reading it out loud as he went along:

The Mercury today exposes TV's Fanny and Danny as a fraud. They boast of their 'dream marriage'. But Fanny, 35, is having it off with her plumber.

Her bit on the side is handsome hunk Clint Dartagnan, 19. In an exclusive interview last night, he revealed their months of non-stop nookie.

The chat show couple even deceived veteran columnist Marina Marshall with their lovey-dovey sham.

On their first wedding anniversary, naughty Fanny told our Marina a pile of porkies about romantic antics with Danny.
'It was me she did all that stuff with,' said the passionate plumber. 'Danny preferred darts.'

'WE DID IT in their dressing room before a show – while Danny was scoring trebles in the pub.

'WE DID IT in a Eurostar loo. Fanny said that made us members of the metre-high club.

'WE DID IT by phone when we couldn't get together – know what I mean?'

'It all started the day I rang her bell with a new ballcock. Now I don't know if I'm coming or going...'

Jack Stack swivelled. 'OK, Bish, take it from there.' His fat felt tip waltzed across the foot of his layout: *How they conned our Marina – See Centre Pages.* 'Terrific. Now I need a shot of the lad right here. Caption: *Plumber Clint...rang her bell.* And the Snowman pic of Marina right here. Caption: *First Lady Marina – Conned.* And' – he went to the set of vetoed pyjama shots – 'this is the beaut I want across five columns. Caption: *Fanny and Danny – Faking it to fool 12 million viewers.*'

His finger stirred the nipple revealed by Fanny's billowing pyjama top. He moved down her arm to Danny's lap.

'Disgusting. Stick a **CENSORED** label over that hand. But not too big, eh?'

Harry's London bureau chief was at the Savoy reception desk. 'We're George and Sally-Jane Theodoulou. Mr Chacewater's expecting us.'

'Oh, dear.' There was pain on the face of the under-manager. 'Afraid he had to call the party off, sir. We've been ringing round all day.' He displayed a clipboard. 'You were the only ones we couldn't raise.'

'No wonder.' Theo sighed. 'That ain't our number.'

Sally-Jane patted her party hair-do. 'Fuck it.'

'More or less what the other forty said.' The under-manager felt for the Theodoulous. Such a handsome couple.

'That's showbiz, I guess.' Theo stroked a neat hip of the black frock Sally-Jane had dashed out to buy. 'Never mind – if we'd got the message, would you have blown a month's pay on this little number? And would the two of us be about to have our first romantic dinner since our last romantic dinner?'

'That was romantic? A shared table at the Pizza Hut?'

'Shared? Well, I'll be damned – I only had eyes for you.'

'Sir, madam' – the under-manager came round the desk – 'allow me to offer you champagne with our compliments while I find you a cosy corner in the Grill.'

The Theodoulous were sipping their second glass in the foyer as they studied the menu and began to feel this wasn't such a calamity after all. Sally-Jane pulled at her husband's arm.

'There – Marina Marshall.'

She directed his gaze to a vision in emeralds, silver jacket and black evening skirt that split interestingly every other step from the revolving doors to the lifts.

'Stockings?' Sally-Jane twitched eyebrows at Theo.

'Lucky Harry.' Theo twitched back.

'Why so sure it's Harry?'

'Who's Harry's date at the ambassador's? Whose paper does Harry suddenly want to own? Why does Harry stand up 40 people? And who just happens along?'

'I'd kill for those emeralds,' said Sally-Jane.

The Mendelssohn violin concerto spilled out into the corridor as Harry, still conducting his sitting room stereo, opened the door to Marina.

'Told you I'd get here before the band went,' she said.

'Confession.' He drew her in. 'Nobody here but Isaac Stern and the Philadelphia – and you and me. I had the desk ring the rest of the world not to come.'

'Confession. I knew.'

He picked up where they left off last night, his hand on her shoulder as he put his cheek to hers. Again, it was half a minute before the freeze-frame unfroze.

'Lovely party.' Marina broke the spell.

'You sure are.'

Isaac Stern and the Philadelphia moved into the cadenza as Harry drew back the double doors to usher her into the soft-lit sitting room. He lifted the champagne from the ice bucket, invited her approval of the non-Californian label and filled their glasses. She took hers to the windows looking out through Embankment trees to the slack-water Thames.

Harry bent to the tray on the low table and lifted a napkin to reveal fat fingers of still-warm brown toast. Flipping open the silver pot, he spooned great blobs of caviare and spread them like blackcurrant jam.

'Come and get it.'

Marina's emeralds glowed as she crossed to one of the deep couches either side of the table. She chose a corner and patted the middle cushion invitingly. Harry parked his blazer and eased tie and top button as he joined her.

Each took a finger of toast and turned to feed it to the other. Nostrils flared as caviare was savoured between tongue and palate, and followed down with champagne before lips smacked for more.

At one such moment, Marina substituted flesh fingers for toast fingers, scooping up caviare to take to Harry's mouth. He closed on them down to the second knuckle and sucked them clean. When, in turn, she fed from his fingers, he felt his brains were about to erupt through the top of his head.

'I'm in love with you, Marina.'

'You don't have to be.'

'Now she tells me.'

Her eyes held his as she removed her ear-clips and set them on the table. The emeralds gleamed like go-lights.

They embraced, his blood surging as her mouth opened instantly to him. Soon, he was freeing her jacket button, roaming warm ribs and coming up to undo her bra. He dedicated a hand to each neat breast and she gasped as the nipples responded. She inclined for him to ease off her jacket but he was already at the gap in her skirt. Now it was he who gasped as his hands discovered stocking tops. On he went, silk smooth above his hand, belly hot and curls crisp beneath it. She began to melt under his beavering, and the secret scent rose from her. He breathed it deep. Eyes half-closed, mouth half-open, she arched to help him slip off her knickers. She shared his rapture at the cameo presented as she sprawled, sweetly disordered: jacket and bra fallen away, unwrapped skirt and slack suspenders framing barbered bush, stockings awry, one shoe half on; only emerald necklace and bracelet still in place.

'You're – ' His throat dried.

'So are you.'

He knelt before her, took her legs over his arms and began to worship with lips and tongue; her moist thighs quivering against his cheeks, her hands stroking back his hair. Her head swayed. Twice, she murmured, 'Come up, darling.' The second time, he got to his feet for her to unbuckle and unzip him, easing trousers and boxers down as one. Harry set hands on hips as she cupped uptight balls and claimed ardent penis.

'Oh, boy,' she said.

His eyes implored. Her lips encompassed. She relinquished him to lie back and draw her knees towards her flushed face. Watching him watching her, she spread slowly, glistening in the low light. She guided him in to the hilt – 'Ah, Harry, that's so good' – and soon he was glistening too. They were hardly touching anywhere but there. Isaac Stern and the Philadelphia accelerated to *molto vivace*. Marina trembled and said throatily, 'Do it, do it, do it.' And Harry did it, did it, did it.

'Oh, boy,' she said.

His face nestled at her neck. He was hers. She smiled. The damsel in distress had found her white knight to rescue the Mercury from the dragon. Just so long as he didn't get to rescue the dragon and slay the damsel.

Bish was dictating to Marina's answering machine the message Jack Stack had dictated to him:

'For God's sake, where are you? Editor's been trying to get you all night. Problem is, Fanny turns out to have a lover – who's gone public and shot your spread full of holes. Editor wants to do you a favour. Drop it. Or at least rejig it. But, as you well know, he's under the cosh from your lawyers. We're just having to do the best we can. Cheers.'

'Should have wished her merry Christmas,' said Jack Stack. 'She won't dare show her face before then.'

Clop.

The Theodoulous came from the Grill in a cognac afterglow as Marina emerged from the lift and crossed to the revolving doors and her waiting car.

Theo saw the same picture of elegance they had seen on the way in two hours ago. Sally-Jane saw a pleasured-in-her-clothes look. And something else was not as it had been.

'So where,' she said, 'are those ear-clips I'd kill for?'

'Lucky Harry,' said Theo.

The moment they got home, he would call Ed Segal. He had witnessed the fate of Chacewater people who thought their first loyalty was to president Harry, or president Bobby before him. It was unwise to by-pass the man who ran the company for them. So the legendary Ed had to be put in the picture about Harry's secretive call for what amounted to a buyer's rundown on the Mercury. And about this parallel obsession with Marina Marshall.

Back at her flat, Marina did not notice the message light on her answering machine. Her head was still full of Harry; her thighs still sticky with him.

She went to the laptop to log tonight's addition to the Chacewater chapter. No tape this trip. She hardly needed one to interview herself:

The trouble with Harry, sighs a current squeeze, is that he means it when he says he loves you. But he doesn't mean what you want him to mean. He doesn't mean, come live with him and be his love. He just means the next bit about proving all the pleasures. And oh, boy, he'll prove them – he'll quite spoil you for other men. But he isn't going to change. He doesn't know how to change. Fuck him and forget him, that's my advice. I hope I take it . . .

Humpty finally got through after being told five times that his brother's boat wasn't yet back at Baynard Cay.

'How are you, Toby? Good catch?'

'Get on with it, Humpty. I'm half-way to the crapper.'

'Just rang to confirm I'll be with you Saturday. Looking forward to it.'

'Don't.'

'Don't come?'

'Come. Just don't look forward to it.'

'Beg pardon?'

'Might have to bring up the subject of retirement.'

'That's a blow, Toby. Thought you'd be in the chair for many years yet.'

'Not talking about my retirement. Talking about yours.'

9

The Bloody Parrot

Dumpty left Humpty snoring at dawn and was galloping a colt into the wind when a motor-bike courier popped the Globe through the Baynard letterbox. Attached was Lord Bull's compliments slip with the message: *Ha! Scooped again, Humpty*. Boxed across the top of Page One was:

THE MERC GETS UP YOUR NOSE – OFFICIAL

The wife of the chief executive of the Mercury told a gathering of VIPs: 'The paper stinks. I wouldn't line the bloody parrot's cage with it.'

Three hundred guests looked on as furious husband Humpty Baynard hurried her from the glittering reception at the residence of the US Ambassador.

Mrs Dumpty Baynard blew her top when a headline-hungry female columnist on the family's downmarket rag streaked naked across the ballroom and had to be removed by US Marines.

Among those shocked by the incident were the Prime Minister, Archbishop of Canterbury, Cardinal Archbishop of Westminster, Chief Rabbi, chairman of the Press Complaints Commission...

A picture of Dumpty in veiled hunting topper flanked the story on one side. On the other was a cut-out coupon with the invitation to present it to a Mercury reader to fill in: *Dear Newsagent – Please cancel my order for the stinking Mercury and substitute the fragrant Globe for a month's FREE trial.*

Humpty winced at this further faggot on the pyre Toby was preparing for him. He tripped over the cat and swore at the bloody parrot. Then he phoned his unsympathetic editor.

'...But Jack, it's a lie. She does line the bloody parrot's cage with it.'

'Who cares, Hump? The Merc's the one selling out today. Everybody wants my Fanny and Danny scoop. Nobody'll buy the Globe to read about your bloody parrot. Calm down.'

'Calm down? *Calm down? CALM DOWN?*'

'Listen, the trick is not to help the Globe keep the story going. Their reptiles will be at your door any minute.'

'They'll get damn-all out of me, Jack.'

'Gag the bloody parrot. Lock Dumpty in the attic. Bind yourself to the mast and stuff wax in your ears. Don't think you can out-smart them.'

'Must go. Doorbell ringing.'

'Don't answer—'

Jack Stack's scream died as Humpty downed the phone, tightened his zebra-striped bathrobe and opened the door. On the step stood this weary young woman looking anything but menacing with a Tesco bag in each hand, and this weary young man weighed down by camera gear.

'Morning, Mr Baynard,' she said. 'We're from the Globe.'

'Prove it.'

'Prove it? We're admitting it.'

'You're wasting your time.'

'Is it true you're in a towering rage with your wife?'

The reporter put down a bag to fish out a tape recorder and switch on. Humpty took it from her and held it to his lips.

'I'm in a towering rage with Lord Bull. Print *that.*'

'You said a few choice words to her?'

'I said a few choice words to Lord Bull. Print *that.*'

'OK, let's talk off the record.' She took back the tape and switched off encouragingly.

'Ho-ho. D'you think I was born yesterday?'

'Chilly out here,' said the cameraman.

'Well, you needn't think you're coming in.'

'Only doing my job, guv. Just one quick snap of the bloody parrot –'

' – and just one quick word with it.' The reporter switched the tape back on. 'And we'll be off.'

'For the record.' Humpty grabbed the tape again. 'It's got no comment to make. Nor have I.'

'I need your wife's side of the story.'

'You need to get up earlier. She left at dawn. Now go away. I've got a plane to catch.'

'To the Bahamas?'

'Who told you?'

'Lord Bull. Will you be coming back?'

'Lord Bull seems to know everything. Ask him.'

'Well, at least tell us what the bloody parrot's called.'

'He wouldn't want his name in the Globe.' Humpty thrust the tape into her hands. 'Now stop harassing me. Clear off before I ring the Press Complaints Commission.'

'It's 020 7353 3732.'

The camera caught Humpty with fist upraised and bathrobe flapping as he slammed the door. The Globe pair tried various windows and keyholes for a sight of the bloody parrot, eventually snapping Humpty as he came into the conservatory and went to the cage. His mouth opened and closed. So did the bloody parrot's.

'Wellington, old son,' Humpty was saying. 'Dumpty wants to divorce me. Toby wants to fire me. But you'll stand by me, won't you?'

'Will I buggery,' said the bloody parrot.

Today's roses were red. Editor and deputy looked on as two flower shop girls carried armfuls to Marina's office.

'Show some respect, Bish.' They stood to attention, hands on hearts. 'Don't see wreaths like that every day.'

Clop.

Mid-morning sun streamed across Green Park into Marina's flat. It matched her mood. She had woken aglow at the prospect of lunch in Harry's river-view suite and an afternoon in that king-and-queen size bed. Oh, boy.

As she went to perk coffee, she noticed the red light that had been blinking on her answering machine all night. She played back Bish's message. The sun went in.

She fetched the Mercury from the pile on the mat, taking in the Fanny and Danny splash on her way back to the kitchen. She sat on a high stool, the paper drooping in her hand. A gallery of grinning

teeth mocked from the celebrity montage lining the walls. She had
been shafted. And it was her own fault. She had broken the twelfth
commandment: Thou shalt leave thy mobile on, whatsoever thou
wishest not to be rung in the middle of.

She phoned Claudia to say she was giving the office a miss today.

'No room anyway,' said Claudia. 'Can't move for roses.'

'And the card says?'

'*Oh, boy.*'

'Book lunch at the Ritz. Dom Pérignon on ice. Tell Harry I'll see
him there at 1.15. He'll say he thought we were lunching at the
Savoy. Tell him I said it's not far enough away from Fleet Street's
shittiest editor.'

The Globe pair had discovered that Dumpty might be found at her
sister's racing stables above the village. They sat in the car for an
hour before she came from the gallops and listened for almost four
seconds before inviting them to get knotted.

The photographer ferreted out a used plastic cup from the well
between front and back seats, overflowing with take-away debris,
full and empty Diet Pepsi cans, muddied wellies, Pampers
wrappings and Globes dating back to the last time the car was
cleaned. He filled the cup from his flask to fuel the reporter as she
spoke to her boss.

'...Went like a dream, Maria-Teresa. Thought he'd never stop.
And Leo's got Humpty with the bloody parrot and Dumpty giving
us the finger...Six hundred words? No sweat. On your screen in
half a mo...'

**Mercury boss Humpty Baynard was sick as a parrot yesterday.
His wife had left at dawn after a row over her publicly
rubbishing his 'stinking' newspaper.**

**And a few hours later Humpty quit the country for a secret
destination. A source revealed he was heading for the family's
Bahamas hideaway.**

**'Lord knows if I'll be back,' he sighed, opening his heart to me
in an exclusive interview.**

**He said he was in 'a towering rage' at the US ambassador's
VIP party when his wife declared the Mercury 'unfit to line the
bloody parrot's cage.'**

'I said a few choice words,' he confessed.

Alone in their grim Hampshire mansion, he tried to console the normally talkative parrot. He was not prepared to say when he might see Dumpty again. And neither was Humpty.

I traced her to her sister's racing stables and invited her side of the story. Her reply cannot be printed in a family newspaper...

Male heads and female eyes swivelled to Marina as she swanned through the rococo splendour of the Ritz restaurant in saffron trouser suit, hair drawn back into a black velvet bow. At a parkside table, Harry rose to greet her. He kissed a warm cheek, and she turned the other for another. In the centre of her place setting lay the emerald ear-clips she had left last night. Her eyes held his as she put them on.

'Some entrance.' He mimed applause and nodded at a couple of heads still swivelled their way.

'I'm giving my greatest performance. You saw that front page – *How Fanny and Danny conned our Marina.*'

'What kind of people could do this to you?'

'Didn't you know? Philip Gibbs's Street of Adventure is now Jack Stack's Street of Assholes.' She reached for the menu. 'Fuck it. Let's sting them with the biggest bill in the history of lunch.'

She chose *pâté de foie gras* with oodles of truffles, and lobster with all the trimmings. Harry said make that for two. The sommelier did not need to be asked to set a back-up bottle in the ice bucket.

'So wise me up about this Jack Stack guy.'

Marina did. She also wised him up about Humpty.

'They're murdering you,' said Harry.

'Do you reckon I should advertise for a white knight?' Her eyebrows went up. And stayed up as she positioned a hand for him to cover.

'How about me?' His hand moved on cue. 'I'm on the lookout for new properties. The Merc would suit us fine.'

Halfway through the lobster, Harry said, 'Marina, great idea. Fly back with me. We'll sail *Miss Print* down to the Bahamas. Drop in on Toby. Wrap it all up in one.'

Marina looked hard at him. Great idea? His old squeeze turning up to get him to hand his beloved paper over to her new squeeze?

'Better to use Humpty. Whisper in his ear that you're after some sort of merger – and he's got a fabulous future if he sets Toby up for you.'

'He'll believe that?'

'You bet. Humpty, being Humpty, will present it as his own idea. And Toby, being Toby, will see right through him. He'll want to talk to you direct.'

'OK, coach. Pity I can't get to see Humpty this trip. Didn't he say he was flying off today?'

'Indeed he did.' Marina pushed back her chair. 'Shan't be long.'

Harry joined the swivellers as she went out and as she came back.

'Missed you.' He eased a foot from a loafer to slip between her saffron pumps.

'Darling.' Her knees squeezed his advancing toe. 'I've rearranged your schedule. You're on Concorde at 5.45. Sitting next to a Mr H Baynard, would you believe?'

'Jeez, Marina, you don't waste much time.'

'Jeez, Harry, we don't have much time.'

'Which means' – he read his watch – 'I need to get moving right now if I'm going to make it to Heathrow.'

'Uh-uh. I've told the Savoy to have your bags ready for my driver. We've got a whole hour before he's outside my flat with the engine running.'

'Oh, boy.'

Male heads and female eyes swivelled to their incandescent faces as Marina led Harry out.

Waiting for the flight to be called, Harry opened the Mercury spread to gaze into the eyes of Marina's picture byline. He had a ready-already grin as Humpty came along.

'Well, hi there. Small world.'

'Getting smaller, Harry.' They shook hands. 'You've made my day – a Mercury reader in the first-class lounge.'

'Got a first-class little paper there.'

'Couldn't have said that when I took over. But I've managed to knock it into shape – against all the odds.'

'Say, what do you reckon the odds against finding ourselves in adjoining seats?'

'Hundred seats . . . got to be 99-to-1.'

'Make it 100-to-1 and I'll risk fifty with you.'

They compared boarding cards. Humpty's face went grey. Harry felt guilty. Five grand must be a lot of money to the guy.

Moments after take-off, the fine-boned stewardess was offering cocktails. Harry proposed dry Martini, straight-up-lemon-twist. Humpty seconded. Harry's spaced finger and thumb signalled large ones, and his circling hand signalled keep 'em coming. Haunches swayed away as the stewardess made the narrow aisle her catwalk. Harry nudged Humpty.

'You horny sonofabitch.'

'Eh?'

'Humpty, that sure was some wink she gave you.'

'Wink?' He peered up the aisle after her.

When she came back with the cocktails, he greeted her with a horny sonofabitch wink. Had he not shoved back in his pocket the bifocals that made him look older, he supposed he would have caught the return wink that Harry now confirmed.

'She means it. You're some stud, Humpty.'

'Takes one to know one.'

'I'll drink to that.' Harry sampled his Martini. 'Wow! Even the gin's supersonic. Me, I'm from bourbon country. Little place on the James. Why don't you stop over on the way back? I'll have my plane pick you up at DC.'

'Couldn't say no to that, Harry.'

Lord Bull was on Jack Stack's private line, chortling as he gave him a preview of tomorrow's thrilling instalment, surmounted by his very own headline: **MERC BOSS LEAVES THE COUNTRY**.

'Crap, Johnnie. Let's face it, you couldn't write a headline to save your life.'

'So what's yours?'

'SICK AS A BLOODY PARROT.'

'You're a real pro, Jack. Globe's not the same without you. How could you leave to work for that prick?'

'Told you, Johnnie. You think you're editor-in-chief.'

'I am editor-in-chief.'

'There you go again.'

Amazing, thought Humpty, how much he and Harry had in common. Scions of great publishing families. Hard drinkers. High rollers. Horny sonsofabitch.

'Y'know, Harry, I could have done without the wife's antics at the party. Soon be the ex-wife at this rate.'

'Johnnie Bull sure made a meal of it.'

'As Scarlett said to O'Hara – frankly, my dear, who gives a shit? The Mercury's the one selling out today. Everybody wants my Fanny and Danny scoop. Nobody'll buy the Globe to read about a bloody parrot.'

'Guess you've got Johnnie worried.'

'Said I was mad to go red-top. Stark, staring, raving mad to hire Jack Stack. But I'm putting on thousands.'

'That, Humpty, is what makes you a great publisher. You stick the bottom line at the top.'

'Where else, Harry?' He drained his glass.

'You wouldn't be fool enough to have your editor pitch the Merc at people like yourself.'

'God, no. If the paper were edited to please me, it would have a readership of one.' He repeated this most pleasing of several such compliments Jack Stack had paid him.

Humpty had tested positive for vanity, stupidity, lechery and thirst. Time to try him on avarice.

'Promise you won't jump down my throat if I say what's on my mind?'

'Course not, Harry. Fire away.'

'You see, I not only inherited Pa's business. I also inherited Pa's team. Great guys, don't get me wrong. But the legendary Ed's 80, for heaven's sake – and I reckon Chacewater Inc. is going nowhere unless I get myself a modern CEO. And, Humpty' – he put a hand on his arm – 'that's got to mean somebody like you.'

'Like me?' He found a fresh glass in his hand and looked up too late to exchange winks with the retreating stewardess. 'Like me.'

'All I'm saying is would you think about it? It'd mean treble what you make in London. Plus all the benefits a major league American CEO gets these days. Golden hello. Piece of the action. Corporate airplanes – '

'Needs some thought.' Mustn't sound like a man on his way to be fired. 'Roots. Family. Friends. Sort of thing.'

' – School fees. Doctor bills. Country club. Five-star vacations. Top-hat pension. Relocation taken care of.'

'I'd want to relocate the bloody parrot.'

'Natch.'

Dinner was being served when Humpty woke. His head was still afloat so he declined the premier cru Puligny-Montrachet in favour of still Malvern. Though after the lobster he was unable to turn aside a twenty-year tawny port with the Wensleydale.

'Humpty. Been thinking. I don't reckon you're a guy who could just turn his back on the family business.'

'Well...' Humpty had by now steeled himself to turn his back not only on the family business but the family.

'We'd get round that if we merged your outfit with mine. That would secure the bridgehead I want into Europe. And you'd run Chacewater Inc. both sides of the Atlantic. Concorde once a week. No problem.'

'No problem.' That stewardess once a week.

'Reason I'm saying merger is that I wouldn't want to put Toby's back up. But you and I' – he tapped his nose – 'we know we're talking take-over.'

'Quite.' Humpty tapped his nose.

One glass more, and he was set to drop the idea into Toby's lap. Then he'd stop over at Chacewater on the way back and they would take it from there. But whatever and what the hell, said Harry, they'd have themselves a real good time. They exchanged horny sonofabitch winks.

Humpty was X-raying the stewardess up and down the aisle. Harry was watching him.

'I wouldn't mind' – Humpty listened to himself slurring – 'getting into her cockpit.'

'So why don't we invite her and a buddy out tonight? You owe me five big ones. Double or quits I can't set it up?'

'Double or quits, it is.'

Humpty swallowed as Harry unclipped to go after the stewardess. He was soon back.

'Break it to me gently, Humpty – is Naff orf some limey expression meaning what I think it means?'

'Can't win 'em all, Harry.'

The beleaguered First Lady of Fleet Street was at her flat, flipping open the new issue of British Journalism Review. It was only weeks since she had sent the highbrow quarterly a cover piece on the beleaguered royals. Who would have thought that, by the time it got into print, she would know just how it felt to be scourged by their tormentor-in-chief?

The fearsome sounds you hear in Fleet Street today echo those of the Paris of Louis XVI. Tabloid tumbrils clatter over the cobbles. Tabloid tricoteuses click their computer mice.

Night after night, the presses thunder mockery and mischief, hatred and contempt at the Palace. And morning after morning, the royals finger their collars to check heads are still on shoulders (and names still on the Civil List payroll). Will editors be satisfied only when Vicki, Nicky, Ricky and Mickey have been dragged to the guillotine?...

The phone interrupted her reading.

'Harry darling! Good trip? How was Humpty?'

'Less and less three-piece as the Martinis went in.'

'Did the bait go in?'

'Hook, line and stinker. When he stops over on the way back, I'll know how right you were.'

'Or weren't.'

'More important, how soon before you stop over?'

'The good news is I've been promised that Max Magnus interview some time in the next week or two – '

'That's good news?'

' – and I could fly on down to you from Toronto.'

'Skip Magnus. I need you more.'

'Come on, Harry. He hasn't given an interview in twenty years. This is the chapter that'll get my book into the headlines. Besides, if you drop out of the white knight game, I'll need a reserve, won't I?'

10

Whaaat-ever...

Rocking his chair gently on the pillared verandah of his pink clapboard villa atop his private cliff, Toby Baynard scanned his private horizon. Brochure-blue Bahamas shallows glinted in the late afternoon sun. Feathery casuarinas fringed the white beach. But the prospect did not soothe. Nor did the gin and tonic. Nor Tauber oozing 'You Are My Heart's Delight' from the stereo.

'*Whaaat*-ever...' sighed Toby.

The word would burst from him now and again, without apparent relevance other than as some sort of protest at his predicament. Indeed, it served to remind visitors that he was not quite over his stroke. He had by now mostly regained use of the affected arm and leg, though a couple of brain switches weren't always engaging. An episode or a person might momentarily slip out of memory. Three weeks ago, he asked someone to set up a surprise farewell party for the last of his live-in nurses, not appreciating that someone was in fact that nurse.

Toby appeared reassuringly prime-of-life in skipper cap, salty beard, bare chest, shorts and sandals. His Harley Street man had spent five days of the blue marlin season at Baynard Cay and pronounced him in fair shape, so long as he let someone else tussle with anything bigger than a triple-tail. The prescription was to keep taking the tablets and keep the back turned on Fleet Street.

But this last week Toby had been doing his fishing in the study. Stacked against its shelves were almost a year of unopened packages of Mercurys, ritually mailed every week along with yards of management printout and buzzwordy bulletins from Humpty. Rip van Baynard had woken too late. The Merc was now recognisable only by the name on its red-top badge. The winged helmet logo had flown. Layout, typography, content and tone were utterly different. The exclamation marks had routed the semi-colons. Wednesday's Adventures of Heidi Hunt mocked Thursday's Marina Marshall column, now as alien as sole Véronique in a fish-and-chip shop.

Toby rocked faster as he readied himself for Humpty's arrival. Between them, the half-brothers had done for the dynasty. After more than a century, Baynard Publishing had run out of publishing Baynards.

Five toots of the horn plus two for luck, from housekeeper Dahlia's teenage son at the wheel of the old Jeep, signalled the entry of Humpty and enough posh suitcases for a cruise. Dahlia's lad was joined by his sister to carry in the luggage and draw identical conclusions about the owner of the face boiling between panama and cravat.

Humpty called out halfway up the verandah steps. 'You're looking bloody marvellous, Toby.'

'More than I can say for the Merc. Looks as though someone's upchucked all over it.'

'Steady on.' Humpty fanned himself with the panama. 'Sales up a hundred thou. Yonks since we had a tale like that to tell.'

Dahlia's daughter offered crystal tumblers on a Georgian tray. Humpty took a gulp, wishing there were less G and more T. He had sunk one or two to shorten the Miami flight, and one or two more waiting for the hop to Abaco island. He found a perch on the verandah rail.

'Sweaty trip.' He wrinkled his nose and flapped his elbows.

'London–Nassau would have made more sense.'

'Thought I'd give Concorde a whirl.'

'The Merc's deep in the red – and the chief exec flies Concorde? You can pay the difference yourself.'

'Marina – '

'Marina what?'

' – flies Concorde.'

'So can you, when publishers are queuing to steal you away from me. Ever stop to wonder why they aren't?'

'Oh, but they are.' Humpty steadied himself against a pillar. 'I'm being head-hunted right now.'

'Someone's pulling your plonker.'

'Not at all. You'd be surprised.'

'Right – I would be surprised. Been catching up with your bulletins.' He drew a note from his pocket. 'Decelerative invoice response. Meaning delay payments?'

'Eases cash flow. Well, our cash flow.'

'Humpty, what language is this?'

'Language of millennium management.'

'And bringing in mad Jack Stack? That's millennium management?'

'Master-stroke, Toby. Robbing the enemy of the smartest tabloid editor in the game.'

'So now someone's hunting your head. Who's the lucky sod?'

'Sorry, Toby. Sworn to secrecy.'

Humpty crossed his heart and lost his balance. His long frame toppled backwards over the verandah rail into the rose bushes.

'*Whaaat*-ever...' sighed Toby.

Under the gaze of the same photo of Marina and the twins that sat on her desk, Toby was dressing for dinner, which in this part of the world meant putting on a shirt.

Before going downstairs, he riffled through the latest management consultancy offering Humpty had brought. He snorted, groaned, laughed out loud – and sucked in breath at the accompanying invoice. He let printout concertina to the rug, and consulted himself for nothing.

Is there any way back for the newspaper I loved? *Not now.* Do I enjoy finding myself proprietor of this chortling bully of a tabloid? Fantabulous!! Funtastic!! Sexational!! *Not one bit.* Even though, if I shut my eyes and open my wallet, it could be Fleet Street's next big success story? *No, thanks.* So why set myself up for maybe a final stroke? *Why indeed?*

The phone rang. 'Hi skipper. It's your favourite peace officer.'

'How you doing, Sergeant Mac.'

'Got a cell guest. Reporter from Miami. Noseying around asking about you. Flashing bills. Flashed one too many. Lost the lot – and his Rolex. I'm giving him a Band-Aid and a bed for the night.'

'What's his game?'

'Just confirmed he's who he says he is. Name of Clarence C Campbell. Reckons he's here to cover Independence Day for the Chacewater papers.'

'Bullshit.'

'Sure. But bullshit ain't against the law. He's free to fly out in the morning.'

'Can't send Clarence C Campbell home empty-handed, Mac. Do him a favour. Happen to mention my doctor just told me to quit the newspaper racket PDQ – and take up fishing full-time.'

'Sure. And I'll do you a favour. Quit the law and order racket PDQ – and be your first mate full-time.'

'You're on, Mac. Say, how about taking *Freelance* out tomorrow? My thirsty brother's going to need a day at sea to blow away the mother of all hangovers.'

Toby went down to the dining room. Dahlia was clearing his thirsty brother's place setting.

'Mr Humpty,' she announced, 'ain't going to make it for dinner. I've washed his face and put him to bed. And said his prayers.'

She had also opened his bedside Bible at Proverbs 20:1. *Wine is a mocker, strong drink is raging; and whosoever is deceived thereby is not wise.*

'Good for you, Dahlia. Wake the man with coffee and aspirins at dawn. Mac and I are going to bury him at sea.'

Toby went out on the verandah to watch sun melt into ocean and subtropical night come down like a roller blind. Why did such a moment seem wanting? Why else but Marina? If only her arm were round his waist again, her head against his shoulder again.

'*Whaaat*-ever . . .' sighed Toby.

Wiping a clammy hand on the sleeve of his dated suit, the chairman of Bogbrush Associates was shown into Bish's office. Thanks to his old mate, Norman Bogbrush was about to hit the big time.

Bish had clearly prospered in journalism since they sat opposite each other on the local rag. Just look at him now. Norman Bogbrush had clearly not prospered in market research. Just look at him now. But yesterday had come Bish's call, inviting Bogbrush Associates to pitch for the Mercury account. My editor reckons those SW1 piss artists aren't worth a million of our research budget, Bish had said. Told him I know an E8 man who is.

Norman had fed his laptop till dawn. Now he set it up on Bish's lap, tilting the screen to display the evidence that Bogbrush and the Merc were made for each other.

81

'There you are, Bish. The Merc needs a programme of headline sociological surveys. Bogbrush delivers.'

'Great, Norman,' said Bish. 'You're playing our tune.'

'Which do you want first then? Sex on the Job, Sex with a Stranger, Sex in Suburbia, Sex on the Move, Sex and—'

'First,' said Bish, 'we want to give you a trial run. See if you'll enjoy working with us.'

'Oh, we will,' said Norman. 'Be like old times.'

'What the editor wants – and wants quick – is a poll of readers' likes and dislikes about our star writers. Who turns them on. Who turns them off. Who scores with the target generation. Who with the geriatrics.'

Norman took back his laptop and typed away. 'Got it.' He lifted his fingers as he looked to Bish for the next bit.

'My editor is betting that the columnist with the worst ratings will be Marina Marshall. Make a note of that.'

'Marina Marshall.' Norman made a note of that.

'Because she's boring.'

'Boring.'

'Snobbish. Out of touch. In a time warp.'

'Snobbish. Out of touch. In a time warp.'

'And he's betting Heidi Hunt will be the readers' favourite by a mile. Why, you ask? Because she's everything Marina isn't. Born of the age we live in and sexy with it.'

Norman echoed as he typed.

'Come back with it tonight and we're in business.'

'Tonight?' Norman blinked.

'No hurry then. Tomorrow morning.'

Spilling out of the revolving doors into the rain, Norman turned up his collar and held his laptop case over his head. To deliver on time, he and his associates – the seven Bogbrush sisters – would poll themselves three hundred time each through the night. But win the Mercury account and they'd be swapping their grim basement in E8 for an ash and chrome penthouse in SW1. The thought made the rain seem less wet.

Brown pelicans watched Toby's 42-footer chug past the candy-striped Hope Town lighthouse. Beyond the coral reef, Sergeant Mac opened the throttles and *Freelance* ploughed twin furrows through the ocean towards the rising sun and, with luck, the rising fish.

Humpty was this morning overdressed in dude safari suit. Toby and Sergeant Mac were in washed-out jeans, goombay shirts and Treasure Cay resort baseball caps on back to front.

Sergeant Mac came down from the bridge to set deep-sea rods in the brass gimbals of the swivel armchairs at the stern. He motioned Humpty to take a seat, readied frozen six-packs of ballyhoo bait and climbed back up to take the wheel so half-brother could join half-brother.

'Sorry if I seemed a little grumpy.' Toby swung in his chair. 'Been looking forward to firing you. But now you're being head-hunted, what's the point?'

Sergeant Mac slowed to an even five knots. He had sighted small, yellowy islands of sargasso weed bobbing on the light sea. Here, the shrimp fed, and were fed upon by fish who would themselves be fed upon, all the way up the predatory chain to the armchair fishermen now about to trail their lines.

'Beats going to the shrink, Humpty. Nothing between us and the horizon. Nothing between us and heaven. Who needs Fleet Street? Who needs the Merc? I don't.'

'Always someone who thinks he does.'

'Such as?'

'Need to give it some thought.' Humpty gave it some thought. 'Might we get a better deal outside the UK?'

'Good thinking, Humpty. A buyer without a stake in Fleet Street would avoid monopolies hassle. How about Max Magnus?'

'Want a horse's head on your pillow?' He looked over his shoulder. 'Rather deal with our kind of guys.'

'Like?'

'Like, er – off the top of my head – Chacewater?'

'Chacewater?' Toby reached under his chair for a couple of cans of beer and passed one to Humpty. 'What makes you think they'd be interested?'

'My spies tell me Harry Chacewater's looking for a bridgehead into Europe. And he's sitting on a mountain of cash. If you like, Toby, I could have a discreet word.'

'Know him?'

'Marina introduced us at an embassy party.'

'Friend of hers, is he?' His rib-cage felt hollow.

'Went to interview him for that press barons book.'

'I used to lunch his Pa whenever he was in London. And that old fox – the legendary Ed. Only know the son from the gossip columns. Bit of a playboy, eh?'

'Normal healthy bachelor, I'd say. Found myself next to him on Concorde coming over. Lot in common.'

The hunter of Humpty's head was revealed. The mission of Clarence C Campbell was explained. They were pawns in a Chacewater Inc. game. So was Harry. The legendary Ed would still be pulling the strings.

'When might you find yourself next to Harry again?'

'Suppose I could take up his invitation to pop in for a swim on the way back.'

'Do that. If he's serious, tell him to come and see me.'

'Hallelujah!' Humpty roared as his line tautened.

'It's a big one,' yelled Sergeant Mac from the bridge. He guessed that anything dwarfing a sardine would be a monster in Humpty's experience. 'Hold tight, man.'

Humpty played the game he had learned as a boy on the banks of the Rother, easing the rod forward then reeling in, again and again. Nothing to it.

Suddenly, Toby was out of his chair and standing by with the gaff as, in a flash of burnished gold, a thirty-pound dorado spiralled out of the water. Toby went to hook it into the open catch-box but missed. The fish flew at Humpty's tailored lap, brought tears to his eyes, and bounced out again into the sea. Still on the line, it took the rod – and Humpty with it.

'Save the goddam tackle, skipper,' roared Sergeant Mac.

'Oh, no!' Humpty's ears picked up *Jaws* music.

Toby, who had moved to offer him the blunt end of the gaff, reversed it to rescue the rod first.

Jack Stack had advised Gloria Mundy that his flat was the most secure place, and after dark the safest time, to work on the Princess Xenia voodoo diaries. But weekdays only. Weekends, he reserved for debriefing Heidi Hunt.

Gloria had arrived tonight with sister Jenny, who was on a nice little earner translating the microscopic Romanian entries made when Xenia shared rooms with her at Cambridge. Jenny lifted her eyes from her magnifying glass to look at Jack Stack like a witch at a cat as he lapped vampire-repellent garlic butter from his take-away Chicken Kiev and chips.

'What's the score?' He dabbed his chin.

'Sixty-six,' said Gloria. 'Third-year diary to come.'

'I'm praying for three figures.'

'Pray for more days like the one before the Boat Race. She hoodoo'd the whole crew at a sitting.'

'The year Cambridge won by a mile?'

'No.' Jenny found the entry. 'The year Cambridge sank. It was her own crew she put the mockers on – they'd ditched Thicky Ricky for a lighter cox and made him cry.'

'Hell, if she'd almost drown nine men over the size of their cox, what's she going to do to the two princes standing between Ricky and the throne?'

'Cat meunière,' said Jenny. 'No, Bat meunière. That red ink doesn't make microscopic Romanian any easier.'

'Stop calling it ink,' said Jack Stack, 'OK?'

11

The Pool

From their heavy gilt frames on the library walls, four Chacewater generations looked to the walnut-faced little man in the wing chair. The legendary Ed shrugged at them. He'd do his darnedest, sure, but this time their boy just didn't want to be saved.

Their boy had gone down to the river to check out *Miss Print IV*, leaving his vice-president with the file on the Mercury. Past and present samples of the paper were strewn on the Indian carpet around Edgar Segal's neat brogues, along with reports, charts and cuttings amassed by Chacewater's London man, George Theodoulou.

Harry's summary, on the back of a Savoy postcard, listed every reason for taking over the Mercury except his real reason. Ed tsk-tsked. Just as well Theo had phoned to wise him up on the Marina Marshall factor. And yesterday, as if confirmation were needed, Mom Chacewater had Mrs Ed over for tea to tell her Harry was nuts about the First Lady of Fleet Street, imagine, and too bad he wasn't man enough for her because this was the woman who could be the making of him.

Ed felt all his 80 years as he read Theo's report telling Harry what Harry wanted to hear. How different from Theo's other report telling Ed what Harry didn't want to hear: *The Merc is at the ass-end of Fleet Street, where the silly season runs January thru December... three words describe its editor: nasty, British and short...*

But the Clarence C Campbell contribution had Ed chuckling. It catalogued CCC's heroic endeavours in pursuit of an insight into the mind of Lord Toby. Two sentences passed on by Sergeant Mac had been crafted into a thousand words, accompanied by long-focus photos of a bare-chested Toby on the verandah. Their graininess asserted the difficulty of the assignment, as the attached expenses sheet asserted its worth. CCC kindly requested Harry to OK his claim for cash payments of $10,500 to 'Confidential Informants'. The pushover president of Chacewater Inc. had kindly endorsed it.

The vice-president was offering a further shrug to the gallery as their boy bounded into the library in Second Fleet sweatshirt, cut-off jeans and trainers.

'Well then, Uncle Ed. How about that for a ripe peach?'

'Harry, it ain't a peach. It's a lemon.'

'Come on. The Mercury could sure as hell make a pile.'

'Pile of what?' Ed's toe stabbed the double-page spread at his feet: **LESBO SKINMAGS IN THE PALACE BINBAGS**. 'Ain't our scene, Harry.'

'I know our scene.' There was an edge to his tone. 'I aim to lift the Merc back into the family market.'

'Then you'd sure as hell lose a pile.'

Harry didn't want an argument with Uncle Ed because he never won an argument with Uncle Ed. He avoided his eye.

'Listen, I've got their chief exec dropping by in a couple hours. Just play along, OK? Kidded him your job's waiting if he sets brother Toby up for me.'

'Harry, you're the one being set up. You'd just be buying their problems.'

'Jeez, Ed. Everything's problems at your age.' Harry moved to the door.

'Hey.' Ed called after him. 'If I wasn't 80 – they wouldn't be problems?'

Ed took off his rimless glasses and, unnecessarily, began to clean them with his top pocket handkerchief. He put them back on and stretched a snake-veined hand to pick up a Mercury and flip open Marina's spread. Was this the face that would do for poor old Chacewater what Helen's had done for poor old Troy?

Not if the legendary Ed could help it.

From his seat by the pilot as the helicopter came down to the croquet lawn, Humpty looked and marvelled. So this was Harry's little place on the James. By comparison, Humpty's little place on the Hamble was a chicken coop.

'Great to see you.' Harry welcomed him with a salesman's double handshake. 'So how'd it go?'

'According to plan. Got Toby nicely teed up for you.'

'And I've got the legendary Ed teed up for you. But keep shtum. I haven't told him I've chosen his successor.'

Humpty was steaming in double-breasted blazer with fourteen brass buttons. He smoothed his already smooth hair as they went into the library. Ed, having heard the helicopter, had stowed away the Mercury material.

'Ed, I very much want you to meet Humphrey Baynard – boss of the London Mercury. And Humpty, this is Edgar Segal – the legendary Ed. My vice-president. My editor-in-chief. And my honorary uncle.'

'Hi, Humphrey.' He couldn't call a guy Humpty. They shook hands. 'Just in from London?'

'Bahamas, matter of fact. Been to see brother Toby.' He looked at Harry. 'Spot of fishing.'

'So' – Ed wondered how much more Harry hadn't told him – 'how's dear old Toby these days?'

'Much improved. But no way back to Fleet Street, I fear.'

'And how's dear old Fleet Street these days?'

'Everywhere but dear old Fleet Street. Nobody left but the Merc. And St Bride's.'

'Ah, St Bride's. Harry's Pa and I were there for your father's memorial service. Place means a lot to us Virginians. It's where the parents of Virginia Dare got married, of course.'

'Of course.' Of course? 'Virginia Dare?'

'You know – first English baby born in America? Ralegh's lost colony? Hey, that smile says you're putting me on.'

'Not at all, Ed. Just never ceases to amaze me – you Yankees knowing more English history than we do.'

'Hereabouts, Mr Baynard' – Ed caught Pa's eye on the wall – 'we ain't Yankees.'

'Never mind. You're all jolly good chaps.'

'Jeez, that the time?' said Harry, without looking at his watch. 'Humpty, let's go take that swim.'

Harry was back in a moment to tell Ed the helicopter was going to be delayed while they replaced the altimeter. Ed said to take all week if they liked; nowhere he was happier to be stuck than old Chacewater House.

'Relax,' said Harry. 'I'm just stringing the jerk along.'

'Sure you are, Harry.'

Humpty reappeared in Palm Beach shirt and Bermudas, long red socks and sandals, panama and Pentax. Harry showed him around and took souvenir shots of him against the backgrounds of the bandstand and *Miss Print IV* and *IV$^{1}/_{2}$*.

'Humpty, she's all set for a trip down to Baynard Cay.'

'Sooner the better. I've convinced Toby it's time to sell, merge, call it what you like. Told him you're the ideal partner.'

'And you're some operator.' He punched an ice-white arm.

The legendary Ed had made his way up to the Sky Room. It was a great place to sit and pull hairs from your ears while an altimeter was being replaced. Meanwhile, you could help yourself from fridge or percolator. And spot a Red Cardinal or two, or maybe something rarer to check out in the Audubon volumes on the shelf.

He perched on a stool behind binoculars mounted at an open panel in the cupola. For a while he scanned the river bank, then swung to the boxwood hedge around the pool. He sharpened the focus to find himself studying not *Cardinalis Virginianus* or anything else in *The Birds of America* – but *Stewardesssis Aeronauticus*, and a pair at that.

The two shortish blondes in shortish airline uniforms, their hair improbably big for their caps, were stationed either side of the pavilion steps as though to offer a gangway greeting. The illusion was assisted by a Tony Bennett boarding tape on the pool sound system.

'Hi, Harry,' they said. And saluted.

'Glad you could make it, ladies,' said Harry, 'Meet Humpty, my good old British buddy.'

'I'm Lula,' said little Lula, raising her sunglasses to take him in. 'Welcome aboard.'

'I'm Lara,' said little Lara. 'Love those socks.'

Humpty raised his Pentax but let it fall when Harry had a word in his ear. No camera from here on in, man. Might be getting some action you wouldn't want Kodak to process.

Little Lara wheeled over the drinks trolley, lifted a bottle from the ice bucket and displayed the label.

'French,' she said as she poured. 'Only way to fly.'

'I'm a BA man myself,' said Humpty.

Little Lara widened her eyes at little Lula.

'Bottoms up,' said Harry and emptied his glass.

Little Lula widened her eyes at little Lara.

Harry reduced himself to swim shorts and, while Humpty took his time about it, nipped into the pavilion to kill Tony Bennett and substitute Mendelssohn. The girls unbuttoned faster as My Heart was abruptly left in San Francisco to make way for the Italian Symphony.

The men now looked like a before-and-after ad for Ambre Solaire. Humpty went even paler as Harry turned him aside to ask who did he fancy first. Or did he maybe fancy them together?

Then the girls were in the water, yelping and waving. Humpty took a chair by Harry at a poolside table and watched them show off their synchronised backstroke, sparkling as the sun caught diamanté shades and gold chains at neck, wrists and just the one ankle. Humpty briefly fished out the bifocals that made him look older. He gulped. Those white bikinis were not white bikinis. Those blondes were not blondes.

Harry nudged. 'Made up your mind, you horny sonofabitch?'

'I'm easy.' Humpty cleared his throat.

'Come on in,' called little Lara. Harry did. Humpty didn't. He sipped his drink, trying not to blink and miss a moment of bobbing breast and gleaming bush.

'Stand by for take-off,' roared Harry.

The girls dragged him under, shrieking when little Lara came up riding his shoulders and flourishing his shorts. She flung them over his head into the pool as he chased her to the pavilion, yelling the Batman theme.

Once through the doors, Harry confessed that he was a reformed character. He'd fallen in love with a lady in London, England. Sure wasn't easy when you got backache if you went without a couple days, but there you go. Little Lara reckoned there was no call to feel guilty about just a little old back rub. Harry reckoned she'd got to be right about that. After four minutes on the massage table, he turned over to present gladsome grin and gladsome groin, tucked hands behind head and told himself it wouldn't mean a thing.

Humpty put away his bifocals as little Lula came dripping from the pool. He handed her a towel to wrap herself but she used it to turban her hair. He could hear himself breathing as she bent to refill his glass, and her nipple stiffened on his forearm. Then her knees were nudging his as she invited him to be a honey and oil her before she began to roast. Drink in hand, she turned between his thighs on an invisible spit while his hands basted her. The vein at his temple throbbed. This was the first fresh flesh Humpty had fumbled since he married Dumpty. He had come to accept that he was destined to die without ever parking in a new erogenous zone.

Little Lula matched his sighs before putting her drink down to scoop oil from her navel and transfer it to his. Having teased inside his waistband, she drew him up, slipped his shorts to his ankles and sat him down again. Her eyes and mouth fluttered as she splayed herself across his lap and trilled that this was little Lula's lucky day. She caught her breath five times while installing him. There followed a flow of commendations for his e-*nor*-mous parts and fan-*tas*-tic performance until he erupted in triumph. Little Lula turned up the ecstasy, rolling her head and telling him she'd never popped her cookies so many times. And, oh-oh, she just couldn't believe this, here we go a-*gain*...

Dazed by unaccustomed measures of sun, champagne and gratitude, Humpty found himself being led into the shallow end. He held on to the ladder to stop the horizon see-sawing. The attentions he was receiving below the waterline confirmed his doubts about the range and quality of his sex life hitherto. Twice in twenty minutes, eh? And that was just him. A blonde head came up grinning. It wasn't little Lula. It was little Lara.

By the time little Lula bobbed out of the pavilion hand in hand with Harry, Humpty was sleeping the sleep of the shagged out. Little Lara borrowed his Pentax for a sequence with little Lula posing with him this way and that; then posed herself with him that way and this. They snapped him with an airline cap over his born-again genitalia, and finished the reel with Harry leaving the springboard for a plunge to retrieve his shorts.

Not even the roar of the helicopter lifting the legendary Ed up and away home could wake Humpty. He was still snoring when Harry saw the girls to their open-top white BMW and gave each a peck on each cheek.

'These uniforms sure do the trick,' said little Lula.

'Great if we got to keep 'em,' said little Lara.

'Just send me the the the tab, baby.'

Marina's bedside phone warbled. She lifted it to hear Mendelssohn's 'Spring Song' accelerating in the background.

'God, Harry. Don't you know it's 3 am here?'

'All I know is you're brilliant.'

'You're waking me up to tell me that?'

'And to tell you the scenario's panning out just the way you wrote it. It's all set up for me to go see Toby.'

'So why aren't you there?'

'I was planning to take the boat down at the weekend.'

'The boat? The weekend? Darling, scramble the Chacewater air force. Helicopter at dawn. Boeing 757 warming up on the tarmac. Ring Toby now. Tell him you're on your way.'

12

Dirty Pictures

Humpty was now resolved to be more of a Harry. Get a sex life. Put himself about a bit. Every other man at the top seemed to be on at least a second wife and to have at least one mistress on the go.

He buzzed his secretary to get the First Lady of Fleet Street on the line.

'Absolutely perfect day for tea in the roof garden, Marina. Care to join me?...Perfect.'

Will you come into my parlour? said the fly to the spider.

Jack Stack headed for the Lifestyle department. Maria-Teresa's still-unconfirmed successor was just getting to her chair six hours after leaving it at 3.30 am.

'Staff beat you to it again, Kitty?' The editor sniffed. 'Ma Teresa used to set a better example.'

'For fuck's sake, Jack. I'm working dawn till dawn. I'm 33 and I look 53.' Her tired hair fell back as she cleared it from her forehead. 'Neglect the kids – my ex is suing for custody. Neglect my lover – he's probably screwing the au pair as we speak.'

'Maria-Teresa was better organised.'

'Fucking Maria-Teresa had a fucking deputy.'

'Yeah, you're right, Kitty. Can't go on expecting you to produce Lifestyle single-handed.'

'Thanks. I really am knackered.'

'I'm moving in Heidi to share your burden.'

'Heidi? Is she really the right person to be number two in Lifestyle?'

'Course not, Kitty. You're the right person. Heidi's going to be number one. Ta-ta.'

Kitty screeched after him. 'Tell her – don't expect me to rewrite her godawful copy any more. That Centrefold Princess crap goes in just the way the illiterate slag wrote it.'

As ever when the lift doors opened at the boardroom floor, Maxine was waiting, hands at prayer.

'Will it be Indian or China, Marina?'

'I'm easy – whichever he's having.'

'Oh, it's always China at teatime.'

Maxine ushered her to the double doors and threw them open. Humpty left his desk, catching Marina's scent and appraising her lemon silk ensemble as he compared her with the jodhpured Dumpty, invariably reeking of Cheval Number 5.

'Hi, Marina. Lots to tell you.' His sun-struck face was a souvenir of that afternoon around the Chacewater pool, as was his sun-struck bottom and his incipient erection.

From the garden six floors up, the view took in the gilded figure of Justice atop the Old Bailey, the dome of St Paul's and the gorge of Fleet Street. In one panorama: purgatory, heaven and hell.

'Dammit,' said Humpty. 'Fountain's farting again.'

'What's new?'

'Wonder why Toby never had it fixed.'

'It made him laugh.'

'He asked after you. Warmest regards.'

'Is he OK?' It mattered. Being up here once more brought everything back. It mattered very much.

'Vastly improved. Mind you, no question of back to work. You'll have to make do with me. Not too terrifying a prospect, I hope?'

'I bet you can be pretty terrifying when you want.'

'When I want.' He lapped it up. 'Bumped into another fan of yours on the plane out – Harry Chacewater. Invited me to pop in for a dip on the way back.'

'Remarkable place.'

'Remarkable chap. Remarkable effect on women.'

'He's not the only one.' Her gaze teased until Humpty looked away. 'And you know it, don't you?' She had him. One more for her collection of glove puppets.

He gestured towards a striped hammock. She took a chair by the low table on which Maxine was now setting the tea tray. Alone on the hammock, Humpty swung annoyingly.

'I'm looking forward to this book – what's it called – *Press Barons of the World*?'

'I hope not. Got to be sexy to sell.'

'Just what I keep telling Jack Stack.'

'You shouldn't encourage the man.'

She tapped him on the back of the hand, the way nanny did. It sent a tingle through him, the way nanny did. He halted the hammock to pour thin China tea into thin China cups poised alongside thin cucumber sandwiches, thin Belgian biscuits and thick Madeira slices.

'Back in a sec.' He rose. 'Something I want you to read.'

He returned with the spiral-bound opinion poll commissioned from Bogbrush Associates. Colour graphics leaped from glossy pages. Method footnotes affirmed statistical substance. The charts rated Marina low against Heidi in every category except popularity with the over-65s. To the question, Would you like her column more often? the Yes percentage was 99 for Heidi against 6 for Marina.

'Don't let it worry you.' Humpty flapped a dismissive hand at the document. 'You've got me on your side.'

She opened a spread dedicated to a dew-lipped picture of Jack Stack's protégée and headlined **What they say about Heidi Hunt.** There were illustrated samples of her Adventures:

CATWALK HEIDI – Supermodels show miaow
REAR-ADMIRABLE HEIDI – Top of the bell-bottoms
GRAND PRIX HEIDI – Dicing for pole position

And there was a run of quotes appreciating her beauty, daring and humour. Mrs CW of York said, 'I like Heidi because she gets my husband up in the morning – do you think she could possibly manage twice a week?'

On the next spread, headlined **What they say about Marina Marshall**, sat the old Snowman picture. It was accompanied by a single complimentary response beginning, 'I've been a Mercury reader since before the war...' Weighed against this was a page of criticisms of her as boring, snobbish and terribly dated. Ms TP of Truro said, 'She's a leftover from the days of debs' delights and cigarette holders.'

Marina threw down the report. 'You're never going to fall for that, are you?'

'Wasn't born yesterday.' He covered her hand. 'Leave it with me.'

'Leave it with you – and what?'

'And I'll have a word with him.'

'A word?' She lifted his hand away. 'Just fire him. The survey is phoney. Why else avoid using a regular market research outfit? Bogbrush Associates? Jesus.'

'Marina, it isn't that simple. Trust me. I have good reason for not rocking the boat at this moment in time.'

'You mean not when Jack Stack's boarded it and run the Jolly Roger up the mast?'

'I mean not when I've found a white knight.' He tapped his nose. 'Someone to put in the investment I need to get this show on the road. Look, I know you've been trusted with plenty of secrets up here. I'm going to trust you with the biggest – I've sold Chacewater the idea of a great transatlantic merger. His dollars. My know-how. Unbeatable.'

'You really amaze me.' Marina was amazed at how amazed she managed to sound. 'But what about Toby?'

'All taken care of.'

'Quite the ringmaster, aren't you?'

'Yes, well. Object of the exercise is to secure the business. Then we can deal with Mr Jack Stack. Meantime, Marina, what might I do to put your mind at rest?'

'This.'

She took him by the hand, led him across the lawn to his desk and buzzed his secretary to bring her notebook.

'Maxine, the boss wants me to draft a memo to the editor.'

'Sir?' Maxine looked at the still-joined hands. Oh, dear.

'Carry on, Marina. Let's hear how it sounds.'

'It sounds like this... You are to shred all copies of that Bogbrush quote survey unquote. You are not to publish any derogatory references to Marina Marshall. And when the Bogbrush bill arrives, it will be met from your salary. Kind regards. There, that about wraps it up.'

'Sir?' Maxine offered him the chance to resume command.

Sniff-sniff. 'Well, stick in the odd 'please', eh?'

Marina continued the insurance of holding Humpty's hand, walking him round the farting fountain and back through the french windows as the typed memo arrived for signature.

'Humpty,' she said as he scribbled, 'to avoid any mishap, Maxine is personally going to put the memo into the editor's hot little hand, aren't you, Maxine?'

'Sir?'

'Carry on, Maxine.'

'I don't know how to thank you.' Marina put her free hand to his left cheek and kissed his right cheek.

'Marina – '

'Humpty?'

' – be nice to get together away from the shop. Dinner perhaps?'

'Lunch perhaps?'

He watched her sway through the double doors. He savoured the hand that hers had held. He touched the cheek her lips had visited.

In the lift, Marina rolled her eyes.

Heidi watched from a chair the other side of Jack Stack's desk as he uncrunched the memo, read it once more, crunched it once more and binned it. He went to the intercom.

'Friendly warning, Hump. Some nutter's sending memos in your name. I just got one. Telling me not to stuff Marina. As if I would. All I want is her head on a plate – you're welcome to the other end. Listen, here's a memo from me. If that bloody woman doesn't quit – and soon – I'm accepting Johnnie Bull's invitation to go back to the Globe and smash the Merc once and for all. Kind regards.'

'Jack,' said Heidi, 'You won't ever want my head on a plate, will you?' She blinked pretend tears.

'Here, kid.'

She went to his side, parking a hand at the back of his neck and her pubic mound against his shoulder. She moved a little in her thin skirt and he could feel wiry curls, almost hear them rustle.

He got Kitty on the phone.

'Listen, Heidi's upset. Says I'm not being fair to you. Says you're the one who should be Lifestyle editor. So I'm giving you the job, right? And putting your pay up ten grand, right?'

'And you want me to rewrite her Centrefold Princess crap for tonight, right?'

'Right.'

'How many grand did you say?'
'Fifteen. Make it sing.'

Bish appeared at the back bench with the last message a tabloid
night editor wants to hear when he's splashing on a decent
quadruple murder.

'He wishes a three-col blurb down the right of One.'

'And tomorrow he'll bollock me for underplaying the sewer
massacre, want to bet?'

Clop.

The blurb came up on the night editor's screen. He put forward
the editor's golden words with an instruction not to improve them:

**The paper that
gives its readers
what they want:
TWICE
AS MUCH
HEIDI!!**

• **Results of a nationwide survey show 99 per cent of readers
want to see more of Heidi Hunt.**
• **Mrs CW of York says: 'I like Heidi because she gets my
husband up in the morning – do you think she could possibly
manage twice a week?'**
• **Well, you're the boss, folks. So we'll be bringing you The
Adventures of Heidi Hunt every Tuesday *and* Friday from now on.**
• **Say Hi to Heidi today on the Centre Pages. She's beautiful.
She's daring. She's fun. She's born of the age we live in and sexy
with it.**

'Let me know which pic,' said the night editor. 'How about one
with a staple – 99 per cent of her colleagues reckon that's what
keeps her brains from tumbling out.'

'Nice day?' Dumpty brought the ritual sherry kit on a silver salver as
her husband slumped into an armchair and eased laces, braces, collar
and tie.

'Lunch at the club. Same old Charge of the Light Brigade survivors.'

'Rang your office at teatime. Maxine said you and Marina were doing it in the roof garden. Couldn't say how soon you'd be finished. I said it's usually seven seconds.'

'Ha bloody ha.'

Dumpty uncapped the decanter and poured two finos. 'What was the bitch wearing?'

'Maxine?'

'Not Maxine.'

'Can't say I noticed.'

'Liar.'

'For God's sake, Dumpty – my poor brother made a point of asking me to give her his regards. All there is to it.'

'Humpty.' She handed him his glass. 'You haven't asked Dumpty what sort of day she's had.'

'Sorry, darling. Nice day?'

'Fucking awful day.'

'Ah.'

'Dropped in to the chemist to pick up your film. She called me to one side. Said she'd be grateful if we took our dirty pictures to some other shop.'

'Dirty pictures?'

'Dirty pictures.' Dumpty produced a set of prints and spread them on the coffee table. 'Dirty pictures.'

Humpty closed and opened his eyes. There was little Lula (or was it little Lara?) riding him like a victorious jockey. There was little Lara (or was it little Lula?) applying her airline cap as his fig-leaf. And there was Harry leaving the springboard in search of his shorts.

'That Harry Chacewater's hung like a horse. You're hung like a mouse. No wonder the chemist felt sorry for me.'

'That shit slipped me a mickey.'

'And arranged for a couple of miniature stewardesses to parachute from their Jumbo and fuck your brains out?'

'Isn't it obvious? Harry set it up to blackmail me.'

'Sell – or he'll send the pictures to your wife?'

'That's about it.'

'So why does he leave you with the undeveloped film? What's left for him to blackmail you with?'

'Ah.'

'Want me to file for divorce?'

'Please yourself.' Please God.

'And make way for Marina? Oh, no, Humpty. She's not having you. I'm sending her the duplicates – '

'Eh?'

' – so if she still plays up to you after this, you'll know it's something bigger than your cock she's after.'

'Dumpty wouldn't.'

'Dumpty already has.'

13

Strewth!!

The Mercury was now the paper Lord Bull reached for before his own. When the first edition dropped, he went straight to the blurb promising Heidi Hunt twice a week – and was dismayed to find himself looking forward to Tuesdays and Fridays. He phoned his editor.

'Kev, you awake?'

'I am now.'

'How can you sleep? Jack Stack's pissing all over you. Why don't you nick Heidi from him? What's she getting?'

'Screwed.'

'Well – ha! – if that's what it takes.'

'Not even for you, Johnnie. But if you don't mind buggering up the Globe salary structure...'

Ten hours later, at the Barbican flat whose mortgage had been wiped out by her Mercury pay-off, Maria-Teresa was on the case.

'Heidi, darling.' She sat by her on a migraine-pattern chaise longue. 'You're so beautiful, so talented. Wasted on those wankers.'

'Jack's done wonders for my image.'

'So? You've done wonders for his. You should hear him telling the lads how he popped your cherry.'

'The little liar.'

'And how you blew his socks off while he was on the phone to the Home Secretary.'

'Foreign Secretary.'

'You're just two tits and a bot to the Merc. That's why I walked out. Couldn't stand them drooling. They've seen more of you than your gynaecologist.'

'Haven't got a gynaecologist.'

'Join us, my darling, and you will have.'

'And a pink Alfa Romeo with ambulance windows?'

'Naturally.'

Heidi said could she ring her mum. Maria-Teresa confessed she wished she'd talked to hers before making career moves. Maria-Teresa left the room. Heidi rang Jack Stack.

'You were wrong about Maria-Teresa. She's really nice. Said I could have a pink Alfa Romeo and a gynaecologist.'

'Kid her you're dikey, did you?'

'Dikey?'

'Only hires lesbians. Show you her jockstrap yet?'

Heidi gave the returning Maria-Teresa a guarded smile and said she'd like to think about it. Maria-Teresa, who had listened on her bedroom extension, said how about lunch to discuss boring things such as a Thames-side loft and a holiday in Phuket, and of course she could take mum.

Heidi was slurring by the time they ebbed out of Le Caprice into the car. The driver opened his window to release tequila fumes, and Maria-Teresa fastened Heidi's seat belt as the girl punched a number into the phone.

'It's me. Listen, Maria-Teresa's offering thirty grand more... OK, hang on.' Heidi covered the mouthpiece. 'Forty?' Maria-Teresa nodded. Heidi passed on the improved bid and came back to her. 'Fifty?'

'Darling,' said Maria-Teresa. 'I'm not sure your mum understands this game. Perhaps if I talk to her – '

'Oh, it's not my mum. It's my editor. Want a word?'

'Two words – the second one is off.'

Predictably, Jack Stack was going to bid whatever it took to stop Heidi crossing the street. So be it – if you can't beat him, spoil her.

'Heidi, I've arranged some special treats to show what the Globe can do for you. First stop, Princess Vicki's own hair stylist. Second stop, her personal beautician.'

'Frocks?'

'Third stop.'

Treats complete, Maria-Teresa dropped Heidi back at the Mercury with the sweetest of smiles.

'Darling, you look out of this world.'

'Ta, Maria-Teresa. You're really nice. Be in touch.'

The message on Heidi's screen said to come to the editor's office at half past four. With a minute to go, Jack Stack was announcing to conference that she had just told the Globe what to do with its offer.

'...and when she comes through that door, let's all put our hands together. That kid's an example to us all.'

The editor led the applause as the door began to open. But his hands dropped and the clapping expired as it swung shut behind her.

Heidi Hunt had suffered a terminal make-over. Long blonde glory was now short black nothing. Teaser top and slapper skirt had given way to boxy striped trouser suit with wing-collar shirt and club tie. Flatties had replaced strappies. Gone were epic cleavage, eyeful thighs, winking navel. This Heidi was never going to get Mrs C W of York's husband up early twice a week.

'Conference cancelled.' Jack Stack thumped his desk and then his head. Bloody Ma Teresa. 'Go on, piss off, the lot of you.' He pointed at Heidi. 'Stay.' He shook his head at her again and again as the executives evacuated.

'Don't like it, do you, Jack?' Eyes moist, jaw trembling, she faced him across the desk.

'I hate it.'

'But it's from the people who do Princess Vicki.'

'You mean Prince Ricky.'

Heidi stumbled sobbing from the room. Jack Stack thumped his head again as he buzzed the Lifestyle editor.

'Kitty my sweet. Your beloved editor speaking—'

'G'day, mate. It's not Kitty your sweet. She's gone to the flamin' Globe.'

'Whaaaat!'

'Just kissed the flamin' phone. Bunged her flamin' stuff into a flamin' binbag. And sang Ave Maria-Teresa all the flamin' way to the flamin' lift.'

'So, who are you? You sound slightly Australian.'

'Good on yer, mate. Pommy bastards usually take me for a bloody Kiwi. Name's Martha. My first day. Kitty gave me a week's trial as the new Lifestyle deputy.'

'Well, Martha, I'm giving you twenty minutes' trial as the new Lifestyle editor.'

'Strewth.'

'Be in my office in fifteen – with a sexy idea for the next Heidi Hunt spread. And on the way, organise a blonde wig for her like the hair the readers know and love.'

Jack Stack sat up when Martha appeared. She was a couple of inches over six feet, most of it in gold leggings and the rest in a green and gold Wallaby rugger shirt with an 8 on the back. She had the straw hair, apple cheeks and parsnip hands of a farmer's daughter. Or son.

'G'day.' Her smile scorched like an outback sunrise.

'G'day.' His mind was already ranging over candidates for his third Lifestyle editor in fifteen minutes. It might have to be Bish.

'Boss, your Heidi blurb was a beaut. I've worked for tabloids all over – and you are definitely the dog's bollocks.'

'Tell me something I don't know, kid. Tell me what's on the next Heidi Hunt spread.'

'No sweat. I'm running a tear-out of that quote from Mrs C W of York with a 96-point streamer, **HOW TO GET YOUR MAN UP IN THE MORNING!**' Martha accompanied the UP with a gesture involving bent elbow, clasped bicep and thrusting fist.

'Love it, love it.' This was like listening to himself.

'I'll have soap celebs telling Heidi what turns their blokes on. And a come-on for readers to send her their tips and win naughty weekends. And I'll shoot Heidi as an ooh-la-la maid bringing in the champagne breakfast. She'll make a great four-col cut-out. Whaddya say, boss?'

'Martha, I say you're a flamin' beaut.'

Georgian Virginia silver and crystal sparkled on Mom Chacewater's lunch table. Her restored town house among the brick sidewalks and gaslights of old Richmond had been Bobby's wedding gift to his bride. Its hillside view of this reach of the James was like that of the Thames from her ancestral home above Richmond, Surrey. Indeed, the resemblance was why the city had been so named, though after a couple of industrial centuries you had to be as romantic as Mom to get the connection.

Her guests today were daughter Janie and son-in-law Chuck, on leave from his London embassy, and the legendary Ed and Mrs Ed. As finger bowls were removed and napkins replaced after the asparagus, Mom tapped a fork against her goblet of Chablis.

'Ed's begging me to break the habit of a lifetime – and talk business before the coffee.'

'At his age, Alice,' said Mrs Ed, 'it's not wise to postpone anything.'

'Hell,' said Ed, 'we all know why we're here. And that call I took as we came in – it was to say Harry's on his way down to Toby Baynard on Abaco island.'

'He won't listen to me, Uncle Ed,' said Sis.

'He won't even talk to me,' said Mom.

'Ed,' said Ambassador Chuck, 'let me ask an innocent question. Can Harry do this deal without the board?'

'In theory – no.'

'In practice – yes?'

'Sure. If Harry does a deal, are we going to repudiate it? Take him to court? Destabilise our stock? Wouldn't that nice Mr Magnus just love it?'

'Face it, Chuck.' Mom sighed. 'If we block Harry, he might bale out altogether. And who's perched on the roof waiting to gobble up his holding?' She palmed the question to the legendary Ed.

'That nice Mr Magnus.'

'Another innocent one from me, Ed.' Chuck came back. 'Could you make a case for Chacewater buying the Merc?'

'Only if we could stomach the Brit pop tabloid scene. This sort of stuff, seven days a week...'

Ed reached down to produce a handful of Mercurys from under his chair. He displayed a spread based on an eavesdropped conversation in which the heir to the throne rated his conquests out of 10:

WHO'S TOPS WITH NICKY
– AND WHO'S BOTTOM!!
TV Tina...........9

Miss World......6

Lady Islay........4

Lord Bosie.......$2^1/_2$

'Lord Bosie?' Sis shook her head. 'Lord Bosie?'

'Better believe it,' said Ed. 'It's what you'll be buying if you buy the Merc. Could Chacewater live with that?'

'I couldn't,' said Mom.

'Nor could Harry,' said Ed, 'if he hadn't fallen for the First Lady of Fleet Street.'

Hollandaise sauceboats docked alongside poached salmon steaks. Silver dishes of petits pois and new potatoes were uncovered. More Chablis was uncorked. And Mom, Sis and Chuck, who had met Marina, told Ed and Mrs Ed how brilliant and how stylish and how handsome and how amusing and how warm she was. They had no difficulty seeing what Harry saw in her. But what did she see in him? Money, sure. But Harry was Harry. You wouldn't want your daughter to marry one.

'Ed will think of something,' said Mom. 'He always does.'

'Heaven knows what this time.' His lips shaped for a soundless whistle.

'Ed.' Mom put a hand on his. 'Harry's not sailing *Miss Print IV* down to Abaco?'

'No, he's flying.'

'Thank God.' Her silence became theirs. 'Ed, I'm getting visions again. Like those of *Miss Print II* blowing up way back when you were hassling with Magnus for those penny ante papers in Maine. And it happened, right?'

'Right, Alice.' Wrong, Alice. The boat blew up before the visions. But blow up her visions thing, and you'd blow her up with it.

'And then I had those visions of the crash that was going to kill Harry's brother, right?'

'Right, Alice.' Wrong, Alice. But she believed it more each time she told it.

'Well, since this Mercury business I'm having visions of *Miss Print IV* going up in flames. Ed, you've got to get Harry out of this.'

It was midnight when Martha burst into the editor's office. Her pendant eyepiece magnifier bounced on her flat chest.

'Flamin' problem, boss.'

'Bang goes my annual early night.'

He lifted his eyes sixteen inches to her as, cigar between teeth, he handed up a glass of champagne.

'Ta, mate.' Martha took an appraising sip. 'Ah, Veuve Clicquot. My favourite non-vintage.'

'Help yourself.' He lifted the lid of his humidor. 'Bolivars on the left. Montecristos on the right – Number Ones, Threes and Fives.'

She took a long Number One, perched on a couch and crossed gold legs.

Jack Stack watched fascinated. A man lighting a cigar was not worth a glance but a woman performing the sacred ritual was a Freudian casebook dream. Martha ran hot eyes up and down and round the Montecristo. Then she closed them, the better to savour its scents of cured tobacco, cedarwood and Cuban thighs. She caressed its length and strength between finger and thumb. She rolled it at her ear. She stripped away its band. He held out a cutter but she nodded it away and circumcised the cap with gold fingernails, balming the exposed end with moist lips. She declined the lighter offered in one fist in favour of the connoisseur's matchbox offered in the other. With the first long match, she seared the cigar at the edge of the flame. With the second, she coaxed it to ignition, anchoring it between her teeth as her cheeks concaved to give it life. She launched a stream of smoke, inspected the evenly glowing end and sighed with pleasure.

'So' – he cleared his throat – 'what was the problem?'

'The ooh-la-la pix.' Martha fished a proof sheet of thumbnail prints from an envelope and handed him the magnifier.

'At least Ma Teresa didn't get her to a plastic surgeon.'

'But, strewth, that flamin' wig. It looks like – '

' – a flamin' wig. Not going to work, is it?'

'So this is what I've done.' Martha produced another sheet of thumbnails. 'Got the computer to mount Heidi heads from old shoots. Works a treat, right?'

'Martha, you're all tabloid.'

She refilled their glasses, puffed at her cigar and settled back as a messenger arrived with the first edition. Jack Stack slid one across the desk for her as he buzzed the night editor.

'Crap headline on the film première pic. No way it's **HAPPY AND GLORIOUS!** Prince Mickey and the girl look bored stiff.'

'It's irony, Jack.'

'Irony bollocks. Make it' – he followed his fat felt tip pen as it moved in Martha's fist – '**SMILE IF YOU HAD IT LAST NIGHT!!**'

Then he buzzed the picture editor.

'Tomorrow, Eddie, get me a spread of famous faces at the moment the cameraman hits them with, **SMILE IF YOU HAD IT**

LAST NIGHT!! Then I want one a day for ever. Starting with the Archbishop of Canterbury.'

Then he buzzed the marketing director.

'I want posters across the land saying, **SMILE IF YOU HAD IT LAST NIGHT!!** And stick an A-board outside Lord Bull's house and at every newsagent on his way in to the Globe.'

The legendary Ed put his slippered feet up on Mrs Ed's lap as he phoned the Chacewater bureau chief in London.

'Hi, Theo. Another favour, please. Drop an indiscreet word into the ear of the Magnus man. Say I'm running you ragged for an inside track on the Merc. Say you're terrified Chacewater is about to buy. Say Harry's into Marina's pants. Aims to make her editor-in-chief, and move you in to bust your balls producing the shit-sheet while she queens it all over town. Say Sally-Jane'll walk out on you if you take the job – and Ed'll fire you if you don't. Theo, it's all a game. Magnus swoops to get in first. And we're home free. Do this for me, Theo. Do it for Harry. And do it yesterday.'

Mrs Ed stroked his toes.

On and on flowed Martha. By the time their cigars were an hour shorter, Jack Stack knew he was in the presence of the second most inspired tabloid practitioner in the world. What more natural than that they should want to add each other to the sum total of carnal knowledge?

But something about Martha held him back. Something wasn't quite right. Nobody could be that flamin' Australian.

14

Pride and Naughtiness

Housekeeper Dahlia disapproved of Harry Chacewater the moment he arrived at Baynard Cay. He had glad-eyed her black and comely daughter much as King Solomon did the nubile Moabites, Edomites, Zidonians and Hittites. As soon as Tulip finished serving dinner, Dahlia had packed her off to Aunt Hyacinth. And on Harry's bedside table she had opened the Bible at I Samuel 17:28. *Why camest thou down hither?...I know thy pride and the naughtiness of thine heart.*

Dahlia's judgement was validated this morning when she took him breakfast. Sitting up to find the tray borne in not by the daughter but the mother, his grin collapsed, as did the tent at his lap.

Toby had taken Harry out to sea on *Freelance*, with a promise that they'd get round to business if the marlin weren't biting. They weren't. And now Marina's past and present lovers were at unease in the fishing chairs at the stern.

'*Whaaat*-ever...' sighed Toby.

'Excuse me?'

'Back of the cabin.'

Harry got up and went, though he didn't need to.

Toby stuck out his foot to swivel Harry's empty chair. He could not warm to this man who wanted to take over his Merc, and with it his Marina. And anyway he preferred the company of journalists to those who manage them, milk them and market them. Those who believe free-range readers are accurately represented by battery-hen focus groups. Those to whom scorn for the slaves of the black art comes easier than sympathy. Those who refer to them as journos, their newspaper as the product, their departments as cost centres, their stories as input. Those who reckon journalists talk too much, laugh too much, drink too much, lunch too much, shag too much and cost too much.

As Harry came back, Toby handed him a can of lager.

'Ever tried to buy up a newspaper before?'

'Can't say I have.'

'Thought not. Shouldn't you have Ed Segal along?'

'I'm not Ed's boy. I'm Ed's boss.' He flipped the ring-pull overboard.

'And whose boy is Humpty? He'd never come up with an idea like this. You feed it to him?'

'I guess so.'

'And who do you guess fed it to you?'

'Thanks for the compliment.' Harry was used to this. He had been pre-shrunk by Dad. By Mom. And by –

'The legendary Ed?'

'No way. Ed's against me on this. He's old Fortress America. Believes we ought to stay out of foreign newspaper wars.'

'Then who's the inspiration?'

'Don't ask – I'm a lousy liar.'

'If you can't tell me' – Toby sighed – 'you've told me.'

'Yeah, well.'

'You're fond of her?'

'Sure. She's really something.'

'*Whaaat*-ever...' Toby stared out to the horizon.

'I'm sorry,' said Harry after a while.

'You're right, Harry – you are a lousy liar.'

Toby swung to catch the eye of Sergeant Mac on the bridge. He made eating signals and opened a fist three times to indicate lunch in fifteen minutes. Sergeant Mac stopped engines and came down to get at the goodies in Dahlia's picnic hamper.

The photos spread over Marina's dressing table had come in an envelope marked Strictly Personal. There was no note but all the circumstances and – sniff – a hint of nosebag pointed to a single suspect. Dumpty must have found these souvenir snaps her husband had been daft enough to bring home. And calculated that, shown what Humpty had been up to, Marina would run a mile.

Marina rolled her eyes. These bimbos in and out of airline uniform were phoney. Too much hair. Too little skirt. And too short to reach an overhead locker. She returned to the shot of Harry dangling between springboard and pool. What was it Humpty said yesterday? Popped in for a dip . . . what fun. So these were the dips. So this was the fun.

Harry would have paid them. Laid them. And with his free hand dialled Interflora to send another field of roses to keep Marina Muggins purring as she packed three new swimsuits to christen in his polluted pool.

To hell with that. She went to unpack.

Aboard *Freelance*, Sergeant Mac was plucking more lager from the fridge to wash down Dahlia's turtle steaks, peas 'n' rice and sweet potato bread. They weren't doing much fishing. Toby was still baiting Harry.

'I'm not selling to anyone who doesn't give a shit about the people who've dedicated their lives to the Merc.' He turned full face towards Harry. 'Do you give a shit?'

'Wasn't me who left the Merc to the mercy of Jack Stack.'

'No, it was your messenger boy, Humpty.'

'But it will be me who spends good dollars bringing the Merc back home to the family market. Saving what's left of the staff you care about.'

Sergeant Mac padded off to fetch Dahlia's weight-botcher special: guava duff with rum sauce. Toby waited till they had done it justice.

'Just tell me, Harry – would you be here if Marina didn't exist? Come on, it's not me you want to merge with.'

'You got a problem with that?'

'Yes – you're not good enough for her.'

Sergeant Mac broke the long silence when he switched on engines to mask a radiophone call from Dahlia. Aunt Hyacinth had just wrung out of Tulip something that happened when she took Harry's bags to his room yesterday. He'd said how pretty she was and all that, and taken her hand and reckoned he could use a little old back rub. Tulip was upset. Dahlia was upset. Sergeant Mac was upset. He called Toby to the bridge to upset him too.

Harry swivelled as Toby returned to his chair.

'Toby, you're sure playing hard to get.'

'I am rather, aren't I? Quite understand if you feel you're wasting your time here.'

'I don't get it.'

'You certainly don't.'

Harry certainly didn't. He shook his head. Some white knight.

Toby called to Sergeant Mac. 'Head for the airport. Harry has to leave right now. Phone Dahlia to have his stuff taken to his plane.'

As Sergeant Mac opened up the throttles, Toby went to the cabin, shut the door and lay on the bunk. He could hear his heart thumping. He felt very old indeed.

'*Whaaat*-ever...'

Marina had decided to send all the pool pictures but one back to Dumpty. Anonymously and in an envelope marked Strictly Personal. She would keep that Harry picture. It would go wonder-fully with his chapter.

Nearing midnight, her phone rang. This time the background Mendelssohn was *Midsummer Night's Dream* – the one he would remember her by.

'Marina. I'm back at the ranch.'

'So soon?'

'Toby gave me a real hard time. Reckon his game is to jack the price up. But he's sure as hell jealous. That torch is still burning.'

'But nobody knows about you and me, except you and me. You bloody idiot. What did you do – draw him a diagram?'

'Didn't need to tell him anything. He told me. Said I wasn't good enough for you – '

'Well, you aren't.'

' – and he gave me the bum's rush.'

'Well, you are a bum. I've seen the happy snaps of you and Humpty taking turns with the phoney stewardesses. Dumpty kindly sent me a set.'

'Marina, I can explain – '

'Explain to my answering machine. I don't want to catch anything.'

She switched on the speaker and glowered in the direction of his pleading voice as though it were his pleading face.

'Listen, Marina, it was you and nobody else who set me up to fix Humpty, right? So that's what I did – fixed him good. Some guys you fix with the green stuff. Some with liquor. Some with tail. With Humpty it's the full deck. So, OK, I had to play along. I roped in a couple of honeys from the journalism faculty. You've got to believe me – I left all the screwing to him. And listen, it was also you and nobody else who sent me off to get a mauling from Toby. Right? So let me call the next play. You go see him. He'll do it for you. We'll get married and – how does this grab you? – I'll giftwrap a new Sunday paper as your wedding present...'

Marina lifted the phone to break in.

'And throw in those bimbos as my bridesmaids? Go fuck yourself, Mr Chacewater.'

She went to her keyboard to add Harry's call to his chapter while it was still boiling in her brain:

Harry's most characteristic intro is, 'I can explain everything...'
Here he is explaining to a now-ex fiancée how he came to get naked
with a pair of pretend air stews in front of a 35mm camera...

The sixth time Harry rang back, he accepted the answering machine's invitation to leave a message.

'Marina, I'm on the next plane to London. We'll straighten it all out, I promise. We can be married in two weeks.'

The seventh time Harry phoned, the line was engaged. Marina was calling the Bahamas.

'Toby.'

'I knew you'd ring.'

'I want to come and see you.'

'To get me to sell him the Merc?'

'To make sure you don't.'

'Come for any reason. Come for no reason. Just come.'

'I'm on my way.'

15

Can I Forget You?

As the Jumbo climbed away from Heathrow, Marina put her watch back five hours to Bahamas time and her heart back a year to Toby time. Turning the watch over to look at his inscription, *Can I forget you?* she fingered it as though it were Braille. She had not worn this watch since they broke up. Nor, until now, had she let herself dwell on that night, or on their time together until that night. The memories had been bundled away with his letters, the message cards with his gifts and flowers, and the cassettes he wanted to do for her what they did for him.

With Harry, it was Mendelssohn. With Toby, it was the Vienna tenor of Richard Tauber. She loaded her Walkman, fitted ear-phones and closed her eyes, the better to let the Kern/Hammerstein magic back in:

> *Can I forget you?*
> *When every night reminds me*
> *How much I want you back again?*

Tauber's *Sacher Torte* tones would go on to remind her with Mozart, Bizet and much Lehár. She slipped off her shoes and curled into the starboard window seat of Row 1, her hand now and again tapping time on the empty place alongside. For nine and three quarter hours, no one but a flight attendant need come by. She would be left alone to think the thoughts she had shut out; recall the images already beginning to flip before her like pages in a photo album.

In the beginning, Toby had been after only one thing: her signature on a contract. She could shake her head now at the vision

114

of herself holding out. Just what kind of girl did he think she wasn't? How long would he go on inviting her to lunch in Mayfair, dinner in Soho but never breakfast in bed? She wanted him in love with her, not just in love with her column. She wanted to be the next wife of Viscount Baynard (motto: *No one touches me with impunity*). Only when she touched him with impunity in a box at the Royal Opera House, half-way through Carmen, was there a start to the making of much love. But his first divorce had halved his fortune and he did not want a second. His wife eventually won a decree anyway, and halved his fortune again anyway. Toby wasn't jumping through that hoop a third time, even to marry the mother of his twins. Her pride hurt, she played the jealousy card...

'*Marina, I had a call from Sibyl – your friend with the pointy head. Wanted me to know what an amusing weekend I'd missed.*'

'*Pity you couldn't make it, Toby.*'

'*Pity you let her fix you up with Carlos.*'

'*Being alone is not exactly what country-house weekends are about, is it, darling? And it's hardly as though I'm your wife.*'

'*Damn you, Marina. You wanted to make me bloody jealous. I am bloody jealous. I do not like what being bloody jealous does to me.*'

'*Calm down, Toby. Nothing happened. He's seriously gay.*'

'*Not according to Sibyl.*'

'*Bitch. You do realise she's after you herself?*'

'*I do realise you put her up to this. I love you dearly, Marina, but I do not love being manipulated. I love you dearly but – hang on, how can I love you dearly when you pull a stunt like this?*'

'*It's no stunt. I hereby resign as your bit on the side.*'

'*Just so long as you don't hereby resign from the Merc. Now that would be a blow.*'

When her phone rang three hours later, she had guessed it would be him to say sorry. Not this time. It was the editor to say sorry. Toby had had a stroke.

Marina was a real pro. Before the editor could wonder who might be the right person to do the stand-by obit, she volunteered. Her headline was, *Last of the Cavaliers* – all the finer an epitaph, she wrote, for the fact that it came from his Fleet Street rival, Lord Bull. Toby, she said, had bequeathed to the Merc the challenge to justify the love, the talent, the treasure he had invested in it; the life he had given it; the life he had given for it.

The obit bore out two classic editorial ironies. The greater the pressure, the better the piece. And the better the stand-by obit, the longer the subject survives to postpone the author's fulfilment.

Since the break-up, Toby had phoned the twins regularly and flown them out for holidays. But there had been only one attempt at contact with her. He had sent a birthday card. It said, *Can I forget you?*

In Richmond, the legendary Ed was on his car phone, taking a call from George Theodoulou in London.

'...Magnus is chasing the bait. Wants the whole schmear on the Merc in 24 hours. Doesn't give a damn that the Brit weekend starts Friday noontime. So his guy's begging me to save his ass.'

'So save it, Theo. Feed the poor schmuck every line of that crap you sent Harry.'

Ed had hardly set the phone down when Harry came on from the cockpit of his 757, awaiting clearance to take off.

'Toby's giving me a hard time.'

'He's doing you a favour, Harry.'

'Do you have to sound pleased?'

'I am pleased, Harry.'

'Ed, I'm going to win this with or without you.'

'Is that so, Harry?'

'I'm flying to London. Going to set up the next play.'

'Have a good trip, Harry.'

At the Mercury, Jack Stack waited twenty rings for Gloria Mundy to lift the phone at his flat.

'Where the hell were you?'

'Long day, Jack. Jenny and I nipped out for a Bloody Mary.'

'Time for that when you've finished the bloody Xenia diaries. How are they going?'

'Terrific. Rivals for Prince Ricky come a cropper most full moons. Do a backward somersault into an empty pool. Punt into the weir. Rollerblade under a London bus.'

'What number bus?'

'Don't know, Jack.'

'Find out. Adds authenticity. And, while you're at it – '

'Er, yes Jack?'

' – let's put together a daily cut-out-and-keep recipe from Princess Xenia's black magic cookbook.'

'Got a good headline: *For guests you want to get rid of.*'

'Got a better one: *Voodoo Foodoo.*'

At Baynard Cay, Dahlia was asking Toby, 'How long will Miss Marina be staying?'

'As long as I can keep her.'

Dahlia had never seen him so happy. He had spent much of the day torturing his English baritone into tenor duets with Tauber. As the old Jeep swung Marina into the driveway, he turned up the volume and sang along with *Ich Küsse Ihre Hand, Madame.* Walking stick as baton, he serenaded his way down the verandah steps and küssed madame's hand.

Marina took off her sunglasses to beam a thank you at Dahlia's lad and win another fan for life as he made a privilege of unloading her cases. In this buttercup frock she had changed into while waiting for the hop to Abaco, she did not look as though she had been travelling half an hour, let alone half a day. She had rehearsed opening lines, rejecting one after another as too sentimental, too profound, too silly. By the time the curtain went up, she knew she had it just right.

'Toby,' she said.

'Marina,' he said.

'I recognised the voice.'

'Mine or Tauber's?'

The better to survey him, she drew as far apart as their linked hands allowed. That fine head was still as commanding as his bust in the Mercury lobby. A year on, he had shed two stone and, in pilot shirt and trousers, appeared to have shed ten years.

'Look at me like that,' he said, 'and you're risking an encore.'

As Toby parked stick over arm and led Marina up the steps, Dahlia watched from the verandah. She had been in this scene twice before. When her mother was housekeeper, and young Mr Toby brought his first bride on honeymoon. Then as housekeeper herself, when Lord Toby brought his second bride. Abaco was too unspoiled for either woman. They spent most of their time around the smart pools and smart people of Nassau. And now, another production, with a new leading ladyship. This time, please God, the one this lovely, lonely man deserved.

Mrs Ed said Max Magnus had phoned and would Ed kindly call back when he had a moment.

'Charming man,' said Mrs Ed.

'Charming like Semtex,' said Ed.

He and Magnus knew much about each other, though they had never met. Nor did Ed know anyone who had met him. The man operated by phone, fax and e-mail, like a spider in his own world-wide web. They last spoke when Magnus asked him to name his price to become his CEO. Even now, Ed could hear the menace in those sincere Aberdonian tones. He took a deep breath and dialled Toronto.

'Hi, Max. What can this old hot-metal man do for you?'

'Ask me what can you do for your boy. What's all this I hear about him eyeing up Toby Baynard's outfit?'

'You tell me – what is all this you hear?'

'Don't be cute, Ed. I've been working years on this. I don't want you guys moving in and upping the ante. Come on. Let's save us both a lot of grief.'

'Gotta tell you, Max. Harry's real set on this.'

'Screw that. You and me, Ed, we've been at this game a long time. Too long to let these Fleet Street assholes use us against each other.'

'Out of my hands, Max.'

'If I don't get the Merc, I'll spend the cash buying up more Chacewater stock. That what you want?'

'I want whatever my boy wants.'

'Believe me, Ed, your boy doesn't want to make an enemy of Max Magnus.'

Harry rang Marina's flat from his 757 as it taxied to its stand at Heathrow. No reply. He tried her office. Claudia sounded as though she wished she'd left her answering machine on.

'...She's away on a job, OK?...Can't help you. Must dash. Dinner party...Sorry, shan't have the faintest how long she'll be in the Bahamas until she tells me. Oh, shit – I never said that.'

Claudia had one call to make before she dashed.

'...Please deliver three dozen dead roses to await Mr Harry Chacewater at the Savoy. That's right, dead roses. No message – the flowers are the message, OK?'

The flower shop trainee noted the order correctly. The manager fired her for being even more stupid than she looked. So, a few minutes after Harry got to his suite, three dozen red roses arrived. No message – the flowers were the message.

Harry over-tipped the pageboy and yelled hallelujah. All was forgiven. Marina had gone to Abaco to fix Toby.

Until she got back with her big surprise, he would fill in time surveying his new empire. He rang the Mercury to find the chief executive had left at his usual 5.15. The Savoy operator found Humpty's home number for him.

'This is Harry Chacewater.'

'This is Daphne Baynard.'

'Hi, there, Dumpty. May I speak with Humpty?'

'No, you may not.'

This night, nothing had been allowed to puncture the enchantment that had Toby and Marina disbelieving they could ever have let each other go. Not all, though, was as it had been. Now and again came reminders of the stroke that had felled him.

As they swung gently on the verandah hammock, Marina counted out eleven chimes from the grandmother clock and automatically checked her watch.

'It's very pretty,' said Toby.

'Isn't it just?'

She took it off and handed it to him. She saw that he did not remember. She bit her lip.

'Can I forget you?' He sang his inscription, not appreciating it was his inscription.

'Go on, Toby.'

'I can't – ' His eyes were full of shadows.

'You can.' She cued him in a contralto whisper. 'Can I forget you? When every night...'

'...reminds me.'

'How much I...'

'...want you back again.'

She clapped. 'See, a little jog, that's all you need.'

'Marina, you're all I need.'

'Of course I am, darling.'

She would like not to have yawned just then. But her body clock was chiming 4 am London time.

'Forgive me.' Toby stood and held up his palms. 'You must be absolutely knackered.'

He kissed her hand and watched her into the house and across the hall to the double stairs. He touched her empty glass to his lips.

From scalp to sole, he ached with longing. But down in the forest, nothing stirred. Simple fact is, his physician had said, the pills that calm our blood pressure do, alas, tend to have a similar effect on our libido. Win some, lose some, eh?

'*Whaaat*-ever...' sighed Toby.

16

Last of the Moccasins

Harry and Theo were on their way to a drink in Humpty's office. Theo was worried: Harry seemed to reckon this was a done deal. Had the legendary Ed pitched Magnus into the game too late to pitch Harry out?

Collecting his boss at the Savoy, Theo walked him down Fleet Street. The Pied Piper of market forces had skipped this way. Mighty newspapers had been magicked off to that joyous land where, as the Piper's poet might have put it, everything is cheap to do and profits put forth a fairer hue; where unions have lost their stings and grey men soar on eagles' wings. And, just as the poet's Piper left behind but one lame lad in Hamelin Town, so the Mercury limped on alone at the bottom end of the street.

Memorials to Northcliffe, Dickens, Dr Johnson and Caxton's apprentice, Wynkyn de Worde, lingered in a lost land. English Heritage façades of old paper palaces were preserved among multi-storey people parks. Historic lanes bore scars left by lorries that once wormed newsprint to monstrous press lines, some entombed in their basements to this day as too expensive to disinter. Discreet brass plates proclaimed the new masters. The Express's shining black citadel had fallen to Goldman Sachs; the Mail's Victorian stronghold to Morgan Bank of America. The Sun/News of the World site, over the medieval crypt of the White Friars, was now home to Freshfields, the law partnership. The Mirror's forsaken fortress was now Sainsbury's HQ. The Telegraph's great clock ticked for Crédit Agricole; the FT's for Obayashi.

Between the Mercury's revolving doors and boardroom floor, Harry was already making proprietorial decisions. Those front-desk bums would get a haircut and a uniform. Those Baynard busts would accompany into instant retirement Humpty and the secretary with the praying hands. The private lift – Harry slipped his collar button – would get air con. But Humpty's suite, Harry would keep the way it was. Full of fine French pieces: how very British. Though there sure was scope for sexing up the roof garden. In place of that goldfish pool, how about a bandstand?

Humpty poured from a pitcher of iced Pimm's into half-pint dimple mugs and proposed a toast.

'Last of the Moccasins.'

'Last of the Moccasins?' The visitors drank to it, looked at each other and back at their host.

'Rest of our ancient tribe have fled. Driven out by the traffic wardens.'

'Traffic wardens?' Harry shook his head.

'See for yourself.' Humpty led them into the roof garden and offered binoculars from the box by the rail. 'I spy four. My chauffeur has to keep circling while I hang about like a spare prick. I'm the only chief exec in the world who gets wet when it rains.'

As they drifted back inside, Theo said, 'Best of the bunch again today. Some editor, that Jack Stack.'

Humpty felt the need to underline that this was his creature; like Mark Antony's horse, doing as bid and well-provendered for it. He reached to the intercom but, finger poised, switched to the phone. The editor's impudence was painful enough without an audience.

'Great paper today, Jack.' He waited for the inevitable.

'Bollocks.'

'What have you got for me tomorrow?'

'A great big hole on the spread. The First Lady has scarpered and left me without her Thursday column.'

'If you can't sort it out, don't hesitate to call me.'

'Been at the Pimm's again, Hump?'

'Have to leave you to it today, Jack. Looking after a distinguished visitor. Harry Chacewater. With me now – '

'Oh, that's the game, is it?'

' – and I want to show him the way we do things. Take him round the editorial floor. Sit in on the conference.'

'And poke bananas through the cage bars? Assholes to that.' Jack Stack hung up.

Humpty carried on. 'Oh, don't worry. He'll understand – he's one of us.' He turned to Harry. 'Up to his eyes in a big story.'

'Let's face it,' said Harry. 'Been to one editorial conference, been to 'em all.'

'Exactly,' said Humpty, who had been to exactly none.

Maxine broke in to ask Harry to take an urgent call from his brother-in-law.

'That was Ambassador Chuck,' said Harry as he returned. 'Thought I'd like to tip you off that tomorrow Beth Macbeth's going to announce a snap election. I guess that's what the editor's up to his eyes in. Look, why don't we get out of your hair? Catch up later.'

Humpty saw them off and dashed to buzz Jack Stack.

'Jesus, Hump. Don't ring me unless you've got a splash.'

'If you're short of a splash, Jack, you don't know Beth Macbeth's calling a snap election.'

'You're right. I don't know Beth Macbeth's calling a snap election. Who'd you get that from?'

'A little bird told me.'

'Not that bloody parrot again.'

An hour later, Jack Stack rang back. 'Love you to bits. What a scoop. I owe you a big drink.'

'Could I ask a small favour instead?'

'The bloody parrot wants a byline?'

'Afraid Dumpty had him put down. Now she's taken against Harry. Won't let me return his hospitality. I can't just leave him all alone in London. Know any nice girls?'

'Certainly not.'

'He has a thing about air hostesses.'

'Yeah, you said he was one of us.'

'Anything but BA. He got badly naffed-off on Concorde.'

'And who's picking up the tab?'

'Tab? Harry's not the sort who pays for it.'

'He'll never know. I'll have us billed for consultancy services.'

'Good thinking – we can claw back the VAT. Do your best, Jack. Lot riding on this. For you and me both.'

You and me both? Click. What could a billionaire American publisher do for you and me both? Click.

Freelance was tied up at the Baynard Cay landing stage and going nowhere. Which was fine by Marina and Toby, lolling under broad brims in the fishing chairs.

'Know what, Marina? I'm tempted to take Harry's money.'

'You're joking, of course.'

'Am I? Imagine being paid all those dollars for the pleasure of seeing him fall flat on his face.'

'It might solve one problem. I could do with a neat morality play ending to his chapter. And it does rather look as though reformation is out.'

'Was it ever in?'

'I did think so for a moment. Till it hit me that all the things I was writing about him were true.'

'Marina, you're losing your touch.'

'Think so?' She left her chair and sat on his lap. 'Go on, give us a cuddle.'

'A cuddle.' He put an arm round her. 'You're too young and lovely to settle for a cuddle.'

'So are you.'

'Hi, there, Jack. This is Harry Chacewater. Just picked up your message.'

'Sorry I couldn't entertain you this morning. Big story. Got it to ourselves. Between you and me – '

' – there's going to be a snap election.'

'Humpty told you?'

'No, I told Humpty.'

'What a tosser. Look, Harry, I can't get away just yet. Why don't we crack a bottle in my office?'

Coming through the revolving doors for the second time this day, Harry felt at home. The front-desk bums saluted him. The Baynard busts looked on benignly. The door of the private lift opened before he touched a button. And the editor was waiting with a glass in each hand.

'Cheers, Harry.'

'Real pleasure to meet you, Jack.'

Harry took a glass and shook the emptied hand, which went on to wave him to a chair. As the hand reached the end of its arc, a messenger appeared and placed in it copies just biked from the dockland presses. Jack Stack passed one to Harry and opened the humidor to him.

Harry lit his Havana as irreverently as a cigarette and turned to the paper. Something wrong. The splash was **PARAS TURN DOWN WIMP MICKEY**. Not the election exclusive.

'Guess I gave you a bum steer.'

'No, I'm only running enough copies of that splash to kid the enemy. Here comes Bish with the real Page One: **BETH POLL SENSATION!!** *The secret only Mercury readers know*.'

Clop, went Bish.

'Better give Harry Chacewater a copy. He's going to be our new owner.'

'Jeez, don't spread that around.' Harry gulped. 'It's only a rumour.'

'Hope not,' said Jack Stack. 'We deserve better than to be owned by a basket case and managed by a nut case.'

'No comment.' Harry put finger to lip.

'Right then, Bish, old son. Couple of things.' He began to go through the paper as his deputy made clipboard notes. 'Leader page just perfect: **THE REAL MACBETH – BY JACK STACK**. But your spread's got cobwebs. Where's that on-the-day feel? I want an instant opinion poll. Friend Bogbrush will deliver before you've hung up the phone. Just make sure he knows my front page cross-ref is: *Your verdict – Beth to make it a hat-trick*. And humanise it. I want talking-head quotes from soap stars who'll be voting for her. OK, get that moving and come back for the rest . . .'

Clop. Bish played along. Jack Stack, having already drip-fed improvements as each page came up on his screen through the day, was staging a repeat performance to wow the next proprietor.

'. . . don't want three leg-over leads on the trot, do we? On 7, it's **SEX CERTIFICATE** *Couldn't stop ourselves say Jacuzzi scene stars.* On 9, **LOOKIE! NOOKIE!** *Bridal suite peephole queue.* On 11, **MIRTH CONTROL** *Beeb bans condom jokes.* Spread 'em around, for fuck's sake. Now 15's a real turn-off. I only use baby pix that make you want to lift the little sod up and say *Aaaah*. That's not an *Aaaah* baby. That's a *Yuck* baby. Kill it. Page 18 needs the odd allegedly in the conman story. And 21's got too many underscored headlines. Change 24 – can't run **COSTA JUMBO DRAMA** against that airline ad on 25. You're all getting too old for this game. And then we come to . . .'

Theo told the taxi driver to go round Trafalgar Square one more time. In the back, he was updating the Magnus man. Marina's flown out to square Toby. Harry's flown in to talk small print with Humpty. Better wise up your beloved chairman before someone else does – and your beloved chairman comes down the phone and rips your throat out. Don't mention it. I'm doing myself a favour.

'... I want more black squares in the crossword. Can't have readers thinking the Merc's too clever for them. And tell those kids on the Diary page there's only one l in air marshal. On 30, either explain why **DOUBLE DEATH DUKE GETS OFF**, or stick a line on the end saying, *For full story, buy a proper newspaper*. And tell sport their inside back's like a bingo card – a number in every bloody headline. Now then...'

It was teatime on the verandah. Marina was layering another scone with peach jam for Toby as Dahlia came out bearing a phone. Max somebody on the line from Toronto.

'You well, Toby?' said Magnus, and did not wait for an answer. 'Let's cut the crap – I'm willing to take the Merc off your hands. How much?'

'What makes you think I'm in the market?'

'I know what's going on in London this minute. Harry Chacewater is talking take-over with your brother.'

'Nonsense.'

'I'm telling you – anything Chacewater will pay, Magnus will pay more.'

'Aren't you taking a lot for granted?'

'Only that you wouldn't want to go to war with Max Magnus. My regards to the beautiful Marina. Take care.'

'How the hell,' said Toby as he put the phone aside, 'does that bugger know you're here? And that Harry's meeting Humpty this minute? And, *Take care* – what's that supposed to mean?'

'... Only two pars for the President's speech to the European Parliament? It's important, Bish. Give it three. And just look at Lifestyle. Who let flamin' Martha have a day off? That antique pic of Ricky wouldn't get past her. And she'd never reverse Vicki. Every woman reader knows the princess parts on the left...'

Clop, went Bish.

Nothing Marina said or Theo reported had prepared Harry for Jack Stack. The man was ace, king, queen, jack and joker. A man to back, not sack. Ed Segal was right about one thing: it would be crazy to drag the Merc back up-market. This was a sure-fire winner. This was fun. This he must have. And Marina? She'd get her own paper to play with. Even Ed would go for launching a Sunday to make the presses earn their keep seven days a week.

'Strewth, boss.' Martha powered through the door in her green and gold shirt with an 8 on the back. Harry side-stepped his chair out of her way.

'Take it easy, Martha,' said the editor. 'Mustn't damage Harry Chacewater. He's going to buy the Merc.'

'G'day, sport.' She gave him a sheep-shearer's handshake until he winced. 'How's your belly off for spots?'

'Australian?' He reset his knuckles.

'Too right. How'd you guess?'

'Wasn't easy.'

'My oath.' Martha loomed over the editor. 'Glad I popped in. I've reversed flamin' Vicki. And grabbed Eddie by the goolies till he got me a today pic of flamin' Ricky.'

Harry watched her go. Enough apple there for an Adam.

Tipping the bottle, Jack Stack found it empty. He drew blanks at fridge and drinks cupboard. His curse might have been a summons. Bish came clopping.

'Hell, Jack,' he said, 'Been trying to think how to tell you this without you storming out and going back to the Globe. Humpty's put a ceiling on all booze orders.'

'That does it. I'm storming out and going back to the Globe.'

He put on his jacket, stuck his humidor under his arm and made for the door. Harry barred his way.

'Don't do this, Jack. I'm going to need you. Listen, Humpty won't be around much longer. And then I promise you champagne on tap.'

'All very well.' He restored the humidor to its perch. 'But what about tonight? He can't just leave us to die of thirst.'

'Jack,' said Harry, 'come back with me. My bar's loaded.'

'You're on. Just need a quick word with the back bench.'

He reached into a drawer to get a number from his little black book, took Bish outside and wrote it down for him. Bish made the call. Two air hostesses at the Savoy tonight, please. Do I mean flight attendants, forward slash, female? Right, love, two of those. What? Not sure you can manage even one on a Wednesday? A double Coppergram? OK, then. Forward slash, female? Yes, please. Contraltos? No, thanks. Access? Very funny.

As the editor led Harry out, Bish switched off the lights with a ceremonious clop.

'Never' – Jack Stack switched them back on – 'let the slaves think I've gone for the night. They'll nod off at the oars.' He turned in the newsroom to call out. 'Back in a tick, Bish. Make it sing.'

The open cocktail cabinet was all that lit Harry's vast suite as he reached for another bottle. The cork flew at the clock that showed five minutes past midnight.

'Jack Stack, where are you?' Harry peered into the shadows. 'Swear I had you when I came in.'

'Here, you drunken bum.' From his stool at the grand piano, Jack Stack waved his cigar like a homing beacon.

'Jack, old buddy.' Harry lurched across a carpet of enemy first editions and leaned under the propped piano lid. 'Can't help wishing you hadn't told Bish and Martha. If a whisper gets to Magnus, it's bombs away.'

'Doesn't frighten me. He's only got one asshole.'

The buzzer went. Harry opened the door, bottle in hand.

'Ello-ello-ello,' chorused First and Second Coppergrams, tucking caps under arm. Untucked hair fell about uniformed shoulders.

'We're looking for two sex maniacs,' cued First Coppergram, cupping an ear.

'You've come to the right place,' said Jack Stack from the piano. His forearm dropped, jarring two octaves as he tipped over the stool to give himself up.

'Right, chummy,' said Second Coppergram. 'You're nicked.'

'What's the charge?'

'Depends. Will you be wanting a song? We do a great "Delilah".'

'Thanks all the same.'

'Please yourself. It's a hundred extra, whether or not. Seven-fifty apiece, all in.'

Second Coppergram fetched handcuffs from her waistband and mouthed the next feed as First Coppergram spoke it. 'You boys going to come quietly?'

'Doubt it.' Jack Stack offered his wrists.

'Your friend doesn't say much, does he?'

'He has the right to remain silent.'

'Assume the position,' said Second Coppergram. 'Have to check for concealed weapons.'

The cuffed punters leaned foreheads against the wall and placed feet astride.

'Aha, just as I thought,' said First Coppergram.

'Aha, just as I thought,' said Second Coppergram.

'Any complaints about police harassment?' said First Coppergram.

'Yeah,' said Jack Stack, 'why has it stopped?'

'Goes up to a grand if you want those cuffs off.'

'For a grand,' said Jack Stack, 'I'm keeping mine on.'

The Coppergrams propelled the punters to a couch, fed them more champagne, downed a glass themselves and – with a synchronised sheesh of Velcro – got on with the job.

'Officer,' said Harry, mindful of Marina as Second Coppergram shuffled him into the bedroom, 'I'll settle for a little old back rub.'

'It's still a grand.'

The hall clock chimed twice. Marina put on a robe and left her room to go to Toby's. He slept on as she got in beside him. Moments later she was asleep too, her body spooned behind his.

17

Pass the Marmalade

They woke at 7.30 to Dahlia's treble-knock at his door signalling she had left the breakfast tray. In pyjama bottoms, Toby went to fetch it, padding from rug island to rug island across the cool parquet.

'How about that?' he said.

'How about what?' Marina sat up.

'Two cups. Two everything.'

'The good housekeeper seal of approval?'

'Dahlia knows what's right for me. She's a real woman. Husband was always smiling. Even in his coffin.'

'Heard that one – they couldn't shut the lid.'

'They should have tried my damn medication.'

Marina put a pillow between her bare shoulders and the brass bedhead as Toby poured her coffee. Black with two spoonfuls of brown sugar, the way she liked the first cup of the day.

'You remember,' she said.

'Comes and goes.'

She put a hand to each bearded cheek as she kissed the other.

'I love you. Pass the marmalade.'

Harry and Ambassador Chuck had trotted to the Royal Albert Hall end of Rotten Row and were giving the horses a breather.

'Chuck, I owe you. That election tip-off really got Jack Stack on my side.'

'Don't tell your sister. She'll kill me.'

'Come on. He's a helluva guy.'

'Helluva shit. Sacked my friend Hugo Cunningham, doyen of the diplomatic correspondents. On the poor guy's first day back after a kidney transplant.'

'So nobody's perfect. But I tell you, that man and that paper are going to make millions for Chacewater Inc.'

'Yeah, if Chacewater Inc. doesn't mind holding its nose six days a week.'

'Seven. I'm starting a new Sunday.'

'Listen, Harry, the best Brit journalists are the best in the world. But, boy, the worst are the worst. How come the ass end of the American press is thick with 'em?'

'Our guys write to showcase themselves to each other. The readers don't come into it. OK, so Jack Stack wouldn't win a Pulitzer – but he sure as hell gives the people what they want.'

'Harry, that's the problem. Did you catch that come-on in Monday's Merc? ***Ever done it with a royal? Give us a ring. We'd love to hear your story.***' Chuck looked back over the busy rear end of his colt. 'Give me good clean horse shit any time.'

Harry tightened his chinstrap, pointed his horse towards Hyde Park Corner and dug in his heels.

'Giddy-up!'

Like a plane in holding pattern waiting for the signal to descend, Marina's fingers circled Toby's midriff. No signal came.

'*Whaaat*-ever...' sighed Toby.

'*Whaaat*-ever...' whispered Marina, and nestled into his shoulder.

When Dahlia brought afternoon tea to the verandah, Marina asked her to stay for a cup. Toby was taking his nap.

'Dahlia, my dear, the breakfast tray was sweet of you.'

'You make the man happy. That makes me happy.'

'He's lucky to have you around.'

'I want him to have you.'

'We've had a few contenders?'

'Sure. That nurse who came out with him after the stroke. And the one who followed. And that accountant who flies in with tax papers and stuff. Real nice ladies. But they couldn't get him to want them – the way he wants you.'

'Not the way he used to, Dahlia. The stroke... the medication... you know...'

'You're very beautiful. Never had to be patient with men. But

I know you will for this man.' She covered Marina's hand. 'It will work out just fine.'

'I'll try.' She covered Dahlia's hand.

'And I'll try. Dish up lots of conch for the pair of you. Sure used to bring out the best in my man.' She widened her eyes. 'And me.'

Upstairs, Toby was in his bathroom eyeing the next six-hourly batch of beta-blockers, weighing the tablets in his hand – and flushing them down the loo. Just like the last batch, and every one of the seven batches since Marina phoned to say she was on her way.

Bish threw open drinks cupboard and fridge to show them stacked again. He conveyed Humpty's undertaking to flay the fool responsible for yesterday's drought. And Humpty's plea for a blitz on everyone else's expenses.

'Especially yours.' Jack Stack reached into a drawer for Bish's latest claim sheet. 'This alleged lunch with the Palace Press Secretary last Tuesday. Bollocks. Last Tuesday, the Admiral had lunch with me.'

'Greedy sod.' Clop. 'Told me he hadn't eaten.'

Dahlia and Marina were living up to their pledges to apply their talents to Toby's numbed libido.

Emeralds afire, Marina came down to dinner with that certain sway of a woman in next to nothing beneath her little black cocktail number. For her part, Dahlia served up the magic mollusc in three guises. Conch restored raw to its pink shell and sharpened with lime. Conch deep fried in egg and cracker crumbs. And conch salad.

Toby hardly noticed what was on the end of his fork as Marina sat opposite in the big bay window. He lifted his gaze from her candle-lit eyes only to lift the Gewürztraminer from the ice bucket.

'Always loved you in freckles.'

'You always loved counting them.' Her fingers flirted with the cluster at her flounced neckline.

'Always loved you in emeralds.'

'In these' – she touched ear-clips, necklace, bracelet – 'unforgettably.'

'Forgettably,' He squeezed his eyes.

'You surprised me with them while I was dressing for a gala night at – '

' – Covent Garden?'

'Yup. And by the time we finally got there – '

' – we were too late to take our seats in the Arts Minister's box until the interval?'

'Yup. They only needed to look at our faces. Oh, darling Toby' – she beckoned him – 'sit by me. Hold my hand. It's all coming back, isn't it?'

'Like that little Swiss hotel where we broke the bed?' Toby moved alongside.

'You waffled in English, French and Italian – and they kept laughing in German.'

They kissed. He stroked her thigh, breathing an extra breath as he felt a suspender clip and remembered some more. She drew his hand up into her hot lap and pressed it there.

The grandmother clock began chiming ten.

By the last stroke, they were on their way to the double stairs. Watching them go up hand in hand, Dahlia thanked the infallible conch. Marina thanked the infallible suspenders. Toby thanked skipping the medication.

18

Divine Approval

Marina woke first. She lay cosily in Toby's arms, thinking how happy she was with this man who loved her for ever. And how happy she could be writing novels under his jacaranda tree instead of struggling to stay sane in the Fleet Street madhouse.

But wasn't she just running away? Not from Harry. You didn't need to run from Harry: he was one you could unscrew as casually as screw. No, she was running from Jack Stack. She bit her lip. He had beaten her. Whether the boss was Humpty or Harry or Magnus or whoever, nobody was going to drop the pilot who now had the Mercury on course for the only sort of success that matters: the sort with a £ sign at one end and a string of zeros at the other.

Toby snoozed on through the treble-knock that announced the breakfast tray. Marina went to fetch it in, and caught Dahlia's eye as she turned at the head of the stairs. They exchanged thumbs-ups.

He woke as she made room for the tray on the bedside table, shunting aside the Bible that Dahlia had left open for them at I Corinthians 7:9. *But if they cannot contain, let them marry; for it is better to marry than to burn.*

'So' – Toby sat up – 'how about it?'

'Is that a proposal?'

'That's a proposal.'

'Not worried how much another divorce would cost?'

'I should live so long.'

They hugged silently for a while, then slipped back under the sheet and eased familiar bodies into a sweet coupling beyond technique.

'Is that an acceptance?' said Toby eventually.

'That's an acceptance.'

He took her hand and caressed the empty ring finger. 'Let's get married Saturday. I'll book the Big Joe steel band. The boys do a great Mendelssohn wedding march.'

'All in all, I'd prefer the Wagner – '

The explosion echoed around Baynard Cay. It rattled the windows, blew leaves off trees and set the dogs howling.

'God,' said Toby, 'what the hell was that?'

'Divine approval?'

They looked out to the landing stage where *Freelance* was vanishing in smoke and flames.

Toby had grabbed his dressing gown and was almost at the door when Sergeant Mac rang.

'You folks OK? That was a mother and father of a bang. I can see the flames from Marsh Harbour.'

'*Freelance* just went up. Meet you at the pier.'

'Stay where you are, skipper. Nothing you can do. I'll raise the fire engine.'

Toby put the phone down, only to pick it up as it rang again.

'This is Magnus.'

'Surprise, surprise.' Toby motioned Marina to listen in.

'I trust my timing is not inconvenient.'

'Max, your timing is perfect. I'm ready to sell.'

'Wonderful. You could not put the Mercury into more respectful hands.'

'I'm not selling to you – you murderous swine. Anybody but you. Marina and I could have been aboard when your bomb went off.'

'My bomb? What do you mean, my bomb?'

Marina squeezed Toby's arm as he hung up. 'Sure it's down to Magnus?'

'Who else wants me to sell to Magnus?'

She picked up a pad and noted the dialogue while it was fresh. She could see it on the page in that elusive Magnus chapter. Heading: *What do you mean, my bomb?*

'Toby, darling,' she said, 'if he rings back, do let me speak to him. I still need to fix an interview. It won't be a real book on press barons if he isn't in it.'

'Journalist.' Toby snorted.

Through his cabin window of the Gulfstream climbing away from Marsh Harbour, Clarence C Campbell could see *Freelance* blazing like a Viking funeral ship.

CCC emptied his hip flask to toast his narrow escape. Arriving at the rental office to return their scooter, he had spotted Sergeant Mac parked opposite. But the officer never looked his way. Just as well. He would not have forgotten giving Chacewater's Miami man a night in the hoosegow. CCC would never have set foot again on Abaco, but he could hardly defy the legendary Ed. Not when the old fixer spelled out that Freedom of Expenses was not implied by the First Amendment: either CCC carried out this little assignment or explained to the FBI and the IRS his phoney $10,500 claim for that Abaco trip he'd made for Harry.

Just why torching *Freelance* was so important to Ed, CCC didn't know and didn't want to know. He didn't think it had much to do with his expenses.

In Toronto, Magnus was asking himself questions. And answering them.

Why does Toby think Magnus blew up his boat? Because someone wants Toby to think that. And why else but to frighten him into selling to Magnus? But why do Magnus such a favour? Why else but to frustrate some other bidder? But there's only Harry Chacewater – so who wants him to miss out on the Merc? Who else but the Chacewater family – and the man pulling their strings for three generations? Who else but the legendary Ed?

Magnus applauded his analysis. Thanks to Toby's defiance, Ed's bomb had not exploded Harry's chances; it had promoted them almost to certainty. Almost.

In Richmond, Ed was taking CCC's call.

'Joe Schmo here, sir. It's done. Heading home to—'

'Don't say another word, Mr Schmo.'

Now Ed rang Abaco. Toby didn't sound at all like a guy who just had the fear of God blown into him. Had CCC hit the wrong boat?

'...Ed, how legendary of you to ring me at the very moment I've got news for you and your boy. Just had a taste of Magnus's business methods. My boat has been blown up before my eyes.'

'God, that's him all right.'

'Marina told me about his track record. Blowing up Pa Chacewater's boat in Maine.'

'Yeah, we took the hint.'

'Magnus doesn't scare me. I'm going to do exactly what he doesn't want – sell to Harry.'

'What can I say?' Ed tried not to sound dismayed. 'Except don't be a hero for our sake.'

'For your sake, keep Harry away from Abaco – unless you want to wreck the deal. The sight and sound of him would change my mind.'

'I get the message.'

'Just make certain Harry gets it.'

Toby turned to Marina as he put the phone down. 'Occurs to me that I mightn't be doing Harry a favour. Could be setting him up for the next Magnus bomb.'

19

Remember Maine

Just before dawn, *Miss Print IV* exploded at her mooring. The smoke turned two Red Cardinals black, and bits of marine toilet came to rest on the dome of Harry's bandstand.

Two hours later, Clarence C Campbell was phoning the legendary Ed from Newport News airport.

'Joe Schmo here, sir. It's done. Heading home to —'

'Don't say another word, Mr Schmo.'

CCC was a worried man. First, Toby's 42-footer. Now, Harry's 63-footer. What was Ed working him up to – the *QE3*?

In a Soho basement restaurant, Harry and Theo were watching blue flames lick the pan under their crêpes Suzette when the mobile trilled. Ed was on the line.

'...Harry, there's only one guy who'd pull a stunt like this. Remember Maine. Don't be dumb. Back off.'

'Remember Maine? Sure do – and as of now, it's my battle cry. Never did get over Pa turning tail like that. Got to stand up to Max Magnus or run scared the rest of my life.'

'Ain't worth it for one more damn newspaper.'

'Ed, I'm not quitting. Marina's out there working on Toby as we speak. We're going to win this one.'

Even now, Ed reckoned, there had to be a way to frustrate Harry. Maybe a more subtle kind of explosion would do it. Since Marina had to be the reason Toby wanted Harry to stay away, how about dropping Harry right in their laps?

Harry was taking a pee when the mobile trilled again. His free hand raised it to his ear. Ed again.

'Harry, it gets worse. CCC just called. Contact tells him Toby's boat has gone up too. I suppose nothing I say is going to stop you racing out there to stop him surrendering to Magnus.'

Jack Stack was at his keyboard, surfing the early pages, when his private line rang.

'This is Magnus.'

'God . . . '

'Call me Max. Feel we know each other. Hear great things about you. Another wonderful scoop today – those naughty mottoes on Prince Nicky's Y-fronts. You've made the Merc a very fine newspaper.'

'I admit it.'

'Good man. I cannot abide modesty.'

'Max, you're in no danger in Fleet Street.'

'But you are.'

'How's that?'

'If Mr Chacewater gets the Merc, you will be out on your ear. The new editor will be Miss Marshall.'

'No chance. She couldn't edit a bus ticket.'

'No chance? If I may speak plainly – one son of the manse to another – Miss Marshall is shagging the ass off him.'

Glug.

'You there, Jack?'

'Just about.'

'Only one way to beat her. Fight his take-over. Use the Merc. Campaign against some foul foreign fornicator gobbling up a grand old British institution.'

'Double-crossing git. If it wasn't for the nice fat pay-off he'll have to give me, I wouldn't hang about. I'd go back to the Globe today.'

'Jack, I have a better idea. I will take over the Merc – and you will stay on. And get the sale to five million.'

'I'll want a massive TV spend.'

'You've got it, Jack.'

'Big bucks for big buy-ups.'

'Name of the game, Jack.'

'Editor on top, management on tap.'

'No prob, Jack.'

'Fire fifty old farts – '

'Music to my ears, Jack.'

' – and replace them.'

'Er, sure, Jack.'

'So we're in business?'

'Up to you now. Chase Chacewater away – and my second cheque for a million dollars, Canadian, will drop on your mat the day I take over.'

'Second?'

'The first will drop the day your campaign starts.'

'Tomorrow too soon for you?'

Jack Stack set down the phone, patted it, put his feet up and summoned Bish.

'I've got something in common with Marina, would you believe? We're both being screwed by Harry Chacewater.'

Clop.

'I want you to hack into her computer again. That book she's doing on press barons. I want her chapter on him.'

'Afternoon, Jack,' said the Prime Minister.

'Beth, thanks for taking my call. I can guess how busy you are right now.'

'Always time for my favourite editor. How'd you get to know the election date before I'd even told the Palace? We were not amused.'

'Never reveal my sources, Beth. That's why you trust me.'

'And I trust your opinion poll. Exactly what I need to hit the ground running.'

'Beth, I've got an election winner for you. An issue to get the voters steamed up. Union Jacks all over it.'

'Bless you, Jack. Got to have something sexier than the public sector borrowing requirement.'

Harry wandered into the editor's office ahead of the messenger bringing the first editions.

'Hi there, Jack. How about a drink?'

'No thanks. Had one yesterday.'

Harry helped himself as though he had already been promoted from guest to proprietor. Jack Stack did not look up from the pages in front of him.

'Come on, Jack. What are we doing for laughs tonight? Got a couple hours to kill before take-off.'

'Don't know about you, Harry.' He ran a fat felt tip around a thin headline. 'I'm editing a fucking paper.'

'Can't edit it all night.'

Fired up by the Magnus revelation and fortified by the prospective Magnus millions, Jack Stack lifted his eyes and got Harry in his sights.

'That the way it's going to be if you get the Merc?'

'Lighten up, Jack. Why don't we fix for a pair of traffic wardens to come and clamp us? My treat.'

'Told you, Harry. Too busy.'

'Sonofabitch. Is that big Aussie sheila around?'

'I'll ask her.' He went to the intercom. 'Harry Chacewater's at a loose end – '

'Tell him to tie a flamin' knot in it.'

'I reckon' – Jack Stack took a cigar without offering Harry one – 'that's Oz for tie a flamin' knot in it.'

'So how about that Heidi Hunt?'

'So how about that Marina Marshall?'

Harry gave him a funny look. Jack Stack gave him a funny look back.

'Listen, Harry. I'll give you a phone number. Just tell them what gender, colour, uniform and quantity you require – and let me get on with my God-given mission.'

'OK, OK.' Harry put up his hands. 'Just as well I'm flying out to get this deal buttoned up while I still love you.'

'Have a nice trip, Harry. And if you run into the First Lady of Fleet Street, tell her not a single solitary soul rang to complain her column was missing this week.'

20

Save the Merc

Marina did not trust the office computer with her book, so Bish had trawled there in vain. After Claudia went home, he looked in the usual hiding place – the pin tray – for a spare key to her desk. Where he found a spare key to Marina's desk. Where he found spare keys to her flat. Where he found her laptop. Where he found the Harry chapter.

Clop. Now he reached across the editor to load a copy disc of that masterpiece of emasculative journalism.

Clop. Now he set before him the photo Dumpty had sent Marina: that snap of Harry dangling between springboard and deep end in search of his shorts.

'*Con Fuoco*.' Jack Stack read out her chapter heading. 'Sounds promising.' It did, the way he pronounced it. He scrolled to locate the sequence:

Harry offered me the sleeve of the Mendelssohn octet. 'There. Con fuoco *– with fire, passion. Reckon he got off on it?' He closed in. His toecap came on to my toecap. 'Marina, you're a beautiful woman...'*

'Harry, go con fuoco *yourself.'*

Clop. Now Bish positioned layout pad and fat felt tip, and opened the humidor. Jack Stack went to work on a cigar and tomorrow's front page. Alongside the masthead he sketched a billowing Union flag, its staff descending to border his headlines:

Beth battles to foil Yank take-over!!
SAVE YOUR MERC
FROM THIS BERK

He roughed the Harry picture across four columns, adding a Stars and Stripes figleaf. He doubled up the text in the remaining three columns, and broke into the middle a cross-ref: ***Harry, go c**∗∗ *f**∗∗∗∗ yourself, says Marina Marshall – See Centre Pages***.

He turned to his keyboard, adding commentary and applause as his words came up on screen.

The Mercury is more than Britain's fastest-growing newspaper. It is a national institution. Like fish and chips.

'And chicken tikka masala.'

But today it is in peril of becoming the new toy of a billionaire Yank playboy. The Merc's sensational success has taken the fancy of bourbon-swilling, bimbo-pulling Harry Chacewater, 27, who quit the US Navy to inherit daddy's publishing empire.

'Jammy devil.'

Thank God, battling Beth Macbeth is leading the fight to keep Harry's mitts off the Merc. The Prime Minister is making the future of your newspaper a key general election issue.

'Well, she is now.'

It is unthinkable that the Merc should fall to a right berk like Harry Chacewater. What next? Surrender Princess Vicki to King Kong?

'Five minutes of her, he'd jump off the Empire State.'

We at the Merc live in the real world. We know that companies are bought and sold. We simply want the Merc to be in the hands of publishers whose values are our values. And that doesn't mean you, Harry Chacewater.

'It means you, Max Magnus.'

Today, in an exclusive report by The First Lady of Fleet Street, we reveal the truth about the man who wants to take you over...

Jack Stack went on to highlight paragraphs in Marina's chapter. 'I want this ... and this ... and this twice ...'

He told Bish to make sure not a word went forward before Humpty's going-home time. Tomorrow, the chief executive would be trembling for his future. Jack Stack wouldn't. Tomorrow, Jack Stack would be a millionaire, Canadian, and on his way to becoming a multi. For extra insurance, he had Lord Bull's return ticket to the Globe.

And he had the Vampire Princess diaries.

He got to his flat at 1 am to find Gloria Mundy and sister Jenny crashed out on the sitting-room couches. On Gloria's face, a smile. In Jenny's arms, the Xenia diaries: three years of black magic that would put the skids under Prince Ricky's bride-to-be.

Jack Stack nudged aside the Chinese take-away debris to set down coffee in three Winnie-the-Pooh mugs. The weird sisters stretched through garlicky yawns as they swung their feet down and into their shoes.

'Mission accomplished,' said Gloria.

He sat alongside her. 'Did we make a century?'

'One hundred and one.'

'Thank you, God.' He put his palms together. 'And the red stuff?'

'Prayers answered,' said Jenny. 'I found an invoice for baboon blood from auntie's delibatessen. Witches recommend it to cool the brew so the magic doesn't evaporate.'

'No law against using it when your ink runs out. I'll print the diary entries in red – and leave it to the readers to make up their own bloody minds.'

'Can't be fairer than that,' said Gloria. 'So when do we kick off?'

'Not yet, kid. The Mercury is in danger of falling into alien hands. I've told Beth to make it an election issue. So this is not the moment to expose the vampire bride she's foisted on the royals. That will have to wait till I've got her back into Number 10.'

'Jack' – Gloria walked to the window – 'I hope the royals don't kick Xenia out for this.'

'They should welcome a witch into the family?'

'She'd be so much at home. Putting the mockers on is what they do. Defiant spouses. Tiresome lovers. Nutty relatives. Fruity butlers. Talkative postillions. Jack, they've been at it for a thousand years. They're world class.'

'Love it, Mrs Mundy. Write down every golden word before you forget. I'll need it all for my follow-up – *The Great Save Xenia Campaign.*'

On her way out, Gloria put an elastic band round the diaries and replaced them under the Wren officer's tricorn on the hall wardrobe shelf. Alongside sat a range of uniform headgear. She shook her head. If the readers were entitled to the private fantasies of Princess Xenia, why not those of their editor? They would so enjoy imagining what had gone on under this Wren tricorn, that Salvation Army bonnet, that barrister's wig, that St Trinian's boater, that nun's cowl and those two City of London traffic warden caps.

21

Hi, Milady

The charred landing stage enhanced the impression that Baynard Cay had been evacuated. At Toby's pink villa, Harry got no answer when he called 'Anybody home?' from the verandah steps, and again at the wide-open doors and again at the foot of the double stairs and again at Dahlia's kitchen. There was a trace of Marina's perfume, but no Marina. Nobody.

As he helped himself to a beer from the fridge, the phone rang. He picked it up.

'I'd like to speak with Lord Baynard.'

'That you, Humpty?'

'Harry! Thought you were still in London.'

'Had to see Toby, but quick. Magnus is closing in. And I needed a change of air. Your Mr Stack was acting real weird yesterday.'

'Even weirder today. You should see the front page. And the middle pages. Man's gone mad. Brace yourself...'

Humpty read him the front page and described the picture.

'What in hell,' asked Harry, 'is a berk?'

'Cockney rhyming slang.'

'Berk for jerk?'

'Berk for what rhymes with Berkeley Hunt.'

'It sure rhymes with Humpty. That goddam picture could only have come from your goddam camera.'

'I'll murder goddam Dumpty. And you'll murder goddam Marina when I've read you her goddam spread.'

'Go on, hit me.'

Humpty hit him. Harry's grunts and groans punctuated the recital.

'Jeez. How could she? How could he? How could you?'

'Sneaky devil waited till my back was turned.'

'Fired him?'

'Not without checking. Say Toby put him up to it?'

'Same difference, Humpty. We're kaput.'

'Wait, I've got a marvellous idea—'

'Spare me.'

'You sue for libel, Harry. Take us for millions. End up getting the Merc for nothing.'

'Asshole.'

'Yes, well…hadn't I better have a word with Toby?'

'Nobody here but me.'

'They must be out fishing. Has the boat gone?'

'Humpty, she's gone all right. The bomb didn't leave much of the landing stage either.'

'The bomb?'

'Don't ask.'

Nodding off on the verandah, two hours and four beers later, Harry was woken by the sounds of a steel band rounding the headland. He stood at the rail to watch a festooned party boat coming into Baynard Cay, the deck crowded with people dancing, drinking, laughing.

The band broke into 'Congratulations' as Dahlia led the way for a tiered wedding cake to be paraded ashore. The happy couple followed; Toby in morning suit, panama and silver-top cane; Marina in cornflower silk and carrying a posy.

The pair looked so good together, Harry almost didn't mind. No sense minding once you'd been told to Go c∗∗ f∗∗∗∗ yourself in asterisks an inch high.

The boat was still noisily disgorging wedding guests, and waiters were dispensing champagne to sustain them on the way up to the lawn. As the band installed itself on the verandah, Harry came down the steps applauding the newlyweds.

'Hi, milady – suits you. Hi, Toby.' He offered his hands and they took them. 'So pleased for you both.'

'Meet our best men.' Marina edged their thirteen-year-old twins forward. 'Olly' – she patted one of the blond heads – 'and Nolly.'

'Nolly and Olly, actually,' said the patted one, dragging his brother away to the ice-cream cart.

'About Magnus—' Harry began.

'Fuck Magnus.' Toby shook his stick towards the damaged landing stage. 'Blew up my boat to encourage me to sell him the Merc. Only one answer to that – I sell to you.'

'Well, how about that? He blew up my boat to warn me off buying the Merc. Only one answer to that – I buy. But we do have a problem.'

'You surprise me.'

'Humpty wants you to ring him. Got a mutiny on his hands. The Merc's launched a Page One campaign to block me. D'you reckon Magnus has blown up Jack Stack's boat too?'

'If he hasn't, I will.' Toby kissed Marina's hand and limped away to phone Humpty.

'Sorry about the dead roses, Harry.' Marina shrugged.

'Dead roses? They sent red roses. I thought I was still in with a chance.'

He couldn't get mad at her on her wedding day. She'd made the right choice, of course. Even now, his eye was peeling the Bahamian beauty in the veiled orange pillbox and the orange two-piece.

'Oh, Harry.' Marina tracked his glance and sighed.

They could hear Toby laughing his way back to them as he threaded through the throng.

'Bloody fool told me not to worry, they sold 50,000 extra this morning. And for his next trick – wait for it – Jack Stack's rigging a vox pop, *Why you don't want an alien taking over your Merc.*'

'He's out the day I'm in,' said Harry.

'Too late,' said Toby. 'Just fired the pair of 'em.'

Harry moved towards the girl in orange. Their eyes mingled. Dahlia watched, shaking her head. The minute she saw that naughty man back at Baynard Cay, she had packed Tulip off to Aunt Hyacinth.

'Guess I fouled up.' The legendary Ed shrugged at Mrs Ed as he came from the phone. 'That was Harry. He's got the Mercury. Over to me to wrap the deal, thanks very much.'

'Did your best, Ed.'

'Hey, I didn't give you the good news. Marina's married Toby. Our boy's off that hook.'

'Mom will be disappointed. She took to Marina.'

'Want to bet that'll be my fault too? Right now I feel 80 years old.'

'Ed, you are 80 years old.'

'Hold on – still two, three weeks before the contract can be ready to sign. I'm not giving up yet.'

'Forget it.'

'Nothing I wouldn't do for that boy.'

'Done too much already.'

Jack Stack felt like a million dollars, Canadian. The six zeros on Magnus's cheque fascinated like champagne bubbles. He was looking at them from various angles when Magnus rang.

'Young man, I congratulate you. Brilliant. What are we going to hit the berk with tomorrow?'

'Max, there isn't going to be a tomorrow. I've just been fired. Toby's selling to Harry. And Johnnie Bull's asked me back to the Globe.'

'Don't join their pension scheme.'

'You mean—'

'I mean my preacher father's favourite text was: *To every thing there is a season, and a time to every purpose under the heaven.* Likewise, Jack, there is a time for Magnus to fail to prise the Mercury from Toby, and a time for Magnus to prise it from Harry.'

Dahlia had gone to fetch the bride a parasol. She noticed the doors to the billiard room closed, and took the wind to have blown them shut. She pushed them open again. Her glance took in two half-empty glasses on a side table and an orange jacket hung over the back of a chair, across which lay an orange skirt. Over the billiard table, between drumming orange stilettos, bobbed a pale bottom.

She advanced on the bottom and swiped it with the parasol. Harry's roar ascended from surprise to ecstasy. His new friend counter-pointed with a run of shuddering gasps as she deployed a hand to hold her veiled orange pillbox in place.

As Dahlia tucked the parasol under her arm, the tip caught the scoreboard and advanced it to 147.

'Did Mr Chacewater leave?' asked Marina as she put up the parasol. 'Haven't seen his face for awhile.'

'Neither have I,' said Dahlia.

Jack Stack was clearing his desk. Into the zip bag reserved for prized items went his humidor, his Editor of the Year awards and his signed photo of Beth Macbeth. Her *Yours aye* had just been devalued by a call from the Number 10 press secretary bleating that the PM could not be dragged into a campaign for or against the ownership of any particular rag by any particular berk.

'Jump in, Bish.' Jack Stack indicated the bag. 'Whithersoever I goeth, thou goest.'

'Not this trip, Jack.' Clop. 'They want me to take over.'

'Don't fall for that. They're just using you while they look around. Acting editors never get the job. Stick with me. Warm kennel. All the Pedigree Chum you can eat.'

'Not acting, Jack. Real, Jack. Three-year contract.'

'Who on earth advised them to pick you?'

Clop. 'Your friend Marina.'

The phone went. It was the Palace press secretary.

'Afraid it's another plea for mercy, Jack.'

'Fire away, Admiral.' The man had clearly not yet heard that the Mercury had a new editor.

'I gather a paparazzo is trying to flog pictures of some Princess Victoria look-alike leaving a police station. This girl apparently spent hours in the cells after a drugs raid.'

'And you're denying it was Vicki?'

'Been at this game too long to dignify that sort of rubbish with an official response.'

'But the last thing you want is any scandal to upset Vicki's betrothal to that Prince Fritz guy, right?'

'Off the record, Jack, all that gossip column bilge about Vicki and Fritz is just that – bilge.'

'Then what I propose to do, Admiral, is buy Signor Paparazzo's grubby little pix and stop them doing the rounds of Fleet Street. I will also see to it that the Mercury doesn't use them.'

'Bless you, Jack. Shan't forget this.'

Clop, went Bish. After five years of hiding his light under this bushel, he was unable to emerge until this bushel had left the field. He settled for a dirty look as Jack Stack turned to buzz the picture editor.

'Don't worry, Eddie – you're coming with me...Sure you can have whitewall tyres. Now listen – as we speak, some pap is on his way with pix of Vicki for me. Bring them with you, OK?'

He buzzed the features desk.

'Martha, pop in. Just opening a bottle of the good stuff to celebrate your wonderful new job. You'll be making history. First Australian to get to number three at the Globe.'

'Sorry, mate, Bish has already signed me up as number two at the Mercury. Do I still get the flamin' drink?'

Heidi Hunt put her head round the door. The blonde glory that Maria-Teresa had got her to crop and dye black was now strangely piebald. Her eyes were big and damp.

'You won't leave me behind, will you, Jack?'

'No, kid, I won't leave your behind.'

Jack Stack's dismissal had not filtered down to the assistant night manager of the Mercury circulation department. So the first edition was duly biked to his flat.

His howl had Gloria running to make sure he wasn't dropping dead before he could make her political editor of one paper or the other.

'After all I've taught Bish.' He thumped the front page. 'You'd think the bugger would have more pride than to start his editing career by stealing tomorrow's Globe scoop.'

EXCLUSIVE: Strip-search princess tells
drugs squad: I'm my lady-in-waiting
VICKI
IN THE
NICKI

Princess Victoria spent five hours in the cells after being nicked in a Scotland Yard drugs squad raid on a Kensington cellar club.

The Yard didn't know they had arrested the 19-year-old princess, who is a role model for the nation's youth. She had misled them by giving the name of a lady-in-waiting, Lady Islay Wight.

The disgrace could put a stop to her rumoured betrothal to Prince Fritz von Blumenkohl, 39, ruler of the postage-stamp Alpine principality.

Vicki, her long golden hair bunched in a rasta cap, was among a dozen society ravers strip-searched for illegal substances. One said: 'There was nowhere the cops didn't look. Vicki couldn't stop laughing.'

The royal purse contained nine marijuana cigarettes. They were confiscated and the princess was released with a caution in her lady-in-waiting's name...

Jack Stack also shook his head at the paparazzo picture. He would have cropped it to make more of Vicki trying to hide her face. He rang the Mercury to be told that Eddie was over the road celebrating his promotion from Picture Editor to Assistant Editor (Pictures). Any message?

Yeah, bollocks.

22

Honest, Truthful and Decent

The bells of St Clement Danes said Oranges and Lemons as the Aldwych traffic lights changed to red. From the pillion of his chauffeured Kawasaki, a moon-helmeted Jack Stack nipped to the pavement kiosk. Now it was the turn of the pile of Mercurys to be made invisible under a handful of Globes.

'Pillock.' The baseball-capped man at the counter resettled the papers.

'Plonker.' Jack Stack moved them back with one hand and raised two fingers of the other as he turned to go.

'C.U.' – the Globes were shifted once more – 'Next Trip.'

At the big window of the editor's office that was at last his, Bish looked up the hill to St Paul's. The meek had inherited the Merc. He was resolved to be a nice-guy editor: the honest, decent and truthful skipper of the happiest ship in the Fleet Street fleet.

Number 10 was on the line to his secretary. The PM would like a word. Did Mr Bishop prefer to be called Reginald, Reggie, Reg – or what?

'Morning, Bish.'

'And good morning to you, Prime Minister.'

'My congratulations. Great challenge. Great opportunity.'

'Thanks, Beth. Much appreciated. Fought like hell to stop Jack dragging you into his private war with Chacewater. The Merc will make it up to you. Promise.'

'Word of a Lancastrian's good enough for me, Bish.'

'Yorkshireman.'

'Even better, lad.'

Clop.

Down river, on the twenty-ninth floor of Globe Tower, Lord Bull put an arm round Jack Stack's shoulder and paraded him the length of the newsroom. Staff looked on like Death Row inmates following the progress of the governor and the man with the cyanide pellets.

'I'm Sally.' The ex-editor's long, tall secretary gazed down upon Jack Stack at the door to his office. 'Can I get you anything?'

'Yeah, a shorter secretary.'

He walked through her into an office occupied by three carpet fitters, two venetian blind hangers, two painters, two plumbers – and one ex-editor.

Kevin O'Connor sat numbly on the throne that was no longer his. He had taken a week's holiday to be out of the way while they readied the 25 per cent bigger office that Lord Bull had promised him for cutting the payroll 25 per cent. He had come back to find his desk drawers being emptied into binbags.

'Great tan, Kev.' Jack Stack raised his voice above the din. 'Been anywhere nice?'

'Golfing on the Algarve.'

'Dangerous, that.'

'Golfing on the Algarve?'

'I mean dangerous to take a holiday. Turn your back for five minutes – look what happens.'

A man came in to unload Veuve Clicquot into the drinks cupboard and three sizes of Montecristo into the humidor. Jack Stack held out a hand for a bottle. As he uncorked it, Sally supplied two trembling glasses.

'Sorry.' Kev hauled himself up to surrender the throne to the new king. 'Sorry.'

Jack Stack took his seat, calculating that, with the refusals of Bish and Martha, he was running short of executive grafters. If he could hold on to Kev, he wouldn't need to go on his knees to Maria-Teresa.

'Can't think why they fired you, Kev. Not your fault you were over-promoted. So – what now?'

'God only knows. What becomes of ex-editors?'

'It's diabolical, Kev. They're doomed to haunt the Fleet Street graveyard for ever. Groaning about declining standards. Moaning about bean counters. Cursing focus groups. Wailing about dockland. Floating in and out of El Vino without buying a round. Materialising at St Bride's memorial services to reproach their successors. And, Kev, I tell you, there are nights when ex-editors swear they hear the phantom presses of old thundering away again. Until suddenly it all goes quiet between editions – and spectral voices sigh for one more chance to sit on the trapdoor with a noose round their necks. It's diabolical, Kev. Diabolical.'

'I'm too young for that, Jack.' He bit his lip.

Plumbers stopped plumbing. Fitters stopped fitting. Hangers stopped hanging. Painters stopped painting. The tools of their trade hung in their hands as they looked to Jack Stack for an act of compassion.

'Listen, Kev. It doesn't have to be the end. I need a deputy. How about it?'

Plumbers, fitters, hangers and painters applauded and looked to Kevin for a symmetrical response.

'Bollocks.' Kev made for the door. 'Give up my pay-off to knacker myself for a thug like you?'

Plumbers, fitters, hangers and painters made disappointed noises as Kev shuffled out to see his accountant.

Jack Stack set off to plead with Maria-Teresa. On the way, his eye fell upon the mouse of a man he had fired from the Mercury Postbag Page, having fired him from the Globe Postbag Page last time round.

'Small world,' said the editor once again.

'Too sodding small,' said the mouse once again.

'What did you call me on your way out the first time and the second time?'

'Can't remember.'

'Try to have it ready the fourth time. Ta-ta.'

Jack Stack stopped at the news desk to check if they'd got the lady-in-waiting in the Vicki story. Not yet. Would be doorstepping her every address if it wasn't for that creep Kev's 25 per cent staff cut.

He found Maria-Teresa finalising overnight feature pages. Honing headlines. Rejigging intros. Purging adverbs. Improving clichés. Shortening sentences.

'You're a real pro.' He took the chair on the other side of her desk. 'Not too many of us around.'

'Don't bother. I'm off back to the Mercury the moment I finish polishing this crap.'

'Forget it. You're going to be my deputy.'

'Like Bish? Pouring your drinks? Knocking the ash off your cigar? Wiping your bum?'

'Come on. Sitting at the feet of the master hasn't done the lad any harm. Look at him now. An actual editor. Couple of years with me, Maria-Teresa – it could be you.'

'Piss off.'

Funny woman. Next stop, Kitty.

'Great to be working together again, kid. Features editor now, aren't you? Well, I'm making you assistant editor.'

'Was that Heidi Hunt I saw coming out of the lift?'

'Associate editor?'

'I'm never going back to rewriting her dazzling column.'

'Deputy editor?'

'Nothing doing. I've accepted an offer from Bish.'

'What's that man got that I haven't got?'

'Martha. And Maria-Teresa. And me. Know what? We're going to bloody murder you.'

Back in his bunker, among the plumbers, fitters, hangers and painters, Jack Stack put his feet up and aimed the TV remote control. Beth Macbeth was in the middle of a press conference, under pressure from the latest cruel-faced aspirant to the role of grand inquisitor.

'... Prime Minister, why are you against American investment in British companies?'

'Wrong, Fergus. I'm all for it.'

'Then what are we to make of the news that you're leading the campaign to save the Merc from the berk?' Laughter.

'Fergus, you're too smart to believe everything you read.' More laughter. 'Or everything you say.' Renewed laughter.

'Actually, we're on live television, Prime Minister. The viewers can see you dodging a serious question.'

'Oh, it's a serious question, is it?' Prolonged laughter.

'Have you not had a call from the US ambassador about this xenophobic campaign against his brother-in-law?'

'You've been off message too long, Fergus. Fact is, the Merc is retracting. I'm sure my friend the ambassador will regard the matter closed.'

'But it isn't closed, is it? A British editor is sacked for standing up against a foreign take-over. He believes the Prime Minister is behind him – but now she is revealed as a friend of the take-over family.'

'You clearly haven't read what I said on the subject.'

'What did you say on the subject?'

'Nothing.' Terminal laughter. 'Next question...'

Jack Stack switched her off. How could Beth Macbeth do this to him? Right, he would detonate the Princess Xenia diaries – and lose her the election.

If Lord Bull would let him.

The Palace was ringing the Mercury to keel-haul Jack Stack. Ah, said a secretary, Mr Stack isn't our editor any more – would the admiral care to keel-haul Mr Bishop?

'Morning, Bish. Best of British and all that. But your Princess Victoria story. Really must express my dismay.'

'Know how you feel, Admiral.' Clop. 'Thank God it's the last time Jack Shit leaves me to carry the can.'

'HM spitting blood. I need help. Vicki needs help. Appreciate anything you can do.'

'I'll give it some thought. Get back to you soon.'

'So grateful. And – while I'm on – why don't I put you and Mrs Bish on the next Palace garden party list? Be nice for HM to meet you.'

Bish buzzed Martha. She twirled in, displaying the new number on the back of her Aussie rugger shirt. She had promoted it from 8 to 2.

'Martha, just had an SOS from HM.'

'Strewth.'

'Jack Stack's farewell splash' – he thumped the paper on his desk – 'looks like ruining Vicki's last hope of a royal husband.'

'A confirmed bachelor? Almost 40? My oath, we're doing the sheila a favour.'

'Problem is, if Prince Fritz backs off, she'll have to marry a human being. Can't have that, can we?' Clop. 'Look at the trouble marrying out has brought them.'

'Things'll get hairy tomorrow, boss. Papers full of Fritz considering his flamin' position. Pride of the House of Blumenkohl. Shame of the House of Buck.'

'God help the Admiral.'

'Got an idea, mate.' Martha vibrated. 'If he'll play, Vicki's in the clear. And you scoop Jack Stack on his first day back at the Globe...'

Bish just had time for a pee before his executives assembled for his debut conference. He re-combed his hair, re-knotted his tie, re-plumped his pocket handkerchief. He had played every supporting role. Jester and butt. Feed and fall-guy. Mixer and fixer. Barman and batman. Wimp and pimp. Now, he was playing the lead.

Martha led the applause as he strode in, taller as editor than he had been as deputy. After years of shrinking to avoid making Jack Stack feel short, Bish could draw himself up to his full five-nine.

He won his first laugh as, taking his seat, he pulled out the cushion on which his predecessor had perched and chucked it over his shoulder.

'Let's make this fun,' said Bish. 'God knows, we put enough into the job. Wreck our marriages. Neglect our kids. Ruin our health – talking of which, I hereby declare this a cigar-free zone.' He inhaled the applause. 'Also an alcohol-free zone. Well, until after the first edition.' Clop. 'I'll tell the management it's cheaper than overtime.'

'Sooner have the fucking money,' said someone.

'Hold it right there.' Bish put up his palms. 'We're also an effin-and-blindin-free zone. No more humiliation, no more insults. Lost too many fine journalists that way. Glad to announce that three of the finest have accepted my invitation to return.' He buzzed his secretary. 'OK.'

In came Maria-Teresa, Neil Robinson and Kitty. Bish moved to shake hands and go clop.

'Not a bad exchange for Heidi Hunt, eh? Let's hear it for the returned exiles. Let's hear it for the freed slaves. Let's hear it for all of us. Let's hear it for the good old Merc.'

Lord Bull's butler opened the doors for Jack Stack to blink his way into a dining room that could have been a Harrods window. The ceiling was starry with spotlights; the walls glowed with illuminated panels of Lalique nymphs. At the far window, Lord Bull was scanning the Thames through a brass telescope on a tripod.

'Just look at that, Jack. Tower Bridge opening. Doesn't it make you want to burst into "Land of Hope and Glory?"'

'Every time, Johnnie.'

'The heart leaps. The eyes fill. The throat dries.' He looked up. 'How much do you think they'd take for it?'

'Some things, Johnnie, are beyond price.'

'Ha! So were you when you were riding high at the Merc. But now you've been fired, look how glad you are to come crawling back for half your old salary.'

'Admit it, Johnnie. You missed me.'

'True. Welcome home. Let's get at the oysters.'

'Have I got news for you,' said Jack Stack as a dozen Loch Fynes were set before him. 'Next week, I shall put the sale up a million. Go on – ask me how am I going to achieve that unprecedented feat.'

'How are you going to achieve that unprecedented feat?'

'**VAMPIRE XENIA!!** *Amazing secret diaries of Prince Ricky's bride-to-be . . .* '

Twenty-four oysters looked up like startled eyes as Jack Stack filled Lord Bull's ears with shock-horror from Princess Xenia's black magic diaries. Double-bubbling cauldron, baboon blood, rhyming ingredients from her auntie's delibatessen in New Orleans, pin-stuck wax images and all. He went on to recite the fate of ring-a-bell names among the 101 victims Xenia had spooked.

'Any spanking?' Lord Bull wondered.

'No spanking.' Aye-aye.

'Ha!' said Lord Bull eventually. 'Astonishing stuff. But Xenia was Beth Macbeth's big idea. Bring down Xenia – and we bring down Beth.'

'Right.' How fast chairmen caught on.

'Can't abide Beth myself. But the other lot would cost me millions.' He wolfed his last six oysters. 'So kill it.'

Jack Stack waited in vain for a grin to take over Lord Bull's fat face. 'You pulling my pisser?'

'No, I'm pulling the story. Saving the nation from an unhelpful change of government.'

'Hang on – Xenia will go on to marry Ricky and spook Nicky and Mickey out of the succession. Imagine – a vampire queen running a thicko king. That what you want?'

'Bring it up again after the election.' Lord Bull helped himself to an oyster from Jack Stack's plate. 'Lost your appetite?' And a second. 'I haven't.' And a third.

Was this how Samson felt, waking to find himself shorn and the Philistines making sport of him? Jack Stack was a captive at Lord Bull's grindstone, sustained by dreams of pulling down the temple – and by that million dollars, Canadian.

'...Jack, buy me those diaries, anyway,' Lord Bull was saying. 'Don't want them falling into less fastidious hands.'

'Problem is' – Jack Stack sniffed – 'it's a deep-throat scenario. They're not up for sale. Someone just wants them published. We can only guess why.'

Guessing why Lord Bull wanted them was not difficult. He had identified a lever to fulfil his dearest ambition. How else could he get Tower Bridge shifted to span the burn through his Scottish moors, opening and closing to amuse his grouse-slaughtering guests?

Marina phoned from Baynard Cay as smiling executives were filing out from afternoon conference. Bish had declared his office a monologue-free zone too. They would now enjoy an hour more to deliver the goods.

'How's the honeymoon, Bish?'

'Bliss. How's yours?'

'Wouldn't dream of interrupting it – except to wish you luck. You're going to be a great editor.'

'I can't thank you enough for getting me the job.'

'Only you and Martha weren't too cowed to come and tell me you liked my stuff.'

'When do we get you back, Marina?'

'You don't. Toby needs me. Maybe I'll do you the odd column. Wouldn't want my last Merc piece to be that chapter Jack Stack stole from my computer.'

Clop.

It was not the skull and crossbones up the mainmast day that Jack Stack had hoped for. He would like his first splash back at the Globe to have been more than a cobbled-up Fritz angle on the Vicki story.

When the Mercury first edition dropped, he set it alongside his own – and crashed ten quidsworth of Havana into the ashtray.

Lady-in-waiting confesses to the Merc:
Girl held in drug squad raid was me
VICKI IS
INNOCENT

Princess Victoria's romance was saved last night when her look-alike lady-in-waiting admitted: 'I was the girl in that drugs raid.'

Until Lady Islay Wight's confession to the _Mercury_, police believed the 19-year-old who gave that name was the princess.

The news was welcomed at Blumenkohl Castle, where her engagement to Prince Fritz, 39, had been put on hold by reports of her arrest...

Bish had biked a copy to the grace-and-favour apartment at St James's where the Palace press secretary was waiting with Lady Islay. The admiral phoned his saviour.

'Thanks, Bish. You deserve to be an archbish.'

If anyone deserved anything, it was not Bish. It was Martha, for the idea. It was the admiral, for selling it to Lady Islay. And it was the faithful lady-in-waiting. for agreeing that one itsy-bitsy fib wasn't much to ask to save Vicki and make the press look fools and liars.

Rollsing home after dinner, Lord Bull adjusted his reading light, the better to look at the first editions. His voice was brimming with port as he rang Jack Stack.

'Merc beat the pants off you, eh?'

'Load of bollocks.'

'That man Bish. Pretty good, isn't he?'

'Pretty good piss artist.'

'Your number two when you had that winning streak here, right? And when you had that winning streak there, right? Ha! Wonder if I picked the wrong man.'

'Listen, Johnnie – '

But Johnnie had hung up.

Heidi Hunt put her head round the door. She looked as depressed as her editor felt. He had flogged himself for nothing all day. Conference was so deadly, he had been glad when Lord Bull's summons arrived in the middle.

'Come in, kid. First friendly knees I've seen all day.'

'Know the feeling.'

'Trouble with coming back – it reminds you why you left.'

'Never mind, eh? Like my new micro?'

'Just perfect for our new chief royal correspondent. Congratulations – '

'Ooh-er.'

' – but I may have to fire you.' He passed her the Mercury. 'You've had the job ten seconds, and you've been scooped already.'

'It stinks.' Heidi held it at arm's length. 'She's put that Lady Islay up to it, hasn't she?'

'Prove it for the next edition – and we're in business.' He snapped fingers. 'OK, kid, your first assignment is to bring me those two big red books from the shelf.'

The new chief royal correspondent made two journeys, using both hands to transport Debrett's *Peerage* and then *Who's Who*. The editor turned to the pages recording seven centuries of Scottish Marquesses of Wight. Lady Islay was the youngest daughter of the current one. Now Jack Stack turned to *Who's Who* for his number, and dialled Wight Castle. He cleared his throat and summoned up the accents of a Highland Heidi Hunt.

'If it's not too late, I'd like a wee word with Islay.'

'It is too late – a day too late. Went back to London after nanny's funeral. Salt of the earth, that woman.'

'So Islay was in Scotland all Tuesday?'

'Who are you?'

'Heidi Hunt.'

'Journalist?'

'Couldn't write to save my life.'

The truth failed to move the Marquess. Down went the phone. Jack Stack immediately dialled the Admiral. On the tenth ring, a sleepy female voice answered.

'Yah?'

'Admiral, this is Jack Stack.'

'Does it sound like the fucking admiral?'

'Sorry to hear about nanny.' Jack Stack took a flier.

'Ah.'

'Listen, Islay.' He held his breath for three seconds; no denial. 'Spoken to Daddy. We know you weren't there.' Again three seconds; again no denial. 'The Merc has dropped you right in it.'

'Fuck the Merc.'

'The Globe wants to clarify the misunderstanding.'

'Fuck the Globe.' Down went the phone.

'Declined to comment,' noted Jack Stack.

He moved out of his chair, bowed Heidi into it and swivelled her to the keyboard. He dictated and she typed, fingers tilted up to keep long nails clear of the keys:

We uncover the great Vicki cover-up!!
HER ROYAL
LIE-NESS
by Heidi Hunt

The Globe today exposes Princess Victoria's plot to save her skin – by sacrificing her lady-in-waiting.

Vicki got look-alike Lady Islay Wight to pretend she was the one caught in a Scotland Yard drugs raid.

And the down-market Mercury fell for the big lie.

The truth? Loyal Lady Islay was 400 miles away at her nanny's funeral. It was fun-loving Vicki who was being strip-searched and held five hours in a cell.

Now all eyes are on Blumenkohl Castle, where Prince Fritz, 39...

'Ooh, you are clever,' said Heidi.

'Save it, kid. I want you to pop over to Blumenkohl and bring me the first interview with *The Postage-stamp Prince Who Broke Our Vicki's Heart.*'

'I can't speak German.'

'Learn it on the plane.'

23

An Excuse and Left

HM looked through the lower half of the royal bifocals at the tabloid splashes on Princess Victoria, then through the upper half at the Palace press secretary.

'Admiral, are you familiar with that saying of Voltaire?'

'The one that goes, *I disapprove of what you say but I will defend to the death your right to say it*?'

'No, the one that goes, *In England it is good to shoot an admiral from time to time – to encourage the others.*'

He nodded himself out. It wasn't press secretaries who needed to be encouraged. It was editors who needed to be discouraged. But nothing and nobody was going to get them to spare the royals. Parliament wouldn't. The proprietors didn't. The Press Complaints Commission couldn't.

As he got back to his desk, Blumenkohl Castle came on the line. Prince Fritz's grand chamberlain must speak with him urgently.

'Herr Admiral, this is Zweibel.'

'Good morning, Herr Zweibel.'

'Colonel-General Graf von Zweibel – '

'Even so.'

' – und Kaldaunen mit Essig.'

'Even more so. What can I do for you?'

'Herr Admiral, I speak to you from a mobile on the battlements. Your press wolves are at the gate. Your long Toms are zeroing in on our bathrooms. Your TV crews are rumbling across the cobbles. The Principality is under siege. What are you going to do?'

'What do you expect us to do – call a meeting of the UN Security Council?'

'Just put out an immediate statement that there is no truth whatsoever in this nonsense about a betrothal.'

'You don't understand how Buckingham Palace operates. If we start denying lies, we'll be up all night every night.'

'You mean, Herr Admiral, that only if it were true would Buckingham Palace be willing to deny it?'

'Ball's in your court, mein dear chap. You could rely on us not to deny your denial. We just hope you aren't proposing to tell the British people their Vicki isn't good enough for your Fritz.'

'His Serene Highness could not be so ungallant.'

'Good to hear it. So why not lower the drawbridge? Invite the wolves in for a schnapps. Tell them any prince would be honoured to make Vicki his bride but this speculation is embarrassing them both. Thank the press for the chance to make clear that a few funny fags could not diminish Fritz's admiration and respect. Dish out souvenir sets of Blumenkohl stamps and T-shirts – and watch the pack slink away to give some other royal a turn in the pillory.'

'And then what?'

'And then nothing, chum. We just sit on our hands. Give Vicki time to fall for an Argentine polo player.'

'Such charades are beneath our dignity.'

Colonel-General Graf von Zweibel und Kaldaunen pocketed his mobile and looked down from the battlements. Two photographers had broken away from the pack to race towards a young woman in a long leather coat approaching the postern gate. She masked her face with a Paddington Bear headscarf as flashes illuminated her.

'Give us a smile, Vicki,' said the first photographer.

'You can't fool us,' said the second.

She knocked three times, then three times more, then once for luck. A peephole opened, bolts were withdrawn and the liveried gatekeeper let her in. This was the entrance, and those were the knocks that seven centuries of young women had used to visit pleasure upon seven centuries of von Blumenkohls.

'*Morgen, gnädige Fräulein. Wie geht's?*'

'Ooh-er.' She referred to the pocket phrasebook she had bought at Heathrow. '*Sprechen Sie Englisch?*'

'Of course.' He looked her up and down, especially down as she loosened her coat and micro-skirted knees twinkled at him. 'Herr Professor will be so pleased to see you.'

'Herr Professor?'

'We say Herr Professor because His Serene Highness has many students. And all so beautiful. Please, your name?'

'Heidi.'

'Come with me, English Heidi.'

All epaulettes and aiguillettes, sashes and stars, spurs and sword, Prince Fritz had just completed this year's sitting for next year's Blumenkohl postage stamps. As Heidi was bowed in, he tightened monocle, clicked heels, kissed her hand and presented her with a bubbling glass of Blumenkohlschaumwein. Lifting his own, he silently toasted the madam who sent him such pretty students as faithfully as her mother had sent papa such pretty shopgirls and her grandmother had sent grandpapa such pretty seamstresses.

'*Prost!*'

She checked her phrasebook. 'And *prost* to you.' She clicked heels, emptied her glass at a swallow and held it out for a refill.

'So, English Heidi. What are you studying?'

'Royal marriages, would you believe?'

She let the long coat slip from her shoulders, and appreciated his appreciation.

'Excellent. I will be your professor.' He rubbed his hands. 'Sit.' She took a gilt chair and he began to pace. 'First lesson: arranging royal marriages is like breeding racehorses. You go to the stud book – and use the blood lines to select your stallion and your mare.'

'What about love, then?'

'Love? Does love come into it with racehorses?'

Heidi shut her eyes, the better to lock into her memory the exclusive interview Prince Fritz was giving the chief royal correspondent of the Globe.

'Note that von Blumenkohl princes don't believe in marrying before the age of 50. That way, we commit a lot less adultery than some royal families I could mention.'

'Never looked at it that way.'

'And it gives us half a lifetime to make love to pretty girls like you.'

'But the papers reckon you're going to wed our Vicki.'

'The papers? If they knew anything, they would know I have met her only twice. The Palace matchmakers sat me next to her at lunch and again at dinner. *Mein Gott*, such an ignorant creature. No knowledge of philately, the ancient world, early music or even colonic irrigation. No vocabulary – my running footmen speak far better English than she does. Everything was cool or yuck. All she could talk about was shopping. She should marry that Harvey Nichols.'

'Shame, innit?' Heidi looked at her reflection in Prince Fritz's monocle. 'You could teach her so much.'

'English Heidi, you are about to reap the benefit of my expertise. I shall treat you to the 77 most mind-blowing orgasms of your life. And, after a light lunch, 77 more. Lucky Heidi – how I envy you.'

His Serene Highness reached under his scarlet tunic. The royal breeches descended to the royal jackboots.

'Come.' Two hands and one shirt tail beckoned.

This was the moment Heidi had so often read about in the Sunday red-tops: when the undercover reporter made an excuse and left. But what excuse? The Sunday red-tops never said. She tried the first to come into her head.

'Oh, gawd. I think I'm going to throw up – '

As Heidi clasped her mouth with one hand and her stomach with the other, Prince Fritz shuffled to a bell-pull. Two flunkeys burst through the double doors, grabbed her coat and bundled her out.

Fritz tsk-tsked. Third one this month. The excitement is too much for them. He folded his arms and waited for the flunkeys to return and pull up the royal breeches.

'That it, then?' Jack Stack snorted at his afternoon conference executives as the news editor lowered his clipboard. 'What about Vicki?'

'Thought you were master-minding that one.'

'Wouldn't need to if my news editor's priority wasn't negotiating a move to the Merc.'

'Well, I'm redundant here, Jack. The chief royal correspondent won't tell me what she's up to. Know what she said?' He went into falsetto for his kamikaze punchline. 'I come under the editor.'

Eyes squeezed. Shoulders rose. The silence challenged that reserved by the Book of Revelation for the opening of the Seventh Seal.

'I do the gags, chum.' The lip curled. 'Just go and ring Bish. Say I can't afford to match his next offer. Ta-ta.'

As the news editor moved to go, his deputy snatched the clipboard of office and took over the chair by the editor's desk. The news editor turned at the door.

'Miserable buggers. You could have laughed.'

The editor's private line rang. He leaned back in his chair and swung his feet up on the desk.

'Guess where I've been,' said Heidi.

'I don't need to guess. You're the Evening News splash – **VICKI RIDDLE BLONDE AT FRITZ CASTLE**. Your face is hidden but the knees are a dead giveaway. So, tell me all . . . '

As he listened, he took his feet down and swivelled to turn his back on conference. They heard him say, 'Colonic irrigation? Nah, colonial immigration, stupid.' Then, 'Pity you made an excuse and left, kid. Have to leave the readers guessing what he'd have given you for lunch.'

Home after midnight, Jack Stack yet again looked at his front page and yet again marvelled.

He had imposed Fritz's postage-stamp head on a model in a costume last worn by the bus driver who played Colonel Popoff in the London Transport Amateur Operatic Society revival of *The Chocolate Soldier*. For this Globe production, the breeches drooped about the jackboots. Vicki was represented by a year-old shot at the moment they broke the news that her favourite pony had been put down.

Heidi Hunt exposes the prince
who broke our Vicki's heart
FILTHY FRITZ!!

After an exclusive ordeal in Blumenkohl Castle yesterday, I can reveal the shocking truth about the prince the matchmakers lined up for Princess Vicki.

My advice to HRH is to say *Auf Wiedersehen* – as quickly as Fritz said *Auf Wiedersehen* to his trousers five minutes after I met him . . .

Harry Chacewater had spent the day putting a potential *Miss Print V* through her paces. He had checked out the hi-fi stack, the fridge, the corkscrew, the shower and the master cabin mattress; all with the assistance of the remarkably long-legged lady lawyer from Richmond who had brought along the Mercury contract.

She had accepted Harry's invitation to take a trip down the James: they could run through the document as they rode at anchor. They rode but they didn't get to run. Harry said he always left the detail to the legendary Ed. Just show him where to put his John Hancock. She showed him.

24

A Fortunate Man

The solicitor who had arrived from London last night to get Toby's signature on the Mercury contract padded from the pool-house. His rainbow bermudas went oddly with the sun-starved skin that bagged his bones.

'Coming in, Toby?'

'Maybe later, Jonathan.'

Or maybe not. Toby was happy in his cane armchair, malt whisky in hand and Walkman loaded with Tauber. From under a broad panama, he watched Marina's limbs gleam as she turned, in emerald one-piece, for another back-stroke length. God, she was beautiful. God, he was a fortunate man. He caught the eyes that had been waiting for his as he woke this morning from the big sleep of a big man who had fought a big fish.

'You,' she had said, 'look very pleased with yourself.'

'I am. Very.'

'Dahlia say something to you?'

'About my fish?'

'Fuck your fish. Yesterday she patted my hand and said, Lady B, you're all melty. You're pregnant.'

'How could that happen?'

'That's what you said last time. I think she's wrong but let's not tell her. It's the only way she'll give us a break from conch.'

'But you do look all melty.'

'I am all melty. She says it's twins again. Girls.'

'We'll call them Polly and Molly.'

'*Whaaat*-ever...' said Marina.

Now Toby rubbed his shoulders where the harness had held him an hour in the fishing chair, feet braced against transom as he battled his biggest blue marlin. He could still feel the rod bending, still hear the line screaming, still see the reel smoking, still smell the scorch as Dahlia's son doused it.

He reached for his Walkman and fell asleep listening to Tauber. Marina's wet face sparkling in the sun as she waved from the pool was the final image on his retina.

Dahlia knew all was not well as she came out with the tea trolley. She abandoned it and hurried to Toby. The glass had dropped from his limp hand. The panama had fallen forward over his slumped head.

Marina ran dripping from the pool, with Jonathan a moment behind her.

'I'll call the doctor,' said Dahlia, already on her way.

Jonathan and Marina set Toby gently on the ground. She bent to try the kiss of life. Jonathan knew she would not accept it was useless until the sad shake of the doctor's head. He picked up the Walkman earphone. The cassette had reached a tinny Tauber duet with Evelyn Laye:

> *Nobody could love you more.*
> *Nobody loved*
> *So much before . . .*

Jonathan looked at Marina. His eyes filled.

Marina broke the silence as they stood around the drawing room, saucered tea cups in hand. She went to the grand piano and picked out the eight-note chorus of 'Colonel Bogey'.

'That's the march-out music he decreed for his memorial service. So everyone goes away with a smile.'

'Just the way he went,' said Dahlia.

'Thanks to Mac,' said Marina, 'he went out on a two-hundred pounder.'

'Glory be.' Sergeant Mac grinned. One-fifty perhaps.

'And thanks to Dahlia.' Marina took her hand and turned to Jonathan. 'She told him she reckoned I was pregnant.'

'Which,' said Jonathan, 'is the reason for the new instructions he taped for me this morning.'

He looked to Marina. She clasped her hands and nodded. He took a pocket recorder from his briefcase, set it on the piano lid and started the tape.

171

'...I was all set to sign the bloody Merc contract and send you home next plane. But you were looking for a nice long weekend in the sun, weren't you? So you insisted on hearing all about my two-hundred pounder...'

'I insisted like the fish insisted.' Jonathan went to fast forward for several seconds.

'...and by then, the contract had to wait till morning. Bit of luck, that. Because Dahlia has divined that we're pregnant. Which makes me ask myself: Is letting the Merc go playing fair by Olly and Nolly and Polly and Molly? So, no sale. I'm transferring my controlling interest to their mother. Let's see if she can make a go of it. If she can't, the proceeds can go in trust for the kids...'

Jonathan stopped the tape again.

'The next bit is a public statement Toby dictated about calling off the Chacewater deal. My firm will put it out later today when they've faxed Harry's lawyers in Richmond.'

'...say that the interest shown by Chacewater and others confirms our belief that the Merc has a great future, blah-blah. We're embarking on a substantial development programme, blah-blah. Marina becomes chairman as of now. That's chairman – not chairwoman, not chairperson, not chair...'

The phone at Marina's elbow rang, and she picked it up before Jonathan could field the call. She heard *Fingal's Cave* in the background.

'Yes, Harry.'

'Hi, milady. I need to talk to Toby.'

'Only wish you could. He died a few hours ago.'

'Jeez, Marina. I'm so sorry.'

'Fell asleep by the pool. Just didn't wake up.'

'Did that lawyer – Jonathan whoever – get there?'

'I'll put him on.'

Jonathan took the phone and let it hang in his hand for a moment while he cooled his anger.

'Yes, Mr Chacewater?'

'I guess you got that contract signed before he—'

'Matter of fact, no.'

'So can someone else sign it?'

'Matter of fact, no. The Merc's no longer on the market.'

'But, man, we had a deal.'

'I regret that Lord Baynard's death has inconvenienced you, sir. Right now, we're all just a little upset too. The next sound you hear will be me hanging up.'

This time it was Jonathan who went to the piano and played 'Colonel Bogey'.

Jack Stack could have done without being summoned aloft to submit proposals for covering Toby's death. The butler indicated a chair and advised that his lordship would be with him presently. The chair was declined, as though continuing to stand would hurry the proprietor along. Ten minutes, and it would be too late for the first edition.

That deadline had passed and Jack Stack was half into the offered chair when the doors opened. Out came Lord Bull. Out too came the braying of the black-tied donkeys and the laughter of the bejewelled hyenas he was entertaining after a first night up river at the Royal National.

'Don't bother to sit down, Jack.' Lord Bull sniffed. 'Shan't be keeping you long.'

His editor set a layout sheet on the table.

Press baron Toby dies
in arms of new bride
HONEYMOON
WIDOW GETS
A BILLION

'No.' Lord Bull wrinkled his nose.

'No?'

'General election on Thursday. That's what the Globe should be leading on.'

'Johnnie, are we out to sell papers or aren't we?'

'Globes, sure. But why arouse our readers' curiosity about the Merc. Not very clever, is it?'

'We'd be showing the Merc up. All they'll run is some sanitised bollocks. The story the readers want is Toby getting shagged to death on honeymoon.'

'Just carry a nice obit on a left-hand page, OK? And forget that crap about leaving a billion. Toby's been draining his fortune for years to keep the Merc going.'

'Don't know why you brought me back if you're going to edit the Globe yourself.'

'Told you, Jack – I want you where I can see you.'

Lord Bull turned on his heel and opened the doors to return to the donkeys and the hyenas. Jack Stack slunk from the presence. He had never felt so short.

'Ed, look me in the eye,' said Mrs Ed.

'I'm looking.'

'Promise me you had nothing to do with this.'

'Promise.'

'I don't believe you.'

'If I don't promise – then you'll believe me?'

25

Bastards Everywhere

Joy lit Humpty's face when he reached The Times obituaries page. The new viscount had waited so long for this. He went to coach the new bloody parrot.

'G'day, your lordship.' He tapped the cage. 'G'day, your lordship.'

'Idle sod.' The bloody parrot tapped back. 'Get yourself a job.'

Humpty shook his head and tried again, as did the bloody parrot. Then he bounded upstairs and into the bathroom where Dumpty lay soaking after her dawn gallop. He held out the folded page for her to read that, because Toby's marriage to Marina was subsequent to the birth of Olly and Nolly, the title went to half-brother Humphrey. And Marina became the Dowager Viscountess to distinguish her from Viscountess Dumpty.

'G'day, your ladyship.'

'Big deal. We won't get a penny in his will. Marina and her bastards will cop the lot.'

'More to life than money.' He reached at a soapy nipple.

She flicked him off like cigarette ash. 'Told you, Humpty – not till you get a job, you idle sod.'

'Did you have to tell the bloody parrot?'

Jack Stack was on the rack again this morning. He had been kept waiting twenty minutes before Lord Bull, having stayed the night, wandered through in dressing gown and cravat. He looked his editor up and down, then thumped Marina's piece in the Mercury open on his desk.

'Brought tears to my eyes. *Last of the Cavaliers – all the finer an epitaph for the fact that it came from his lifelong rival.* How do you think I feel, reading my words in the damn Merc?'

'Could have read them in the damn Globe if you hadn't been too busy partying to write me a piece.'

Lord Bull went to the window to swing his brass telescope on its tripod and check on Tower Bridge.

'Ha! Tower flag's at half mast. They must be reading my mind.' He turned to level the telescope at his editor. 'God knows where you'd go this time.'

'How about the BBC lunchtime news? I'd tell the nation I quit because you killed the Princess Xenia diaries.'

Round the door appeared a languid blonde, still in her first-night finery. A Cartier watch glittered as she drew hair clear of her high-boned cheek.

'Bye, Johnnie.'

'Bye, Clarissa.'

'Vanessa. Bye.'

She was waiting for the lift when Jack Stack joined her.

'Hi, Vanessa. What do you do?'

'Let rich bastards spank me.'

'Snap.'

With three days to go, Beth Macbeth's fate was in the hands of the Don't-knows. The Opposition leader's husband was already looking at wallpaper catalogues. Beth was desperate for some inspired insight into what might yet move the electorate her way.

Jack Stack took her call while watching a TV news clip of the morning press conference. She wasn't doing herself any favours. While being charmed by the Beth at his ear, he found himself wincing at the Beth on the screen:

'Am I at all rattled by the polls, Andy? Do I look at all rattled, Andy? Do I sound at all rattled, Andy?'

'Jack, dear. You mustn't think I'm off you over that Save the Merc thing. Silly boy. It's all in the game.'

'Am I ashamed there are only two women in my Cabinet, Kirsty? Is your editor ashamed there's only one in hers?'

'Do pop round, Jack. Please. I desperately need to consult my favourite editor...'

On the way to Number 10, he stopped off at his flat to lift the Wren tricorn, ease the elastic band holding the three Xenia diaries, and put one in his inside pocket along with Gloria's typed transcripts.

The Prime Minister's heels clacked across the chequered hall floor. Disraeli looked down his marble nose as she took Jack Stack's elbow to steer him past the Chippendale hooded chair and the pot plants into the Cabinet room. She took her seat, the only one with arms, at the centre of the long oval table and motioned him to sit the other side of the brown baize.

'That's where I put the Foreign Secretary. Got to keep both eyes on that bastard.'

'World's full of 'em, Beth. Bastards everywhere.'

She went to the galleried tray at her elbow and lifted the decanter with the worn silver collar that said Sherry.

'Not too early for you, is it?' She filled two glasses. 'I fear it's too late for me. You've seen the polls.'

'You're looking at the wrong ones.'

'I wish.'

'Beth, the polls that matter are those that tell you what the people want. They want murderers to hang, OK? Promise an immediate referendum on bringing back the rope – and you're home.'

'I'd never convince the colleagues.'

'Bollocks to the colleagues. They won't dare disown you on the eve of the election.'

'Or 24 hours later if I win.' She looked at her man-size Rolex. 'It's my big ITN interview at 6.30. Why don't I take a chance and spring it there?' She allowed herself her first chortle for three weeks.

'Beth, it'll make the lead on every TV and radio news bulletin all night. And the splash tomorrow in every paper in the land. You'll absolutely walk it on Thursday.'

Twenty tumblers and ten water carafes rattled as the Prime Minister slapped the baize and embarked on a jig half-way round the Cabinet table to embrace her saviour.

'Unless – ' said Jack Stack.

'Unless?'

'Unless Princess Xenia's diaries get into orbit.' He fished from his pocket the sample volume and the transcripts, and held them out to her.

'My God,' she said several times in the next few minutes. From the walls, Churchill, Pitt and Walpole looked on as their successor slumped bonelessly into a chair and threw down the diary. 'My God, what a meal the gutter press will make of this.'

'Yeah, so will the tabloids.'

'Can you imagine the headlines, Jack?'

'Just about.'

'They'll shatter HM. Could be the last straw.' Her speech began to move up through the gears. 'Jack, the voters know Xenia was my idea. So they'll take it out on me. Fair enough – that's showbiz. But our monarchy is the enduring symbol of our nation. My duty is to preserve it – at all costs. Not thinking of myself, you understand.'

'I do. I do.'

'Thinking of you, Jack. Say the royals decide enough is enough – we're outa here. You'd be left with a republic. Not much fun being a tabloid editor then, eh?'

'It's the nightmare scenario.' Would life be worth living without the royals to scourge? Compared with them, the privacy of your average gone-tomorrow politician was hardly worth invading. 'But do I look the sort of editor who'd suppress a story with such overwhelming public interest?'

She stroked her chin thoughtfully at him. 'I'd be grateful. Very.'

'Y'know, Beth' – the baize muffled his drumming fingers – 'I've always fancied being a press baron.'

'Course you have, dear.' She put a hand to his cheek. 'But we couldn't do it in one jump. First, a knighthood, yes?'

'Sir Jack Stack?'

'Sir Jack Stack. Trips off the tongue, doesn't it? Then, keep playing your cards right – and who knows?'

He pondered for six seconds. 'You've talked me into it.'

'That's it, then – as soon as you deliver the diaries.'

'One now.' He set it back in her hand. 'One the day the honours list is published. And one on my way back from the Palace with the ribbon round my neck.'

They shook on it. When the reinforced front door closed him out, Beth leaned back on her side of it and mouthed Jack Stack's maxim. Bastards everywhere.

He emerged, fixing cigar between teeth like Winston on this very doorstep before him, and offering a V sign to the waiting cameramen.

'It's only Jack effin Stack,' said one.

As the pack lowered lenses and turned away, he reversed his fingers at them. Only Jack effin Stack? Who else had single-handedly ensured the return of the effin government and the effin gallows? Who else had just saved the effin throne?

At the Palace, half an hour later, the PM was advising HM that the rhyming ingredients were about to hit the fan. HM was listening as in a dentist's chair; eyes shut, mouth issuing only dry gurgles.

'How,' asked HM eventually, 'can we stop the bastard? Do you suppose Xenia could deny the diaries are hers?'

'You mean lie to the public?'

'Something like that.'

'Wouldn't stop them being denounced in full.'

'Beth, could she go for a copyright injunction?'

'And announce the diaries are genuine? Bigger headlines still. Easier to buy the reptile off with a K.'

'A knighthood?'

Not since Lady Bracknell uttered the word 'handbag', had two syllables been invested with such lofty incredulity.

'An ordinary knighthood.'

'Plain Sir Jack Sewage?'

'Buys us time till after the election. Then I'll rush through a privacy law. Ban hunting with newshounds.'

'That won't bother the editors, my dear. They'll stampede to be the first Fleet Street martyr. Never mind Sir Jack – he'll be Saint Jack.'

'Ah, but I'll have criminal sanctions against the press barons. They won't risk being banged up without a butler for five years.'

'What about hanging?'

'Funny you should mention that. It's on my list.'

Once the PM had gone, HM had a quick word with the Almighty before summoning the Private Secretary.

'She'll have to go.'

'The opinion polls do rather seem to agree with Your Majesty.'

'Bugger the opinion polls. I mean bloody Xenia.'

26

Coronet of Weeds

Lady Islay Wight sat under a willow on the river bank below Windsor Castle, plaiting buttercups and daisies into her hair. She looked a vision of Pre-Raphaelite innocence in white muslin, though her head was seething with a plot to destroy Jack Stack. Thanks to him, Vicki had been ordered to ditch her for a lady-in-waiting with no sense of humour.

A hundred yards up the Thames, three Eton College boys looking more like two and a half Eton College boys lolloped down the meadow to the boat-house. Between the giant oarsmen nicknamed Gog and Magog bobbed the cox nicknamed Tab, short for tabloid, on account of his ambition to follow in the family footsteps.

To this end, Tab Baynard had written Dearest Aunt Marina a letter of condolence, with a PS asking if the Merc might have a vacation job for him. Dearest Aunt Marina had been touched; promising a word with Bish and inviting Tab to recite a little Kipling at the forthcoming St Bride's memorial service for Dearest Uncle Toby.

As picture editor of the College Chronicle, Tab had permanently at his neck the Pentax with which his father had done so much damage around Harry Chacewater's pool. At an institution for boys bred to be the other side of the lens, Tab's wish to become a Fleet Street snapper was regarded as pretty disgusting. Gog certainly thought so, and was delighted to have been roped in for the plot by cousin Islay.

Tab coxed his pair into the stream and let go his rudder lines for a moment to level his Pentax at the vision in white muslin. As he framed her against the Round Tower, his memory clicked along with the shutter. Of course. It was Vicki. He had snapped her at the Eton–Harrow match.

This was the moment Islay was waiting for. She gave Tab a royal carriage wave as though to confirm his assumption. Then she walked down from the willow, stepped out of her shoes and into the river. He lost her as she went under.

'Brakes!' he shrilled. 'Body in the water!'

Swans paddled clear as Gog and Magog dug their blades in. Tab drifted the boat towards the spot where the vision had disappeared. It was half a minute before he sighted her again. She was floating on her back with her dress fanned out. Eyes closed, limbs limp and in her coronet of weeds, she could have been modelling drown'd Ophelia for the Millais masterpiece. Gog and Magog were agog at the transparency of the soaked muslin that was all she wore. Tab raised his camera.

'Paparazzo!' sneered Magog. 'How much do they pay for wet tits on Page Three?'

'Enough for wild duck at Monty's,' said Gog.

'Avec Château Lafitte '65,' said Tab. 'They're not just any old tits, you know. They're Princess Vicki's.'

'Vicki's!' chorused Gog and Magog, a semitone apart.

'Glug-glug,' said the vision, opening one sly eye long enough to cue the rescue sequence, and the other sly eye long enough to wink at cousin Gog.

'Hold on, Princess,' said Magog and went over the side. What was his Royal Life Saving Society certificate for, if not the saving of royal life?

Supporting her under the armpits, he back-stroked to the bank. Tab rode the boat up the reeds and leaped out for more shots. He snapped Magog administering the British kiss of life, and being rewarded with the French kiss of life.

'My heroes.' The revived vision got to her feet, spraying them as she swung her hair. Two butterflies and a moth fluttered beneath the muslin.

Tab captured the gallant Gog pulling off his T-shirt to drop over her head. The logo on the front read, Coxed Pairs Do It; the one on the back, Coxless Pairs Don't. She wriggled under it until the wet dress fell about her ankles for her to step clear.

'Now that you've saved one's life' – the T-shirt hem rose astonishingly as she pushed her arms into the sleeves – 'one can hardly ask you not to sell the pictures to Jack Stack for an absolutely fabulous sum.'

'Oh, but I'm a Baynard,' said Tab. 'Got to give it to the Mercury. Mr Stack's now at the Globe, you know.'

'I know, darling. But he'll pay you the most. Especially with some juicy quotes.'

'You're too kind, Princess.' Tab fished out pocket notepad and pencil. 'Dad says if you don't give the scum a quote, they interview your bloody parrot.'

'Actually, one's forbidden to talk to the press.' She put a knuckle under each eye, then laughed. 'So attribute it to that Palace Insider one's always reading about. Quote: Vicki's in despair. Can't go on living like a bird in a cage. Just wants to end it all. They're out to marry her off to some pervy old stamp collector who lives in a place with no Marks and Sparks. And they won't let her choose her own ladies-in-waiting. OK, boys – get going or you'll miss the first edition.'

'We'll see you home,' said Magog.

'I am home.' She indicated the Round Tower.

Tab's Pentax followed her as she danced up the slope. At the top, she flipped the tail of the T-shirt at her saviours and disappeared into the Castle.

Forty brace of grouse hung upside down in the cellars of Lord Bull's Scottish hunting lodge. They testified to a good day on the moors. Seven brace of reds still on the snooker table after he and his chums had been playing an hour testified to a good night on the port.

Lord Bull eyed the exit-poll election forecast on the wall-mounted TV. Beth Macbeth's promise to let the people decide on hanging had done the trick. She had her return ticket to Number 10. He picked up his mobile, motioning the chums to gather round while he had some sport with his editor.

'Here's your headline, Jack – **THE ROPE BRINGS BACK BETH**.'

Jack Stack could hear the port slurping as the chums creased themselves.

'It won't sell as many as my headline.'

'I don't agree.'

'Wait till you've heard it – **JILTED VICKI SUICIDE BID**. And I've got ten pages of exclusive pix of her being saved from drowning in the Thames.'

'Kill it, Jack. I'm not publishing paparazzi pix of the royals. Against the Press Complaints Commission code.'

'Bollocks to that. These aren't pap pix. They're taken by an Eton boy who happened to be rowing past.'

'Let's put it to the Press Complaints Commission. I'll ask the chairman as soon as he's potted the pink. Hang on... Well, it looked like the pink to him... Right then, I've asked him. He agrees with me. So lead on the election, OK?'

'If you insist on that, Johnnie, I shall have no alternative but to tender my resignation.'

'I do insist.'

'In that case, I shall have no alternative but to withdraw my resignation.'

The call ended against a background like sitcom laughter running fast forward.

Heidi Hunt's head came round Jack Stack's door, followed by the rest as he beckoned her in.

'Lord Bully been getting at you again?'

'Thinks he can edit the paper from the bottom of a decanter in the middle of a grouse moor. He reckons he'll fire me if I run these pix.' He slid them across the desk to her. 'But, you watch, he'll forgive me when we sell an extra quarter-million.'

'Would you believe it?' Heidi looked up from the pictures. 'That silly cow again.'

'Yeah, can't keep silly Vicki off the front page.'

'It's not silly Vicki. It's silly Islay.'

'Told you – don't say Is-lay. It's Eye-lay.'

'That's what I'm telling you, innit? It's Eye-lay. You can't see further than the boobs and pubes. She's more like Vicki than Vicki – till you look at those sly eyes.'

Jack Stack looked at those sly eyes, and those sly eyes looked back at him as he rang the Palace press secretary.

'Admiral, sorry to disturb you.'

'No problem. Phone was ringing anyway.'

'Just thought you ought to know. Some schoolboy is here with a set of pictures showing Vicki being rescued from the Thames this morning.'

'Impossible. She's in Wales. Nanny's funeral.'

'God, they're dying like flies.'

'HM's decided. Period of invisibility required. Strictly between you and me, the princess has been aboard a warship all week. Good enough for you?'

'Aye-aye, Admiral. I wouldn't touch this one with yours.'

'Much relieved, Jack. But hadn't I better ring round? Little creep might try to sell his snaps elsewhere.'

'Leave it to me. I'll fix him.'

Jack Stack grinned at Heidi as he went to the door and curled both index fingers to invite Tab into his parlour.

'Come and meet our chief royal correspondent, Heidi Hunt.'

'How d'you do, Miss Hunt.'

'Ah.' Miss Hunt looked into the choirboy face and was touched. She had never before been addressed as Miss Hunt. 'Seen a lot of Vicki, have you, dear?'

'Ra-ther.'

'Ooh, look,' said Heidi. 'He's blushing.'

'Miss Hunt,' said Jack Stack. 'These pix will make Tab Baynard famous. But I'm going to do him a big favour. I'm not running them in the Globe.'

'Sir?' Tab's jaw dropped.

'Have a cigar.' Jack Stack offered the humidor.

'I don't smoke.'

'Yes you do.' He cut a Corona, stuck it between Tab's teeth and lit a match for him. 'Son, never forget you're a Baynard. The new generation of the greatest family in Fleet Street. Uncle Toby will turn in his grave if your scoop appears anywhere but the Merc. And Auntie Marina will never give you that vacation job.'

'But the Princess particularly wanted you to have it.'

'Even so, Tab. Even so. I just can't let you do it. Your dad was good to me. I owe him. So off you go to the Merc. And God bless you.'

'And God bless you, sir. And you, Miss Hunt.'

'And you, dear.' Miss Hunt set the choirboy face between gold fingernails and kissed its forehead.

'Tab,' said Jack Stack, 'a friendly tip. Keep that cigar in your hand when you see the editor. Mr Bish will realise we've not been talking peanuts. Tell him what I offered you – and say Auntie Marina told you the Merc always pays best.'

'What did you offer me?'

'A hundred grand. Plus half net syndication.'

Jack Stack buzzed the night editor.

'Splash head coming up. **THE ROPE BRINGS BACK BETH!** Just the one ejaculation mark...What d'you mean, Lord Bull won't like it? I don't give a shit whether he likes it or not. I'm the bleeding editor.'

Bish could hear himself breathing. These pictures were a godsend. He imagined chairman Marina's face tomorrow when he met her off the plane with the news that the Merc was out-selling the Globe for the first time in history.

He called Martha in to tell him how brilliant his ten-page layout was and how bold of him to reduce Page One election coverage to a cross-ref. Instead, she went all quiet.

'Bish, it's not like flamin' Jack Stack to let Tab leave the building with the scoop of the flamin' century.'

'Cobblers. Tab walked out because Jack tried to rip him off. A hundred grand plus half the net. I'm giving him two hundred plus sixty per cent – and we'll still make a million world-wide.' Clop.

'Boss, let me do a quick check with the Admiral. That Lady Islay could be playing look-alike games again.'

'Can't trust the Admiral.' Clop. 'He'll put out a statement all round saying it was only an accident...HRH simply tripped over a twig...never in danger...swims the Matterhorn twice a week. It'll torpedo my scoop. To hell with that.' Clop.

'Please, boss. Look at those sly eyes.'

'Sly eyes, bollocks. Marina's nephew was there – with two Etonian witnesses. Vicki herself gave him the quotes.'

'Please. We looked a right flamin' twit last time.'

'Surprised at you, Martha. Ask yourself – would Jack want to rip Tab off if the stuff wasn't kosher?'

Clop.

27

The Going Rate

Eyes swung to Marina as she swanned through the exit barrier at Heathrow. In autumn-leaf shades, from one-off headscarf to millionairess shoes, she might have been leaving the Ritz rather than an overnight Jumbo.

'Morning, milady.' Her chauffeur touched his peak.

'Morning, Joey.' She almost said they had been on first-name terms too long to switch. But chauffeurs knew best about such things: deny your enhanced status and you deny theirs.

Clop, went the man at Joey's side.

'Hello . . . Bish?'

He was much changed since she last saw him, before his elevation to the editocracy half a dozen chapters ago. The fat glasses had been replaced by contacts. Savile Row had horizontalised his sloping shoulders. Jermyn Street had added devilment to his neck; Wimpole Street, caps to his teeth; Curzon Street, a hairy halo to his head.

'Oh, what a beautiful morning, Marina.' The Yorkshire vowels were cooler too.

He took her elbow, clocking lucky-devil glances as he steered her to the nearest news-stand. Extra supplies of the Mercury were arriving while the heaps of rival tabloids stayed high, their election headlines uniformly screaming, **THE ROPE BRINGS BACK BETH**.

'Bish, are you going to tell me – or do I have to buy a Merc to find out?'

'You have to buy a Merc to find out.' Clop. 'Could be the one that takes us ahead of the Globe.'

She joined the queue, dipping a gloved hand into the thresh reaching for a Mercury. As she lifted one, Bish plonked down the required coins and smirked.

The see-through drown'd Ophelia picture filled his front page under the headlines:

Jilted princess sensation:
10 pages of exclusive pix
VICKI SUICIDE BID

'All this' – Bish aligned his cheek for a kiss – 'and a Baynard byline too. Promising lad, our Tab.'

'Jesus.' The paper froze in Marina's hand. 'Those sly eyes.' She drew Bish clear. 'Sure it's Vicki, not Islay?'

'Absolutely.'

'Sure as you were last time it was Islay, not Vicki?'

Clop.

As the Bentley she had taken over from Humpty headed for town, Marina told Joey to tune in to the radio news channel

'...Palace statement...no truth whatsoever in the Mercury story...girl in the pictures is Lady Islay Wight...simply tripped on the river bank...Olympic class swimmer...never in the slightest danger...quotes pure invention...'

'Your bloody nephew,' said Bish. 'He can forget the vacation job. And that bloody Martha. She's for the high jump.'

The phone trilled. Cockney foghorn tones filled the car.

'Let me talk to your beloved chairman.' Jack Stack waited for Joey to pass the phone. 'Hi, Marina.'

'Hi, asshole.'

'Guess what I'm leading the Globe with tomorrow.'

'**MERC EDITOR CASTRATED**.'

'Close enough. I'm printing a claim form for your readers to demand their money back – '

'How thoughtful.'

'And I'm providing your Freepost address.'

Marina gave Bish a look and elbowed him off the shared armrest as she put the phone down. It rang again. This time it was his secretary.

'Bish. End of the world situation. BBC and ITN here. Sky coming at 1. *Desert Island Discs* at 2. Palace demanding a Page One apology plus a donation to Battersea Dogs' Home. Seven hundred and two readers want you to ring back. I've phoned your tailor not to come in, right? Eight hundred and eight. Your astrologer's cancelled lunch – I'll tell the Groucho you won't need your table. Oh, and Tab's outside with two huge Etonians, saying they won't budge until they get their two hundred grand. And please ring Mrs Bish. Microwave's gone dead. One thousand and one—'

'Tell flamin' Martha to sort it out. It's all her fault. And don't let my Groucho table go. I still have to eat.'

'And the Evening News is just in. Nice picture of you. That Snowman one you had done. I'll read the story—'

'Don't bother.' He looked at Marina. 'It's all lies.'

'One thousand two hundred. And Martha's here now. Says she's got to talk to you.'

'Tell her to save her breath. I want her resignation on my desk by the time I get back.' Clop.

'I flamin' heard that.' Martha was on the line. 'You're not dumping on me, you turd. You ordered me not to check with the Admiral. If the boss doesn't flamin' fire you, mate, I'm off to the Globe.'

'The boss just flamin' fired him.' Marina seized the phone from Bish, who slumped into his corner and closed his eyes. 'Darling, you're not going to the Globe. You're taking over the Merc.'

'Strewth.'

'Print the damned apology – with a blob par on the end saying I've accepted Bish's resignation and you're the new editor. Send a cheque for ten grand to the fucking dogs' home.'

'Hell, Marina, I'm not printing a flamin' apology. If the Merc's going to turn dingo, you might as well keep Bish.'

'Hear-hear.' Bish was still alive.

'Hold on, Martha. Hey, Joey – pull in at Ken High Street Tube. Mr Bishop is leaving us.'

'Please, chairman.' Bish spoke into her hair as she leaned across to open the door. 'Please.' He turned his head as his first foot touched the ground. 'Try to see it from my point of view – '

Marina pulled the door to and returned to the phone. 'Martha, you were saying?'

'Tough it out, boss. Let's have a go at Vicki and Islay for playing silly buggers with the great British public. Get the readers to suggest a suitable punishment. First prize: Live like a spoiled princess for a week – with a lady-in-waiting to squeeze your flamin' toothpaste.'

'Pity the Battersea Dogs' Home has to miss out.'

'Too right. Let's endow kennels in the names of Vicki and Islay – and keep the bitches in Winalot for a year.'

'You're sounding like Jack Stack.'

'Gee, thanks.'

Marina lifted the armrest and put her feet up across the back seat. She was enjoying this. Now she had dispatched her first editor, she knew why so few escaped the chop. Chairmen got off on it. Theirs was a power denied Crown, Parliament, High Court and Press Complaints Commission. Only a chairman could pull down an editor grown so almighty that the merely mighty despaired.

Bish wished he had bought an evening paper, if only to hide behind. Every other passenger on the Tube seemed to be looking at that Snowman picture of him between the mocking faces of his executioners and below the headline, **VICKI'S LADY SLY-EYES FOOLS MERC AGAIN**. From time to time, people would look up, and Bish would turn away to be confronted by his reproachful reflection in the window.

He did not get out at Blackfriars. Not wise to go back to the office in such a rage. Flamin' Martha had deliberately obeyed his orders: how like a woman. Her triumph would be complete if he went in and throttled her. She was a big lass though; she might throttle him. Either way, it wouldn't do much for his prospects. Or would it? No call for nice-guy editors these days.

Bish picked up a discarded paper from the next seat, covered his head with it and let the train take him round the Circle Line again.

Maxine had had to go: too creepy for Marina. So Claudia, now the chairman's personal-assistant-actually, was at the boardroom lift doors to greet Arnold, Marina's overweight solicitor, and Jonathan, Toby's underweight one. They were here to bring her down to earth about the arithmetic of her inheritance.

Arnold presented his inevitable gladioli. Marina opened her inevitable champagne. She filled three flutes, offered two – then set them down again. The body language was all wrong.

'Do I pour it back?'

'We're not quite at that stage.' Arnold smiled weakly. 'But just as well you've been in the game too long to believe those billionaire headlines.'

'Oh, but I did.'

Marina sniffed. Journalists were the original suckers for stories too good to be untrue. Bish was not the first to hazard his career rather than entertain doubt.

'Toby will leave around a hundred million,' said Jonathan. 'Before tax.'

'Hardly enough for me to play at press barons.'

'He drained his fortune to keep the Merc going. Even on that last tape, he's about to commit a chunk of your hundred million. He'd never go to the City for funds – the City would want its own man in the driving seat.'

Marina walked out into the roof garden and twice round the farting fountain. She needed a solitary moment to rearrange her life from filthy rich widow to merely rich widow.

'Jonathan,' she said at the french window on her way back in, 'I could sell and pocket the lot – yes?'

'Yes. Though not exactly what Toby had in mind.'

'What would it fetch?'

'We'd already got Chacewater up to four hundred million. Magnus might top that.'

'Toby wouldn't let Magnus into Fleet Street. Neither will I. Let's do what Toby wanted. Let's give it a go.'

'For how long?' Arnold was concerned enough to suspend a handful of nuts halfway to his mouth.

'For as long as it's fun.' She laughed. 'It's fun so far. Fired my first editor. The fool who wouldn't check that phoney Vicki stuff.'

'Phoney or not.' Jonathan worked his eyebrows.' It had the 7.26 from Brockenhurst rocking all the way in.'

'But you've seen the evening paper. We were conned rotten. Wouldn't that make you drop the Merc?'

'What for? I buy my tabloid for a giggle. Fortifies me for the broadsheets. One look at the wrong girl in wet muslin, and I'm ready for a page of law reports. What are you giving the 7.26 for an encore?'

'Another giggle. I'm putting the flamin' boot in to Vicki and Islay for playing silly buggers with the great British public.'

'Love it,' said Jonathan.

After two trips round the Circle Line, Bish emerged from Blackfriars, blinking at the daylight. The evening paper story had moved on and the news-stand poster now said **EDITOR AND ROYAL LADY SACKED**. The pro in him appreciated the penny-catching quality as he waited his turn to have his pennies caught. And, unfolding the paper and following the story to Page 2, the victim in him drew solace from the box headlined *The hot seat*.

It recorded that over three decades the going rate for Fleet Street editors averaged one every nine weeks from one newspaper or another. Among the 176 changes listed, 26 names (five of them women) appeared twice, four were in three times, one four times and one five times. He had edited three papers, on two of which he replaced his replacement before being replaced a second time.

Bish braced himself to go back to the office to say goodbye to his old colleagues and his new Jag, empty his desk and secure his pay-off. He came through the revolving door to find his way barred by a security man.

'Now we don't want any fuss, do we, Mr Bishop?'

'I only came to say goodbye.'

'That's what they all say, guv. The last but one wanted to say it with a Kalashnikov.'

'But I've got to collect my things.'

'Course you have, guv. Martha's had them all nicely packed and ready for you.' He lifted two black binbags out from behind the desk.

'Well, could I use your phone to call a taxi?'

'My pleasure, Mr Bishop.' The security man looked round him and saluted. 'Afternoon, milady.'

Bish turned to see the doors revolving behind Marina as she swept in to come upon this tragic cameo of her ex-editor between the binbags that contained all that was left of his career.

Dear God, she thought, I might as well have put the poor creature in a third binbag. How little I know about this forlorn figure whose fate I have decided. I see the poor wife weeping by that dead microwave. Unable to break it to the poor granny that she cannot now end her days in that five-star seaside retirement complex. Unwilling to tell the poor kids they must be withdrawn from St Hilda's. All their little friends are going to be ballet dancers and dentists. Have I doomed them to follow their father into the Street of Shame?

'Marina, they won't let me in to say goodbye.' Clop.

'Nonsense. Come on up with me.'

'You're all heart.' He picked up the binbags.

'I should leave them here.'

In the lift, she said, 'Don't worry. I'll see you get your contract paid up. A year, is it?'

'Three.'

Martha looked up from the editor's chair to see the pair of them in her doorway.

'Just popped in to say good luck,' said Bish.

'Good on yer, mate.' Martha came round to shake hands. Her Aussie rugger shirt now had a big 1 on the back.

'When I fire you, Martha' – Marina sounded less jocular than jugular – 'you'll expect a farewell drink.'

Martha broke out the champagne.

'This'll kill you,' she said. 'Just heard Jack Stack's getting a flamin' knighthood.'

'Don't make me laugh.' Marina laughed.

'My oath. Got it from a cobber who's shagging a Downing Street secretary. I nearly threw a seven.' Martha crashed fist into palm. '*Sir* Jack? The scumbag who set Bish up with the Lady Islay pix? It's wicked.'

'*Sir* Jack?' Marina shook her head. 'The creature who tried to destroy me? It's disgraceful.'

'*Sir* Jack?' Bish went clop. 'The creep who pimped to cure Harry Chacewater's backache? It's obscene.'

'Really?' said Marina.

'I was there. He went to his little black book and ordered a double Coppergram from an escort agency. That's his thing, girls in uniform. Keeps the hats as souvenirs.'

'A lot of it about.' Marina could see those pool snaps.

'If I could get hold of that little black book' – Martha rubbed her hands – 'I'd fix him good and proper: **WHAT A DIRTY KNIGHT!** With a nice big second deck, *Why they mustn't make this saddo a Sir*. And on the spread, *Ladies of the Knight*. Just imagine.'

'I'm just imagining,' said Marina.

She made a mental note to add the Coppergrams to her Harry chapter. She had been burnishing the book as she lazed by the Baynard Cay pool in black one-pieces befitting a widow. It was ready but for two more of those merciless profile interviews with press barons. One with Magnus. The other with herself.

'Bish,' said Martha, 'You must have had a note of Jack's escort agency numbers in your desk somewhere. Let's get those binbags up and flamin' dig them out.'

'Er – ' He looked at Marina.

'Like to keep the Jag?' she said.

Clop.

'Don't answer it,' yawned Mrs Bish. 'You said at least we wouldn't get calls at three in the morning any more.'

'Hello.'

'Keeping busy, Bish?'

'Yeah, Jack. Ceramic hob last night. Mower tomorrow. Guttering Thursday. Dishwasher Fri—'

'Got a better idea. Come and be my executive editor.'

'Do I get a parking space under cover this time? Don't want to ruin the Jag.'

'Let you keep it, did she? In appreciation of what?'

'Loyalty.'

28

Eee-aaaouw!

'First indication?' Marina's Harley Street gynaecologist poised his broad nib. 'Pregnancy kit?'

'Sort of. A Bahamian lady with the gift. You look all melty, she said. It's twins again. Girls.'

'Didn't happen to give you the Derby winner?'

'No. Dahlia disapproves of gambling.'

'Well, let's see, shall we?'

'Let's ... '

He was completing his notes as Marina came back from the dressing room.

'We'll get ultrasound to tell us if Dahlia's right about quantity and gender. But – two months on – even a gynae man might just have guessed you were pregnant.'

'Two months?'

'Getting on for three now.'

'Eee-aaaouw!'

'Bit of a surprise?'

'You might say that.'

Eee-aaaouw, indeed. It wasn't Toby. It was Harry. That night at the Savoy? She somehow didn't think so. She just knew it was that after-lunch quickie at her flat, when they sealed his appointment as her white knight. At that time, intoxicated by their conspiracy, she might even have married the man, kidding herself she could domesticate his libido. But those pool babes, those Coppergrams, and what Dahlia told her about Tulip and about that wedding guest in the orange pillbox, proved what Marina surely knew all along.

She was glad she had been fated to see Toby out with a smile on his face. And it had put a smile on hers to find herself bequeathed the independence of a multi-millionairess, the status of a viscountess, the power of a newspaper proprietor. Playing such a widow beat playing Mrs Harry Chacewater in buckskin and jeans at the Shenandoah Apple Blossom Festival, wheeling Polly and Molly in a twin buggy and wondering what Harry was up to in his bandstand.

As Marina came from the consulting rooms, Joey nipped round to open the car door.

'Where to, milady?'

'Good question.'

Meanwhile, back at the Mercury...

Maria-Teresa was setting a gift-boxed orchid on Martha's blotter and saying how wonderful, this crest-of-the-wave feeling all over the office, and thank heaven for some inspirational leadership, and how about me as your deputy? Martha was promising Maria-Teresa the flamin' job the moment she came up with the flamin' words and music for the Dirty Knight exposé.

Meanwhile, back at the Globe...

Bish was tipping off Jack Stack about Martha's intended hatchet job, and saying how about setting the bloodhounds on her first? Jack Stack was reckoning there had to be something phoney about that accent. Bloody flamin' this and bloody flamin' that. What was all the kangaroo crap covering up? Check her out Down Under. And down under.

Meanwhile, back in Toronto...

Max Magnus woke at the bleep of his bedside fax. He reached for his horn-rims and whooped as he read the emerging message. After weeks of getting nowhere, the private inquiry agency he had commissioned to look into the blowing-up of *Freelance* and *Miss Print IV* had something to submit other than expenses.

The agency had got lucky when it set about checking local airport car rental records around the times the boats were torched. One name had now come up on two lists. A Clarence C Campbell from Miami had returned his hired scooter to Marsh Harbour the morning Toby's boat went up, and a Clarence C Campbell from Miami had returned his hired car to Newport News the morning Harry's boat went up. The agency awaited further instructions.

Magnus preferred to take it from here himself. Within one minute he had Clarence C Campbell's listed home number. Within one more, he had the answering machine advice that right now CCC could be reached at the Chacewater Miami bureau. Magnus dialled the number provided.

'Clarence C Campbell, please.'

'You've got him.'

'Sir, this is the US Navy Department.'

'Hi, Navy. What can we do for you today?'

'I'm Petty Officer Samuel J O'Hara, Second Fleet security. Real sorry to take up your time, sir. We're out to trace an Iraqi snoop who flew in to visit our area a few weeks back. Now he'd be using fake ID, natch. So my chief reckons if we work through every passenger list and eliminate every bona fide – we'll end up with the alias of big daddy from Baghdaddy.'

'No problem, Mr O'Hara.'

'Not for you, sir. We got thousands of names to clear. OK – do you confirm you are the Clarence C. Campbell who flew out of Newport News on – let me see – August 25?'

'Sure do.'

'All rightee. For the record, who can verify?'

'My editor-in-chief up at Chacewater Inc. That's Edgar Segal on 804 226 3000.'

'Shouldn't be necessary, sir. Nice talking to you.'

To give himself time to get to Ed first, CCC had made the plausible error of supplying Petty Officer Samuel J O'Hara with the number of Richmond International Airport.

Ed was in the garden with Mrs Ed watching the kids menacing great-grandpa's rhododendrons when CCC came through to his mobile. Ed said it all sounded pure routine. But he was concerned at the panic in CCC's voice; so much so that he didn't kick his butt for forgetting he was a reporter and failing to tap Petty Officer Samuel J O'Hara about the obvious story – **NAVY HUNT IRAQI SPY**.

'Doomsday, Ed?' said Mrs Ed.

'Not yet. Tomorrow maybe.'

Ed sat small in his garden chair. Just as well it was the Navy and not the Feds checking out CCC. One law enforcement mitt feeling his collar, and the poor schmuck would sing. Oh my God, would they send a guy of 80 to jail? For arson and conspiracy, they sure would. And all for nothing. A tear trickled down an ancient cheek as he watched his great-grandchildren play.

Meanwhile, back in Mayfair...

'It's Harry,' said Claudia as Marina came into the flat. 'Want him?'

'No,' said Marina. 'Put him on.'

'Hi, milady. How you doing?'

'Fine.' She could hear the *Midsummer Night's Dream* overture in the background. 'You?'

'Just great. I gather Fleet Street's putting on a big memorial service for Toby. Thought I might come over. Pay my respects.'

'Kind of you.'

'Marina, maybe we could get together. Lunch, dinner, whatever. Talk some more about that deal we were about to sign for the Merc.'

'Still interested?'

'Interested? Jeez, Marina, I can't stop thinking about you. I—'

'Bye, Harry.' She turned to Claudia. 'And when his damn roses start descending again, just dump them, OK?'

29

Fair Stinkum

Having asked the caller with the Geordie accent to say 'urgent' and 'personal' again but slowly, Martha's secretary was now explaining that she couldn't put her through without a name. Just say it's Arthur's mum, said the caller.

Martha muffled the phone against her rugger shirt as she waited for a hovering Maria-Teresa to take off.

'Hello, Mum.'

'Hello, Arthur.'

'Martha.'

'Listen, pet. Just had a lass at the door asking about you. Said it's for some radio series on women at the top.'

'Strewth.'

'Said she'd looked up your birth date in the parish register – and there was only an Arthur born at this address on that day.'

'Bloody oath. That's dropped me right in the dunny.'

'Did my best, pet. But she knew for sure Martha was Arthur the moment she spotted that photo on the mantelpiece of you in your swimming cozzy. She was real nice, though. Said the sex change was a brilliant career move.'

'Too right. The sheilas are taking over Fleet Street. Arthur was going to be a down-table sub for ever.'

'Aye, but why'd you have to make Martha Australian?'

'To improve me flamin' image.'

'Hope I did right, pet. Didn't want the lass to think I had anything to hide. Let her borrow the photo.'

'Mum, they don't use photos on radio.'

'That's a relief. I was worried you'd be angry.'

'What name did she give?'
'Heidi something.'

'A tenner says that's Martha,' said Jack Stack when his private line
rang. And a moment after lifting the phone, he was holding out his
palm to Bish for the money.
'You know why I'm calling you, Jack.'
'Yeah – and you know why I'm calling you Arthur.'
'Pommy bastard.'
'I'm a bastard? Not me who's been flashing money around the
escort community for the dirt on a fellow editor. You chequebook
journalist, you.'
'Not me who sent Heidi to nick photos off an old mum's
mantelpiece. You blackmailer, you.'
'True, Arthur. I'm all set to expose you as a phoney.'
'Nothing phoney about it. I've had the flamin' op.'
'No flamin' op can turn you into a flamin' Aussie.'
'Or you into a flamin' knight.'
'Tell you what, Arthur. Ask me nicely, Arthur – and I'll spike the
whole disgusting story, Arthur.'
'Exactly the generous offer I was about to make to you.'
'That's nicely enough.'
'Fair dinkum, Jack.'
'Fair stinkum, Arthur.'

'Chairman on the line, Martha.' Maria-Teresa passed the phone.
'Let's run the Dirty Knight stuff tonight.'
'Tonight? It's not ready, Marina. Got to be checked out.'
'Checked out? God, you're no Jack Stack, are you?'
'But Marina—' She looked at the dead phone and crashed it down.
'Women bosses,' said Maria-Teresa on her way to the door.
Four minutes later, she was spreading the Dirty Knight layouts
across the chairman's desk and feeding her pictures from the file.
'...and here we have a model posing in the top half of Jack's
favourite uniform. Note the artful tricorn.'
'Caption: *Keep it under your hat.*'
'Brilliant.' Maria-Teresa scribbled it on the spread. 'And here's
Jack being presented with his Editor of the Year award by the Prince
of Wales.'

'Caption: *A verray, parfit gentil knyght?*' The chairman took the pen and scribbled it down herself.

'You're a star, Marina.'

Mischief lit up Maria-Teresa's face. Let Martha tell the chairman that red-tops were no place for Chaucerian allusions, much though a medieval Mercury would have jumped at Ye First British Serial Ryghts of Ye Dirty Knyght's Tale.

'And here' – Maria-Teresa held up another picture – 'is an arresting shot of Sir Jack's double Coppergram. Cuffs optional.'

'Hey, wouldn't they make the perfect heraldic supporters either side of his knight's coat-of-arms?'

'I'll get the art desk to mock one up. Oh, Marina, it's such fun with you around.'

'Tell me – what's holding Martha back?'

'She and Jack.' Maria-Teresa sighed. 'You know.'

'She'll have to choose. If she won't publish tonight, I'll appoint an editor who will.'

At long last only a stab from the throne, Maria-Teresa waltzed back to the editor's office. 'Cheers, Martha.' She poured champagne for them both.

'What are we flamin' celebrating?'

'Me getting out of the chairman's office in one piece. God, she really put me on the spot. Demanded to see the Dirty Knight file.'

'As if you're the sort of deputy who'd by-pass the editor.'

'As if. But she's crazy enough to run it tonight. I said Bish knew better than Martha. Look what happened to him.'

'Good on yer, mate. You've set me up to tell the flamin' boss to go take a running jump.'

'Only trying to help you, believe me.'

'Trying to help me in the back. That I believe.'

Martha stormed out to the lift. Her finger hovered at the 6 button for the chairman's floor but she changed her mind and pressed G. She was going across to St Bride's to leave a message on the Almighty's answering machine.

Please, a little miracle...

Scotch at one elbow, press secretary at the other, the Prime Minister was enjoying the Varsity match on television. She cursed when a scrum in front of the Oxford posts was interrupted for a newsflash.

Reports were coming in of an airliner disappearing in a Force 9 gale over the North Sea. Aboard were the cast of *Sunnyside*, Britain's top soap, on their way home from collecting eleven golds at the Copenhagen TV Festival.

'Don't just sit there, Derek,' said Beth Macbeth. 'Rush out a statement from their number one fan.'

'Their Number 10 fan,' giggled the press secretary.

'Quote,' said the Prime Minister. 'I never missed an episode, whatever crisis was howling about my head. Had the RAF fly videos out every day at Summit conferences.'

'Quote,' said the press secretary. 'When the awful news came through, it was as though the sun had gone in. I find it hard to believe it will ever shine again.'

'My favourite was that postman, Wee Willie McGinty – '

'Wee Wally McNulty.'

' – he'd just have had my note that he's in for an wee MBE in the honours list. I'd have made it a wee OBE if I'd known.'

The newscaster was now adding unconfirmed reports that the plane had crashed into the sea and sunk within seconds.

'Terrible,' said the Prime Minister.

'Wonderful,' said the press secretary.

'Eh?'

'Let's release immediately not just Wee Wally's wee MBE but the entire honours list. You're worried sick about flak coming at you over the Jack Stack knighthood. Tonight, he'll be lucky to get more than a paragraph.'

'It's an ill wind,' said the Prime Minister.

'Force 9 gale,' said the press secretary.

Martha got back to her desk to find her prayers had not been in vain. One call to Marina, and nemesis should back off for a few days anyway.

'Would you believe it, chairman? All set to go on the Dirty Knight – and the flamin' *Sunnyside* disaster drops on us.'

'What flamin' *Sunnyside* disaster?'

'Switch on your telly.'

'Wow.' Marina took in the drama as Martha went on.

'It'll fill 1, 2, 3, 4, 5, 6, 7, 8, 9, 10, jack, queen, king. Funerals every day for a fortnight. ***River of tears. Sea of flowers. Ocean of*** *sorrow*. TV blacking out the 7 to 7.30 slot every night, except for the ad breaks. So forget everything else until after the Westminster Abbey memorial service.'

'OK, Martha. Hold it for the day of the Investiture. We'll nuke the bugger on his way to the Palace.'

Jack Stack simmered as he waited for Lord Bull to take his eyes from the three TV screens spewing non-stop *Sunnyside* coverage.

'Shocking, Jack.'

'Yeah.' Was it for this exchange that the chairman had summoned his editor in the middle of handling the biggest disaster in the history of soap?

'How come I didn't know this was on the cards?'

'You're not that sort of lord yet.'

'I'm talking about your bloody knighthood.' Only now did he mute the TV sets and look at his editor. 'I could have done you a favour, Jack. Told you to turn it down.'

'Thought you'd enjoy pissing on a knight.'

'You've certainly pissed on your career. Red-top editors can't join the bloody establishment. You'll lose all credibility. Readers will wonder what the PM's rewarding you for.'

'Services to journalism.' He turned. 'Paper to edit, OK?'

'Oh, Jack.' Lord Bull called after him. 'Whatever happened to the Princess Xenia diaries?'

The editor turned and locked eyes. 'You killed them.'

'No, I said bring them up again after the election. Fancy you forgetting.'

'Fancy me forgetting to tell you they turned out to be fakes.'

'Fakes?'

'Fakes. Wasn't even human blood.'

Again, the editor turned to go. Again, the chairman called after him.

'Playing for a peerage now?'

'That how you got yours?'

The first editions dropped. Fleet Street was on the high that goes with a colossal production feat against the clock. But then came Radio Copenhagen with a flash that survivors from the crashed plane had been spotted. Within minutes, it was clear that the entire cast of *Sunnyside* had been picked up – except for Wee Wally McNulty.

The presses came to a halt while page after page was seamlessly updated. Off came the black borders. The *Sunnyside* disaster became the *Sunnyside* miracle – except for Wee Wally McNulty. Mourning became joy – except for Wee Wally McNulty. Fleet Street was soon on the high that goes with a colossal remake against the clock. And then, as editorial teams slumped knackered for the second time this night, Wee Wally McNulty was picked up too.

The news of Jack Stack's knighthood survived it all as a mere bubble on the surface of the Bermuda Triangle way back in the book: the final resting place of corrections, retractions, clarifications, amplifications, and adverse adjudications of the Press Complaints Commission.

30

Something Appalling

As Chairman Marina had commanded, the Mercury's Dirty Knight exposé nuked Jack Stack on the morning of the investiture. But not before he could hit the take-that-you-bastard button to unleash in the Globe's later editions:

Story the Mercury dare not print
SEX-SWAP
EDITOR
SCANDAL!!

Martha had not hung about for the mushroom-shaped cloud. She had taken the next Jumbo out of Heathrow.

Maria-Teresa's first act as acting editor was to kill the message left on her screen: *Rot in hell, you brown-nosed dingo.* Her second act was to wind down the editor's chair to suit five-four rather than six-two. Her third act was to pop her head round Marina's door.

'All the same, chairman. Can't help feeling sad for her.'

'Me too. Know what I said? Martha or Arthur, you just take all the time off you want. Maria-Teresa will mind the shop till you feel like coming back.'

'Oh, doesn't it make your flesh creep that she used to be a man?'

'So did half the editors in Fleet Street.'

Jack Stack's electric-blue morning suit, with toned-in cravat and polyester carnation, had last been hired for a jockey's wedding. Tourists at the Palace railings cheered as his chauffeured Kawasaki slowed to bear him through the great gates. He rocked his head inside his moon helmet and waved his topper at them.

As the bike drew up, a footman who had already opened the doors of 63 Investiture Day limos went through the motions for a sixty-fourth. Jack Stack parked his helmet over the outstretched hand and joined the queue.

Upstairs in the Green Drawing Room, apart from lesser folk attending for lesser honours, the knights were being rehearsed in the ancient ritual by an ice-pale gentleman usher:

'One advances to the marker – *so*. One bows – *so*. Just the simple Coburg nod. Down-pause-up. None of that *Three Musketeers* stuff. Then forward to the footstool – the twin of this chappie here – *so*. Steady oneself on the hand rest – *so*. Plant one knee – *so*. Await the sword tap on each shoulder. Upon rising, incline the head for the garlanding – *so* – as HM places the ribboned badge around the neck. One then receives a few well-chosen words. One doesn't linger. Two short steps backward – *so*. A final bow. Down-pause-up. A right turn – *so*. And exit . . . '

Jack Stack doubted that those few words would be as well-chosen as those he and Lord Bull exchanged last night when the Mercury dropped. God, Jack, I could do without an editor who pays Copper-grams to cuff him. God, Johnnie, I could do without a chairman who pays Vanessas to spank him.

The knights in formal black distanced themselves from the knight in electric blue. He flipped up his tails and sat on a gilt chair to await the call. It was going to be a long wait. The Lord Chamberlain had advised that Vicky, Nicky, Mickey and Ricky might well bolt the moment their great tormentor appeared, so it would be as well to put him last on the list. And to give the official video camera operator the day off.

In the gallery of the ivory-and-gold ballroom, the Royal Marines orchestra was playing a medley selected by the Master of the Household in the hope of raising a smile on grim royal faces as particular honours were dished out. 'A Little Night Music' to mark the dubbing of a little knight. 'Got to Pick a Pocket or Two' as a Tory party fund-raiser collected his gong.

Two bars into 'Something Appealing, Something Appalling', the baton commanded a pause for the Lord Chamberlain to proclaim the accompanying citation.

'For services to journalism.' His lordship's eyes rolled. 'Jack Stack.' His lordship's nose, which until now seemed retroussé beyond further disdain, turned up to display nostrils like a sawn-off shotgun. 'To receive the honour of knighthood.' His lordship's lips formed a silent word. 'Asshole.'

Jack Stack's lovable-cockney face glowed and his shoulders see-sawed as he advanced up the red carpet to the throned dais. He bowed. He knelt. HM raised the ceremonial sword.

This accolade that garlanded neither Milton nor Kipling, nor Dickens nor Donne, nor Galsworthy nor Goldsmith, nor Blake nor Burns, nor Keats nor Shelley, nor Trollope nor Conrad, nor Johnson nor Jonson – nor even Shakespeare for 14 comedies, 13 tragedies, 10 histories and 154 sonnets – was about to be bestowed upon the author of My Royal Weathercock, Knickerless with Nicholas, Filthy Fritz, Yankee Nudle Dandy and the double ejaculation mark.

The blade trembled in the hand of the sovereign whose family this creature had comprehensively shat upon. The five Tudor-uniformed Yeomen of the Guard gripped halberds. The two Gurkha orderly officers gripped kukris. The six royal corgis rumbled and bared their teeth. So did Vicki, Nicky, Mickey and Ricky. So did the 400 family and friends of recipients seated in the ballroom. Their ice-pale gentleman ushers had briefed them not to applaud their favourites but had said nothing about giving tabloid tyrants the bird.

Vicki could take no more. She burst into tears and fled the ballroom.

Now the sword began to descend, gleaming in the light of the great chandelier as it hovered about Jack Stack's bowed head.

'No!' roared HM. 'No, no, no, no, no, no!'

Jack Stack supposed these must be the few well-chosen words the gentleman usher had mentioned. He waited for HM to take the knight's badge from the velvet cushion borne by a knee-breeched page and set the red-and-white ribbon about his neck. But HM was handing the sword to the Lord Chamberlain and leading the family out. The orchestra shifted into 'Always Look on the Bright Side of Life'.

'Does that mean' – Jack Stack lifted his head – 'I don't get the effin knighthood?'

'I'm afraid it doesn't,' said the Lord Chamberlain. 'But it should do – it's your fault Xenia's got the push.' Jack Stack was converting this information into tomorrow's headlines as his lordship took the insignia from the cushion and garlanded him.

'Arise, Sir Jack. Now you're up there with Winston Churchill. Fucking ridiculous, isn't it?'

Spotting TV crews and the press pack thronging the Globe portico, the chauffeur vroomed the Kawasaki round the back. Sir Jack reached his desk to find every news medium in London had e-mailed, faxed and hand-delivered its offer to top all other bids for an exclusive interview.

'What do we tell them?' His secretary held up a sheaf of messages in each fist.

'We tell them bollocks.'

Over at the Mercury, Maria-Teresa was up in the chairman's office for the nineteenth time today.

She had left eighteen times, still only acting editor. This time, she was more confident. She was about to present a Page One layout that looked straight from the fat felt tip of Jack Stack. It was straight from the fat felt tip of Jack Stack. He had phoned to congratulate her on the well-deserved promotion he was about to ensure she got. Just imagine yourself as myself, he said. She did, taking his dictation with cigar between teeth and saying bollocks a lot.

Now her fat felt tip flew across the layout pad on the lectern by Marina's desk. Headlines were inscribed, pictures outlined, text indicated and a tear-out of yesterday's Page One sketched in. The fat felt tip did not falter for a moment, nor go back to cancel half a line:

NO SIR!!
The great dub snub:
HM walks out on
the Dirty Knight

'Love it, love it, love it.' Marina vibrated with glee. 'Maria-Teresa, you've got the job.'

Ten minutes later, the Dirty Knight was on Marina's line.

'Can't wait to find out what you're going to do to me. Shall I prepare for the rope, the stake, the chair? The garrotte, the guillotine, the gas? The bullet, the needle, the axe?'

'In that order.'

'I suppose a little mercy's out of the question?'

'Expect the mercy you showed Martha.'

'Why blame me? I wouldn't have retaliated if you hadn't made her fire first. It's your fault she's gone. Your fault you're left with Ma Teresa.'

'She's done me a terrific Page One.' Marina described it. 'Eat your heart out, Jack.'

'I left my heart at the Merc. Can't stand by and watch you splash the wrong story. Just had a tip-off from a very, very high source – don't ask how high. Got a pen? Got a pad?'

Marina picked up the fat felt tip and drew a front page to Jack Stack's dictation.

'OK, OK,' she said. 'What's the catch?'

'No catch. I just love doing Page Ones.'

'And doing yourself a favour.'

'Sure. And the day I get Johnnie Bull to pay me off, I'll do you a favour. Return to the good old Merc and make you the greatest press baron of them all.'

'I knew there was a catch.'

Marina admired the page for some moments, then folded it away as she buzzed for Maria-Teresa to come back up for the twentieth time.

'Darling,' she said. 'Just had a tip-off from a very, very high source – don't ask how high. So you can begin your editorship by scooping the Street.'

She led Maria-Teresa to the lectern. The fat felt tip flew across the layout grid. Headlines were inscribed, pictures outlined, text indicated and a tear-out of Xenia's engagement announcement sketched in. The fat felt tip did not falter for a moment, nor go back to cancel half a line.

Exclusive: Palace sensation
RICKY
JILTS
XENIA

Maria-Teresa gave Marina a funny look. 'Needs a double ejaculation mark, don't you think?'

Jack Stack had been busy. By late afternoon, every news desk in print, TV and radio was on to the Admiral to check an exclusive tip-off from a very, very high source – don't ask how high – that the engagement of Ricky and Xenia was off.

'As you well know,' said the weary Admiral to yet another reporter, 'we aren't in the denial business.'

'Meaning it's true?'

'Meaning we're not in the denial business.'

'Are you in the confirmation business?'

'Goodbye.'

The Number 10 press secretary had nothing to say on the record. But off, he made sure every caller went away with the clear impression that Beth Macbeth was appalled at the royal dismissal of the Commonwealth princess she had sponsored. No, the PM had not been told the reason. And if you were about to ask whether the Palace old guard had won an infamous victory, then Number 10 couldn't help you there either.

It was the only story that mattered. The Jack Stack investiture bollocks was shunted further and further towards the sports section.

Gloria Mundy came into his office and shut the ever-open door. He was slaving over a hot keyboard, cooking the block-buster for which all the rival Xenia front pages and all the newscasts would serve as appetisers. She trembled as he turned from the screen.

'Jack, the diaries...' She dried.

'Brace yourself, kid. They're fakes.'

'You knew?'

'All along. Didn't want to upset you.'

'I found out when I had the red ink analysed. It was real blood, all right. Not baboon's. Not Xenia's. But my sister Jenny's. The diaries are hers. I'm so sorry.'

'It happens.' He returned to the keyboard.

'And it wasn't microscopic Romanian – it was microscopic backslang. Jenny speaks it like a native. *Ecnirp Ykcir* for Prince Ricky. *Noobab doolb* for baboon blood. *Elbuod-elbbub* for double-bubble.'

'*Noobab doolb ... Elbuod-elbbub ...*' He typed some more.

'Poor Jenny confessed. She was driven by jealousy. It ate away at her. Sharing rooms with someone so much more brilliant and beautiful, generous and kind, wealthy and sexy than she could ever hope to be.'

'And so much taller, I bet.'

'How'd you guess?'

'Lot of it about. Look at Bish. And Humpty. And Harry. And Martha. And Ma Teresa. And Johnnie Bull. All double-bubbling with heightist fantasies about me.'

'I've let you down, Jack.'

'Bollocks.' He tapped away some more. 'Is it Jennie with an I and an E?'

'Jenny with an Y.'

'Here we are, kid – '

ONLY in the Globe: Voodoo diaries
that spooked Prince Ricky romance
VAMPIRE XENIA
FAKE SENSATION!!
by Gloria Mundy, Political Editor

No prob. It was genuine Xenia diaries that he had got his K for not running. Who was going to complain about him running fakes? Not Beth Macbeth – she came out of it all as the good guy. Not Lord Bull – the diaries would keep his sales soaring for a fortnight. Not Xenia – she was squeakier clean than Maria von Trapp. And surely not the Palace – he was one of them now.

31

The Short and Curlies

'Hello, Mum. Guess who?'

'Martha?'

'Arthur.'

'Where are you, pet?'

'Australia – always said I'd come here one day.'

'You sound different.'

'Had the op reversed, man. Got me Geordie accent back.'

'That Marina's been on every day. Sends her love and says she needs you. The Merc's falling apart.'

'Tell the lass thanks but no thanks. Say, if I were her, I'd send for Sir Jack.'

Marina's visit to the gynaecologist was routine enough to leave her twenty minutes early for this appointment with her solicitor. When a taxi driver swore at her double-parked Bentley, she told Joey to come back later. It was such a nice morning, she'd wander down to the river.

She tucked her Mercury under an arm and crossed into Embankment Gardens. Talk about bums on seats: dossers had taken over every bench. Some lay like corpses. Others only half-embalmed took up only half a bench, leaving room for anyone who cared to sit by a pig-eyed wino with his entire rotting wardrobe on his back. One group were studying the morning paper over a late breakfast of laced Newcastle Brown.

Meeting readers was never a good idea for press barons. It imperilled their delusion that they know what readers want because they are readers themselves. Those who ran broadsheets stood to discover they were typical solely of multi-millionaires who played right-handed French horns, restored salvaged U-boats on the Medway, patronised Anglican livings and considered Simone de Beauvoir ill-served by her translators. For tabloid chairmen, descending from their golden coaches to go among the baying customers was to court terminal self-reproach. Could it be our fault that these brutes we feed a daily diet of violence and vulgarity behave like brutes fed a daily diet of violence and vulgarity?

It was no comfort to Marina that the Embankment Gardens derelicts were all reading the Globe. Well, reading a Globe: one copy had been divided among the community. Here, in a snapshot survey, was the explanation why the punters were deserting the Mercury. Jack Stack's Page One bait this morning was **GAYS BASH BISHOPS**. Maria-Teresa's was **EURO REBELS DEFY GOVT**. No contest.

Marina recoiled as a long hand in a frayed sleeve flapped the Globe spread at her. Headline: **SCANDAL OF THE SIXTH FORM LAP-DANCERS**. Picture: a lolly-licking Lolita. Caption: *Bottom of the class.*

'Ere y'are, darling.'

'And here you are.' Marina offered her Mercury like a Salvation Army missionary.

'No, thanks. I've read it. Took almost two minutes. Boring, boring, boring. The Merc's lost the plot. Headlines too mini – 48 point page leads, I ask you. Pix too dinky – hardly any over three cols. Pages too samey. And dead below the fold. Jesus, is anyone in charge of the clattering train?'

'I imagine,' she said, 'you used to be a journalist.'

'Used to be.' He noisily assembled a spitball and, saving her presence, turned to eject it away over his shoulder. 'These days I'm on the Merc.'

'Oh, really? Doing what?'

'Dogwatch. Midnight till seven. Always worked nights. Only way to avoid the bosses.'

'If you were the boss, what would you do?'

'Bring back Jack Stack.'

A grinning bag-lady in a scarlet balaclava staggered towards her, one mittened hand at an invisible rail. Was she on the staff too? Marina side-stepped to the greasy grass and accelerated up-wind to Arnold's office.

Her disaffection was peaking. The horrors of tabloid war were survivable only if you were winning. She wasn't. Up-yours journalism was exciting only if your sales were up too. They weren't. Laugh-a-line newspapers were fun only if the bottom one was smiling. It wasn't.

Pity she couldn't bring back the magic without the magician. Jack Stack had never stopped pitching for the job. He phoned her flat every night as the first edition dropped. As intended, Marina echoed his vivid critiques to devastate a Maria-Teresa already second-guessing herself into a strait jacket. And every morning too, Sir Jack would be on the phone, telling Marina her last edition was even crappier than her first. The desperate Maria-Teresa lauded and magnified the chairman's every misjudgement. Marina's good taste bestrode the editorial floor like the angel of death. In their thousands, the readers were turning to the Globe.

The brutal arithmetic was the single item on the agenda this morning. Arnold shook his heavy head at the latest printouts.

'Marina,' he said, 'you're trying to take the Merc up the down escalator. It's bring-back-Sir-Jack time.'

'Oh, no it bloody isn't.'

'Then it's take-the-money-and-run time. Grab Chacewater's cash. Go and write books under your jacaranda tree.'

Marina went to the double-glazed windows and stared down at the weirdly silent traffic. Arnold waddled across to join her.

'OK,' she said eventually, 'I'm ready to sell.'

'Fine. I'll call Harry before you weaken.' He frowned. 'Say he wants to know about the sales position?'

'Unlikely. He probably invented it.'

'Well let's not give him time to ask questions. I'll say he's got until the weekend. Then I'm instructed to advise other interested parties. If he lets it go to market, he'll be fighting it out with Magnus.'

'Magnus? I wouldn't sell to him if he were the last press baron on earth. I can still hear our boat going up, and then that voice on the phone. *This is Magnus. I trust my timing is not inconvenient.* Shiver, shiver.'

Mom Chacewater's hammock swung gently in her garden high above the James river as Ed finished talking to Harry on his mobile.

'That,' she sighed, 'sounded an awful lot of dollars. Cheaper to marry the girl.'

'He still insists he's doing this to thwart Magnus. Wants it wrapped before the guy can move in.'

'Ed, I wish Harry would give up on this.'

'So does Magnus. Else why fight us so hard?'

'Else why blow up all those boats?'

Ed said he needed the bathroom. There, he used his mobile to engage the Chacewater London bureau answering machine: Theo was to tip off the Magnus man that the Mercury quadrille was on again. The message ended with the sound of the loo flushing.

The remarkably long-legged lady lawyer from Richmond had brought Harry the Mercury contract for signature. Apart from the date and the substitution of Marina's name for Toby's, the document was exactly the same as when she brought it last time. So was their day. Again, with her assistance, Harry had put his new *Miss Print V* through her paces. Again, with her assistance, he had tried out the hi-fi stack, the fridge, the corkscrew, the shower and the master cabin mattress. Again, she had showed him where to put his John Hancock.

It was almost dusk by the time they came ashore. The butler greeted them with the message that Magnus had called six times, unsatisfied by the repeated assurance that Harry was not yet back. When the seventh call came, Harry was in his study, telling the remarkably long-legged lady lawyer that he would never trust that man an inch, and if she listened in on the extension she'd likely hear just why.

'How's the new boat, Harry?'

'Max, don't even think about it.'

'You should be making that speech to the legendary Ed.'

'What are you talking about?'

'You employ a Mr Clarence C Campbell?'

'CCC? Sure.'

'He's the guy who blew up your boat. Ed told him to. So you'd think it was me – which you did. And back off the Mercury deal – which you didn't.'

'I can't believe I'm hearing this.'

'CCC also blew up Toby's boat. Ed told him to. So Toby would think it was me – which he did. And accept my offer – which he didn't.'

'Max, you're crazy.'

'Think so? My agents have been investigating this for weeks. Airport car rental records confirm CCC was there on both occasions. And I have on tape the guy's admission it was Ed who sent him. So who do I pass this stuff to first – the FBI or the FBI?'

'Sonofabitch.'

'Come on. I haven't blown up anybody's boat. Wasn't me who blew up *Miss Print II* to scare your pa out of Maine.'

'You can't pin that on Ed.'

'Why not? It's what he does. He probably did the *Titanic*. I ought to finger him before he murders somebody. But, Harry – '

'Here it comes'

' – there is a favour you could do me.'

'Pull out of the Mercury deal? Forget it. There's no way Marina will sell to you.'

'Harry, you're right. You go ahead and do the deal.'

'I don't get it – '

'Right again. You don't get it – I do. You sign the contract. Then you sell to me. And Ed's off the hook.'

'Waiting for me to say thanks? Don't hold your breath.'

'Don't be like that, Harry. I'm paying you with the Chacewater Inc. stake I've built up. You're pulling off a brilliant coup to frustrate my ambition to take you over. Mom, Sis, Ed – you'll be their hero. Goodnight to you.'

Harry shrugged at the remarkably long-legged lady lawyer. She shrugged back.

'Wow, what an operator. He's sure got you by the short and curlies.'

'Guess so. But, y'know, Ed did these things for only one reason. He loves me.'

'And you love him for it, don't you, Harry.'

'Sure do.'

32

The Sacred Torch

The Prime Minister's Jaguar pulled away from Number 10 for Fleet Street, where she was to deliver the address at the St Bride's memorial service for Toby Baynard. She turned to her press secretary and patted his hand on the armrest.

'Just think, Derek. All the reptiles under one roof. Oh, for a friendly bomb.'

'God help the bomb,' said Derek. The phone trilled. He fielded the call. 'One sec, Marina.'

'Beth,' said Marina. 'Must tell you – just in case it affects your speech. We're selling the Merc.'

'To?'

'Chacewater – '

Beth glanced at Derek. Like her, he was recalling that **SAVE YOUR MERC FROM THIS BERK** front page, starring Harry with a Stars and Stripes figleaf.

' – it was Toby's last wish.'

'Ah.'

'Can't let Jack Stack dictate to us, can we?'

'Perish the thought.'

'And we don't want Max Magnus in Fleet Street, do we?'

'No fear. He's all right where he is – on the top shelf.'

'Believe me, Beth, this is good news. The Merc will get the investment it needs. Launch a new Sunday. Maybe a London evening too.'

'The more, the merrier. When's it to be announced?'

'Noon tomorrow – mustn't upstage Toby's big day.'

'Dear me, no.' She handed Derek the phone to replace.

'Dear me, no.' He mimicked her.

'Perhaps I'll tone down my blah-blah about the sacred torch of British press freedom burning bright.'

'Don't tone it down.' He snorted. 'Tone it up. The sacred torch of British press freedom is not for sale – except to the highest bidder.'

The PM sighed. She expected flak in the Commons about our American friends grabbing this last slice of Fleet Street. Still, could be worse. Could be our European friends.

'Derek, set up a dinner for Harry. Invite all the press barons – Americans love a sniff of ermine. Ambassador Chuck. Prince of Wales. Got to get the bugger on side.'

'How about a dozen Page Three girls?'

'You're pathetic.'

'Beth, we're all pathetic.' He removed his hand from under hers. 'Shit-scared of the press. Else you'd be promising them a privacy law with criminal sanctions. It's what you promised HM.'

'I'd have promised anything to save Xenia.'

'But it didn't, did it?'

'Xenia thinks it did. Lovely thank-you note from her yesterday.'

'In red ink?'

'Red something. She's in Louisiana. And getting engaged to the Governor. He's running for Vice-President.'

'Hang on, Beth.' He dialled his opposite number aboard Air Force One, flying the President to New Orleans for his party convention. 'Karen? Derek. Is the chief dining at the governor's mansion tonight?... Well make sure he wears an amulet and doesn't eat anything... Name Xenia ring a bell with you?... Yes, *that* Xenia...'

Occasions like this proclaimed the endurance of St Bride's as the village church of Fleet Street, whose weary and heavy-laden have come unto it through the centuries.

The organ played Bach's *Toccata and Fugue* as the pews, which all faced inward like choir stalls, began to fill with practitioners of the black art. The sun reached in through unstained antique glass, haloing heathens who would run a spoiler on the Second Coming if a rival outbid them for First Rights. Everyone seemed to know who everyone is or was, or might have been. They had observed each other at their finest and foulest. Hired each other and fired each other. Succeeded each other and preceded each other. Harried each other and married each other. Screwed each other and screwed each other. Eyes flashed across the marble aisle as a past mistress assessed a present mistress. Eyes glazed as an editor blanked a columnist he had reduced to a half-columnist.

The Prime Minister and her press secretary took their places in the first pew alongside Marina. She was telling them she wore this cornflower outfit on her wedding day. No one was in black. It was not a morning for mourning but to give thanks for the life of Toby Baynard.

In through the north porch shuffled a smallish, sixtyish stranger with antler eyebrows.

He stood aside from the queue announcing themselves to the name-takers whose lists would occupy a column of pearl type at 14 lines to the inch in tomorrow's broadsheets. His name would not be there. The antler eyebrows lifted from time to time as he put a face to a name or recognised a voice he had heard on the other end of the phone from Toronto. Though they would not know his face, the several whose newspapers he had sought to acquire over the years would not have forgotten the sincere Aberdonian tones of Max Magnus.

The Humpty-Dumptys reached the name-takers.

'Viscount Baynard. With Viscountess Baynard. And our son, the Honourable Toby, better know as Tab.'

'Now do get it right.' Dumpty demanded attention. 'The happy widow' – she pointed towards Marina's pew – 'is properly styled the Dowager Viscountess. Looks the part, don't you think?'

'Sergeant and Mrs Mac from Baynard Cay,' announced Dahlia. It was three weeks since she had married Sergeant Mac, who now wore that cocky smile he envied her late husband. 'And this is my daughter, Tulip.'

Tulip caught Tab's eye. He blushed at what he was thinking, and fiddled at tie and fly. Dahlia moved to block his line of vision. She thanked heaven for Marina. But for her, Baynard Cay would have gone to Humpty, and young master Tab would be out there every vacation, panting to pluck the nubile Tulip.

'Ha! Lord Bull of the Globe.'

'Ambassador Charles T Bergdorf. With Mrs Bergdorf. And our niece, Miss Honey Chacewater.'

Honey caught Tab's eye unbuttoning her. He blushed some more. She mouthed two syllables at him.

'Harry Chacewater. With my mom, Mrs Alice Chacewater. And

the legendary Ed and Mrs Segal. And George Theodoulou, our bureau chief, and his lovely wife, Sally-Jane.'

'Lord Holborn of the Herald.'

'Admiral Sinjin Standfast. Big S, little t. Big J, little o-h-n.'

'The ghost of Kevin O'Connor, once editor of the Globe.'

Ed was telling Mrs Ed that King George III asked Benjamin Franklin's advice when lightning blasted eight feet off this tiered-wedding-cake steeple. Ben said to install one of his conductor rods with pointed ends. But King George knew better – he commanded blunt ends. It confirmed the colonists' belief that they couldn't lose against such a loony tune. And a dozen years later, Ben Franklin was drafting the Declaration of Independence.

'Well, I never knew that,' said Mrs Ed.

'Well, you know now,' said Ed.

'Lord Bridewell of the Gazette.'

'Sir Jack Stack. Highest-paid editor in the Street. With Mr Reginald Bishop. Highest-paid barman in the Street – '

' – and with Miss Heidi Hunt,' said Miss Heidi Hunt.

Heidi took Sir Jack's arm and smiled a Mona Lisa smile. He was hers. She had made him fire Gloria Mundy and set fire to his little black book. Moved into his flat. Added to his rack of uniform headgear a Virgin airways cap and an Esso hard-hat. And she had told mum Tara, 44, and dad Gustav, 49, that this little church was where they'd very soon see their little Heidi become Lady Stack. Ooh-er.

Sir Jack and cronies found space in a rear pew. Magnus settled alongside. The antler eyebrows turned the other way as he whispered to a neighbour:

'Have you heard? She's sold the Merc to Chacewater.'

The neighbour passed it on. The antler eyebrows lifted, and stayed lifted as the word rippled through the congregation like a Mexican wave. It reached the Number 10 press secretary, who whispered it to the Prime Minister, who whispered to Marina that there seemed no point keeping the secret until noon tomorrow when everyone knew it at noon today. The whisper came round to Bish. Who turned to tell Heidi. Who turned to tell Sir Jack. Who turned to complete the circle.

'Have you heard? She's sold the Merc to Chacewater.'

'That's correct, Sir Jack.' The antler eyebrows were already levelled at him. 'But tomorrow at noon it will be announced that Chacewater has sold it on to me.'

That voice. 'You'd better be who I think you are.'

'I am.'

The antler eyebrows twitched and Magnus handed over an envelope. Sir Jack lifted the flap and peeped at a cheque for that promised second million dollars, Canadian.

'And each time you put the sale up a million, there will be a further such token of my appreciation.'

Now the congregation rose as the cinnamon-gowned choristers proceeded to their central stalls and offered the harmonies of heaven to the disciples of discord.

And now Olly and Nolly came forward to share a recitation of Kipling's *If* — which Tab would have performed *If* — he had not made the Mercury look foolish over the fake Princess Vicki suicide story. Everyone saw Toby in them.

And now a tenor and a soprano rose to sing his adored Tauber/Laye duet:

> *Nobody could love you more.*
> *Nobody loved*
> *So much before.*

Throats were cleared, eyes dabbed. And now the Prime Minister moved from her place to deliver the address. At the brass eagle lectern, she surveyed this diaspora come home to EC4 from SE1, W8, E1 and E14. Such a respectable congregation. Was this some other Fleet Street than the one out there?

The one that tells the nation which royals to love and which to hate, whoops at their follies and weeps at their funerals.

'I am so grateful to Marina.' She nodded to her. 'Such an honour, such a privilege, such a pleasure to be asked to speak on such a day in the history of Fleet Street...'

The one that sees public office as justification for inspecting the sheets of those who undertake it. The one that doorsteps the minister's loyal spouse and snaps the minister's bewildered children.

'The noble Viscount Baynard was plain Toby to journalists and inkies alike. I was glad to count him a close friend. I valued his wise counsel in our never-ending battle against those who fear press freedom and would have the newspapers in reins, even in chains...'

The one that hounds anyone on the box, from quiz-show host to magician's assistant, who falls foul of a code of private morality that the press does not require of its own.

'I confess I am hooked on newspapers. I can't even wait till morning for my daily fix. I have the first editions biked to Number 10. Such an advantage to read your horoscope the night before...'

The one whose gleeful invasions of sexual privacy send Parliament into frenzies that have thus far fizzled out but will, one day, boil over and imperil the freedom to expose real scandal.

'And on this inspiring occasion, I make to you the solemn pledge I made to Toby. As long as Beth Macbeth is prime minister, the press need never fear for its freedom. Your rights and duties are our precious heritage.'

She looked up from her notes. She spotted Ambassador Chuck and guessed that the man next to him was Harry, not readily recognisable without that Stars and Stripes figleaf. This was her opportunity to cancel Jack Stack's insult as publicly as it was issued.

'Up to his last moments, Toby was working to safeguard the future of the Merc. His health would never let him return to Fleet Street. But he was concerned to preserve the paper – and everything it has come to stand for. He was about to repose it in the hands of one of the most distinguished publishing houses in the English-speaking world. What better moment than this to give you the news that Marina has fulfilled Toby's last wish...'

Harry, Mom, Sis, Ambassador Chuck, Honey, Theo, Sally-Jane and the legendary Ed and Mrs Ed shut their eyes tight. This fool was about to proclaim them saviours of the Mercury, unaware that in 24 hours it would become known that they had used it to save themselves.

Outside, two stretch limos pulled up and waited with engines running, ready to get the Chacewater clan away to Heathrow and their private 757 home to Virginia.

It had been Harry's idea to get Chacewater's entry into Fleet Street off on the right foot by turning out in strength at St Bride's. But when Magnus came into the plot, Harry dare not let Ed find out until it was a done deal. He could not risk him wrecking it – and himself in the bargain. And at two o'clock this morning, the remarkably long-legged lady lawyer from Richmond had called to say Magnus had delivered – and was on his way to London to announce his take-over at noon tomorrow.

Harry had broken the news to the family halfway through breakfast. Suddenly he was their hero. In exchange for the Merc none of them wanted, they had grabbed back Magnus's menacing parcel of Chacewater stock. Ed had given him a that's-my-boy wink. Then Harry had said, Oh, and one more thing, guys. He'd had just about enough of this game – he was going back to the Navy.

'. . . So, on this day we thank God for Toby, let us welcome his successor – Chacewater Incorporated, of Richmond, Virginia. Harry's one of us already. The sacred torch is in safe hands. We know they're safe because Toby chose them. He can rest happy.'

Now all rose to belt out 'Glory, glory, Hallelujah!' The Chacewater group did not join in the Battle Hymn of the Republic that defeated its Confederate forbears.

'Told you all along' – Ed muttered through tight teeth – 'this just ain't our scene.'

He would be glad to get away. In the business pages back home, the Magnus deal would play as a smart move by Chacewater. But here it would go down as a cynical double-cross. The legendary Ed would get the credit both sides of the Atlantic.

And now the rector blessed this gathering of all religions and of none. The choir sang the *Nunc Dimittis*. The organist allowed Toby his last chuckle, playing two bars of the Beethoven funeral march before breaking into 'Colonel Bogey'. As the old buffer had planned, the congregation sprang back into the world with a smile on its face.

Dahlia was the first to greet Marina. They hugged, and Dahlia whispered that it sure didn't show yet. Marina said she was moving out to Baynard Cay before it started to, and wouldn't be back until she'd given birth to Polly and Molly and a best-seller novel about a dysfunctional Fleet Street dynasty.

Harry edged towards her but his way was blocked by Maria-Teresa in a purple trouser suit. She offered a waxy hand. Theo intervened to take it and tried to tug her aside. She jinked round him.

'Hi, Mr Chacewater. I'm your editor. No time to lose. Sales dropping like a stone. The Merc needs a whole new image, I've got thousands of ideas. Free for lunch?'

'Maria-Teresa,' said Theo. 'This is not the moment, OK? We'll get back to you.'

Harry took Marina gently by the elbow and walked her out into the little churchyard.

'You look sensational.'

'I know,' she said. 'It's called pregnancy.'

'Well, how about that?' Harry shook his head. 'So when's the happy event?'

'Events, plural – I only do twins. And about nine months from the fifth of July. Or maybe the sixth.'

'You mean – '

'I mean.'

'So how about becoming a Navy wife? I'm rejoining the fleet.'

'Been a widow three whole months. First proposal so far.'

'Don't say yes till I've told you something.'

'I wasn't going to say yes. But what's the something?'

'Look, Marina. I had to get back Magnus's stake in my company. Only way he'd part was to trade it for the Merc.' He held up his palms. 'It's done. Announcement tomorrow.'

'Harry, you're a shit.'

'From your point of view maybe.'

'Reason I sold to you was to keep Magnus out of Fleet Street. If I'd sold to him, I'd have made a lot more. He's got the Mercury on the cheap. And he doesn't have to blow up any more boats.' She flapped hands. 'Shtum! I'm sure this is him.'

'Good day to you, Marina.' Antler eyebrows twitched at her. 'And good day to you, Harry.'

'Max.' She clasped his arm. 'I'm happy for you.'

'So much to talk about. Come to Claridges for tea. Earl Grey, is it not?'

'If it wasn't, it would be. I want that interview.' She was shaping his chapter as she spoke.

'Marina,' he said as he beckoned Sir Jack, 'I'm sure you'd like to congratulate my new editor.'

'Wish me luck,' said Sir Jack.

'If you insist. Bad luck.'

'Harry,' said Magnus, 'if you're around for the announcement tomorrow, come and help push the boat out.'

'I'll be pushing my own boat out. The new one.'

'Taking the legendary Ed?'

'You bet.'

'Very wise, if I may say so.'

The church had emptied. Old-timers were retracing steps to their ancient whisky-and-watering holes. They barged once again through the cowboy saloon doors of El Vino. Or looked in vain for familiar faces at the Wig and Pen. Or paid homage at the site of the Stab (short for Stab-in-the-back, though its sign said White Hart). But nowadays, Fleet Street pubs were full of City types: the money-changers had been cast into the temple. They looked askance at the return of these hot-metal legionnaires, slapping backs, prodding ribs and hooting about the good old days of male ascendancy, pussycat management, union tyranny, untidy desks and lunch without end.

The prime minister's car was being overtaken on the Embankment by the Chacewater limos when the phone went for her press secretary. His office had picked up a buzz that Harry was selling on to Magnus.

'Derek,' she said, 'set up a dinner for him. Invite the press barons – Canadians love a sniff of ermine. High Commissioner. Prince of Wales. And Wee Willie McGinty—'

'Wee Wally McNulty.'

'Him too. Lots of Scots. Got to get the bugger on side.'

'How about a dozen of his Wild Wives?'

Sir Jack patted the pocket in which Magnus's cheque was warming his heart. He told Heidi he'd see her later, ignited a Montecristo and danced into Fleet Street. His chauffeured Kawasaki awaited. He took the proffered helmet, lifting the visor to accommodate his cigar as they accelerated up the hill.

The bells of St Clement Danes were saying 'Oranges and Lemons' as the traffic lights changed to red.

Sir Jack nipped from the pillion to the pavement kiosk. He lifted a handful of copies from the Mercury pile to dump on the Globe pile.

'Asshole,' said the baseball-capped man in the kiosk, and put the Mercurys back in place.

'Up yours,' said Sir Jack, and sat Mercurys on top of Globes again and himself on the pillion again.

He turned as the bike vroomed him away. This time, the man in the kiosk already had his own two fingers up.